THE 100 SOCIETY

THE 100 SOCIETY

CARLA SPRADBERY

Hodder
Children's
Books

A division of Hachette Children's Books

First published in Great Britain in 2014
by Hodder Children's Books

The right of Carla Spradbery to be identified as the Author
of the Work has been asserted by her in accordance with the
Copyright, Designs and Patents Act 1988

2

A Catalogue record for this book is available from the British Library

ISBN 978 1 444 92008 6

Typeset in Berkeley by Avon DataSet Ltd, Bidford-on-Avon, Warwickshire

Printed in the UK by Clays Ltd, St Ives plc

The paper and board used in this paperback by Hodder Children's Books
are natural recyclable products made from wood grown in sustainable forests.
The manufacturing processes conform to the environmental regulations
of the country of origin.

For Chas

Grace Becker searched the star-flecked horizon for something to focus on, anything to stop her from looking down as she inched her way along the ledge. Pressing her back as close to the brickwork as she could, she used her fingers to feel her way along the outer wall of the bridge.

Somewhere in the darkness – ten, maybe even twenty metres beneath her – was a railway track. If she slipped, a few broken bones would be the least of her worries.

She paused, rested her head against the wall and closed her eyes. The cool bricks provided a momentary distraction from the heat that was quickly building beneath her Balaclava. Grace curled her toes, checking the ledge beneath her feet. She didn't dare move them any further forwards; the tips of her trainers were just a few millimetres from the edge. If she curled her toes to find nothing firm beneath, she knew she would be unable to move.

Nearly there. Just a few more steps.

Grace opened her eyes and immediately realized it had been a mistake to stop. The horizon started to tilt and her head began to spin, her skin prickling with sweat.

'Don't get too comfy there, princess,' said a voice on the ledge beside her. 'The middle of the bridge is the highest point from the ground. Have a quick look down and check, will you?'

Instinctively, Grace bowed her head just as a train exploded into existence beneath her. She flung her head back, gasping as it cracked on the wall behind her. The train thundered below, a seemingly endless stream of carriages clanking over the tracks she had been trying so hard not to think about. After what felt like a lifetime, the final carriage emerged from under the bridge and carried away the noise that had filled the night air. Next to her, the silence was broken by the unmistakable sound of stifled laughter.

'You think that's funny, Trick?' Grace asked between gulps of air. 'Would it have been funny if I'd fallen?'

'Well, perhaps not funny in the conventional sense.' He shuffled towards her, almost close enough for their arms to touch.

'I hate you. You know that?'

'Come on,' he said, laughing softly. 'You're nearly there.'

The single streetlamp on the bridge above was shrouded in darkness, the bulb inside having been broken earlier by a well-aimed rock. Staying out of sight was one of their most important rules, although, with the darkness beneath her almost palpable, Grace had begun to wonder if safety should feature a little higher on the list.

Trick's silhouette moved on the ledge beside her and, even in the shadows, she was able to make out the sharp outline of his jaw, the smooth curve of his bicep beneath his shirt. Moments later, his fingers curled around Grace's arm and instantly she felt safer.

'OK?' he asked. 'Are we ready?'

Grace nodded.

Trick shrugged his rucksack from his back. 'Light?' he called, as he began to unzip the various compartments.

A shaky torch beam appeared, cutting through the darkness between the bridge and the steep bank to their left.

'Damn it, Pete,' Trick shouted. 'This job is hard enough already. Any chance you could keep the torch still for longer than a second?'

'Sorry,' Pete called from the shadows. 'Faith thought she heard something.'

'It's OK, Pete,' Grace called back through gritted teeth, her fingers pressing a little more firmly against the brickwork. 'You're doing fine. You too, Faith,' she added as an afterthought, thinking of the friend she had dragged along to keep watch. Though Pete and Faith were on the bank, concealed by the shadows and hidden among the trees and bushes, she could hear their murmurs as they

3

talked quietly between themselves.

The torch beam steadied and the wall next to Grace was brought to life in an explosion of colour. Slowly turning to face the wall, Grace trailed her fingertips across the paintwork, as though the graffiti might somehow make the bricks feel different.

Trick's bag clanked as he reached inside to pull out a can of spray paint. 'There,' he said, checking the label in the beam of Pete's torch. 'Midnight Black.' He offered Grace the can.

Steadying herself on the ledge, Grace shook the aerosol, pulled the lid off and, with a final glance at the half-lit wall in front of her, began spraying.

There was something about having a can of paint in her hand that relaxed her. Suddenly it was all worth it; the fear, the danger, the risk of being caught. She allowed herself to move back from the wall a little, each stroke of paint becoming more confident as she focused only on her work and on the picture that was slowly taking shape in front of her.

With a final flourish, she lowered the can and stepped back to get a better look at her work – but her foot dipped into nothingness.

Her hands instinctively shot forwards to claw at the brick wall, but there was nothing to grasp.

In that instant, she knew it was all over.

She closed her eyes, anticipating the stomach-lurching fall she knew was coming – and then a strong hand took hold of her forearm and pulled her almost effortlessly back on to the ledge.

'What the hell was that?' Trick's words came between deep breaths and, with her body pulled close against his, Grace could feel that his heart was beating just as fast as hers.

'I slipped.'

Trick exhaled. 'No kidding. And you almost took me with you.' He turned to look down over the ledge. 'Let's just finish this thing and get the hell out of here.'

Grace nodded, unable to form any more words as the adrenaline continued to surge through her. With a shaking hand, she raised her can and began spraying again.

The lines were a little uneven, but Grace was willing to let it slide if it meant getting off the bridge sooner.

Trick turned to Grace and lifted his Balaclava. 'Done. Now what do you say we get back on to solid ground?'

Grace opened her mouth to reply, but before she was able to speak, the torch beam swung away and they were plunged into darkness.

And then a piercing scream filled the air.

Instinctively, Grace flattened herself against the wall. The aerosol fell from her hand and clunked once beside her feet before falling over the edge. The distance between her and the railway tracks below suddenly seemed to double in height and she clutched at the brickwork, sure that she wouldn't be so lucky if she slipped a second time.

5

'What happened?' Trick whispered. 'Where did Pete go with the torch?'

'I don't know. I can't see anything.'

For a moment all was quiet, then came the clanking of paint cans being dropped into a bag and the sharp sound of a zip being pulled closed. Listening intently, Grace frowned at the shuffling sound beside her, realizing that Trick was making his way along the ledge to where the bank rose sharply up to meet the bridge.

'Where the hell are you going?' Grace whispered.

'I'm getting out of here.' There was a dull thud as something heavy landed on the bank beneath Trick. His bag.

Grace was just able to make out Trick's silhouette, leaning away from the bridge. He steadied himself and Grace realized he was about to jump.

'Trick, wait . . .'

Without a word, Trick stepped forwards and disappeared into the darkness. Grace held her breath, waiting for a sound, a sign that would tell her that he was OK.

'Don't just stand there,' his voice called up from the shadows. 'Go!'

Grace continued her way along the ledge, her heart quickening with every step.

Then footsteps sounded on the bridge above.

Grace froze.

It could be anyone, nothing to do with them. But the way the footsteps were moving – slowly, from one side of the bridge to the other – told Grace that this person was looking for someone.

And there was only one person left to find on this bridge.

Barely even daring to breathe, she squeezed her eyes closed, her head pounding in time with her heart.

The footsteps drew nearer, growing louder until they came to a halt somewhere overhead. For a moment there was silence and Grace imagined a figure leaning over the wall above her, peering down to where she stood holding her breath. She flattened herself against the bricks, pushing herself as far into the shadows as possible. A strange sound came from above, a sharp scraping that was followed by a burst of orange light. Then, only a metre or so to her right, a lit match fell from the bridge, the flame tumbling quickly into the darkness before disappearing.

It was quickly followed by another match, this one falling in a wider arc, as though the person above had flicked it with some force.

What were they doing? Using the light from the matches to search the ledge? Why not just bring a torch?

Grace tried to flatten herself further against the wall, ignoring the way the rough bricks scraped her cheek through her Balaclava.

It felt like hours, but it must have only been seconds before the footsteps started again, this time continuing across to the other side.

Now was her chance.

Grace started to move, shuffling her feet along the ledge with as much speed as she dared until she reached the bank. As quietly as she could, she stepped from the ledge on to the verge, slowly backing away as she watched the figure moving along the bridge. He wore a hooded top, his face concealed.

He stood for a moment, leaning over the wall to look down before striking another match and tossing it into the blackness. Then he crossed back to Grace's side of the bridge. Again, he peered down, searching the ledge that Grace had been on only seconds before.

It was time to leave.

Grace turned, only to see a face inches from hers. She tried to scream, but a hand reached out to cover her mouth, the other taking her by the arm and pulling her towards the trees.

She pulled away, but the grip grew tighter as the other person spoke.

'It's me,' Pete whispered, slowly removing his hand from her face.

With both hands, Grace gripped at Pete's jacket. 'You scared me.'

'Sorry, but you were about to scream.'

Grace glanced over her shoulder at the stranger on the bridge. 'What now?'

'Now we leave.'

Securing her hand in his, Grace let Pete guide her along the bank.

'This way,' he whispered, squeezing her hand tightly. He pulled her deep into the thicket of trees, until the air around them was clogged with the scent of earth and fallen leaves. The bank was steep, the ground thick with tree roots, and on more than one occasion Grace stumbled, her trainers slipping in the dirt, but Pete was strong and his hand simply tightened around hers, lifting her back to her feet. Finally, they stopped and there was no sound other than their breathing.

Grace pulled off her Balaclava, relishing the cool air against her face. 'You think he's still there?' she whispered. 'What was he doing with those matches?'

'I don't know.'

'Where did Faith go? What happened?'

'She kept telling me she could hear something, that she thought she could see someone moving behind the trees. I went to take a look and the next thing I know, she screams and runs off back towards school.'

'You think it was the person on the bridge?'

'Who knows? I didn't see anyone until I made my way down from the bank.'

Grace shivered. 'I hope she's OK.'

'I'm sure she's fine,' Pete said. He placed an arm around Grace's shoulder and rubbed her arm. She leaned into him, grateful for the warmth. 'We should probably wait here a while though, just to make sure.'

Grace looked up at Pete, at the way his blond hair caught the moonlight. 'Thanks,' she said.

'For what?'

'For not leaving me.'

Pete shrugged and pulled her closer. 'Hey, it's what I'm here for, right?'

'I mean it, Pete. You're a great friend.'

He looked down at her and, just for a second, Grace thought she saw the lines of a frown etched across his forehead. 'Thanks. You too.'

They stood together in silence, waiting and listening until Grace could no longer stand the cold. 'He must have gone by now,' she said, her teeth chattering. 'Shall we head back?'

'Sure,' said Pete. 'If that's what you want.'

They made their way back along the bank, grabbing on to tree trunks for support. When they emerged from the thicket of trees, the bridge was empty.

'Looks like we're in the clear,' Pete said.

Grace tried to rub some warmth into her hands. 'Can we just get back to school now? I want to check on Faith.'

'Don't you want to see?' Pete flicked on his torch and shone it against the bridge, lighting Grace's artwork.

Grace stared. 'I didn't get the detailing on the tail quite right.'

Pete laughed softly and, even in the darkness, Grace could tell he was shaking his head at her. 'Always the perfectionist.'

'How will I ever get better if I can't criticize my own work?'

'You've done ninety-six of these things. Ninety-six! How can you still be questioning whether you've got the damn thing right?'

'Because I've got four more to do. The last one has to be perfect.'

'It's a graffiti tag, Grace. Hardly comparable to your final art project.'

'Actually, it's *more* important.' Grace took the torch from Pete, chewing her lip as she took in the work she and Trick had created. A dragon chasing its own tail. 'You sure it actually looks like the letter Q?'

'Yes, I'm sure. Would I ever lie to you?' He reached out to brush a strand of hair from her face and this time, he was definitely frowning. He opened his mouth to say something, but before he could, a twig snapped loudly behind them.

Pete turned, shining the torch beam into the darkness. Then came another crack, and another. Someone was moving quickly between the trees.

The beam swung wildly from side to side as Pete searched the shadows. Then the light picked out a hooded figure, disappearing behind a tree only metres from where they stood.

For a moment, nobody moved. Grace could just about see the outline of the figure behind the tree, his head turning from side to side as he looked for an escape route, but the only way out was to get to the road.

And that meant going through Grace and Pete.

11

The figure darted towards them, almost colliding with Grace. Pete grabbed at the stranger's arm and they struggled together, their feet slipping in the mud.

'Pete, let him go!' Grace cried, but it was too late.

With a final shove, the stranger pulled himself free and sent Pete flying backwards, disappearing into the darkness as he tumbled down the bank, his fall punctuated by the sickening sound of branches cracking beneath his weight.

Grace covered her mouth and turned to look at the silhouette standing before her, his shoulders rising and falling in time with his breathing. He stared at her for a few seconds, the glint of his eyes the only thing visible beneath his hood. Then he turned and ran into the shadows, leaving Grace standing alone on the steep verge.

Holding on to a tree for support, Grace leaned down and peered into the darkness below.

'Pete? Pete, can you hear me?' She stepped down the bank and her foot slipped, setting off a small avalanche of dirt and stones. She reached back and grabbed at the trunk to steady herself before continuing, inching her way slowly down the steep verge as the ground crumbled beneath her feet.

A low groan emerged from a bush to her right and she looked over to see a hand reaching out from the tangle of branches.

'Pete? Are you OK?'

'Yeah, but I think I've lost my torch. Can you give me a hand?'

Grace shuffled across to the bush and grabbed Pete's

hand. He pulled himself up, cursing loudly as the branches snapped against him. Wincing, he reached up to touch a shadow on his left cheek.

'Is that blood?' Grace asked, leaning in to take a closer look.

'It's fine. Just a—' His words were drowned out as another train blasted out of the tunnel below, filling the night air with noise.

Grace's hand tightened around Pete's as they huddled together, watching it rumble past.

Grace shuddered. 'You could have been down there,' she said.

For a moment Pete said nothing, then he tugged on Grace's hand. 'Let's just get back to Clifton.'

Grace stepped on to Pete's cupped hands and pulled herself up the wrought-iron fence. 'You really think Faith made it back to school?' she puffed, swinging a leg over the top of the railings.

'She definitely ran off in this direction,' Pete said, trying to secure a foothold against the railings. 'And I can't imagine anywhere else she would have gone.' He started to pull himself up, but his foot slipped against the metal.

'Come on,' Grace whispered, glancing nervously at the expanse of darkness behind Pete. Though she had already started to convince herself that the person on the bridge had nothing to do with them, she couldn't help but wonder if he was still lurking out there somewhere.

'I'm trying.' Pete secured a hand around one of the metal spikes that ran across the perimeter of the fence, designed to look like arrow heads and certainly *not* designed to be impaled in the legs of students breaking in and out of the school. His feet scrabbled against the railings as he reached up to grab at another spike.

'Ah ha,' he cried triumphantly, pulling his body up the rest of the way and carefully hooking a leg over. 'See? Just a simple matter of physics.' Gripping the spikes tightly, he manoeuvred his other leg over the fence and lowered himself down to the ground.

They crept towards the trees that lined the perimeter of the school grounds, keeping their bodies low and concealed within the shadows. Somewhere nearby, Sylvester the night watchman would be doing his rounds and Grace was quite aware that it would take a much better liar than her to explain why she was breaking back into school in the middle of the night.

To their right, Clifton Manor rose up into the night sky, a building that was a hotchpotch of doorways, arches and leaded windows, topped with sloping slate roofs and chimney stacks. Spiralling metal steps made up the fire escapes that coiled up the outside of the building. To Grace's left, the bell tower of St Nicholas' church stood behind another row of trees, in the disused and overgrown churchyard adjacent to the school grounds.

Since a fire had destroyed the school's reception at the beginning of the previous year, there had been a step up in safety and security, including the placement of security lights around the school grounds, hidden along the rooftops and around a number of the huge brick chimney stacks. Before they had set out on their first tagging mission, Pete had located them all and drew a map to show the paths they should take to avoid them. Now Grace knew the paths as well as she knew the boy who had drawn them.

She weaved her way through the trees towards the back of the school, pausing when she heard footsteps. Turning back to Pete, she raised her hands, indicating he should stop. They stood silently for a moment until Sylvester turned the corner of the main building, whistling as his heavy boots crunched along the gravel path that surrounded the school. He came to a stop under one of the streetlamps and pulled out his cigarettes, then slid one from the packet and held it between his lips as he patted his jacket pockets. In the shadows, his tall, thin frame looked somehow even wirier than usual, barely wider than the post he stood next to. His hand disappeared into a pocket, then re-emerged with a box of matches that he held up to his ear and shook.

Grace raised an eyebrow. Sylvester had always struck her as being a bit of an oddball and as she watched him strike one of the matches, staring at the flame intently before lighting his cigarette, she wondered how none of her friends could see it too.

Sylvester raised the match up in front of his eyes, the orange glow illuminating the sharp features of his face. Then he flicked the spent match into the bushes and continued on his way, alternating his whistling with deep drags on the cigarette.

'OK, let's go,' Pete said, starting to move again. 'We need to get back into the dorms before Sylvester notices the fire-escape door is unlocked.'

Grace nodded and stepped on to the pea-shingle driveway that curved around to the back of the dormitories. This was the riskiest part, crossing the gravel to get access to the fire door they had left unlocked by taping down the latches. Grace's foot sunk into the stones and she winced as they shifted, the crunching louder than usual in the silence of the night. With the smell of cigarette smoke clinging to the air around them, Grace could tell that Sylvester was still close by.

'Shh.'

'I'm trying to shh,' she snapped, taking another step. Her foot didn't land as heavily this time and she started to move a little faster, placing her feet as flat on the ground as she could. Barely able to hear Pete behind her, she glanced over her shoulder to see him pitching silently across the gravel.

'Let me guess,' she whispered. 'Just a matter of physics, right?'

Pete smiled. 'Exactly.'

Grace reached the fire door, bright white and contrasting horribly against the old brickwork of the building. She gave it a gentle nudge and when it opened she exhaled with relief.

She pushed the door slowly, peering down the dimly lit corridor. The hallway was empty, filled only with long shadows created by the dim night-lights that lined the corridors.

When Pete stepped in behind her, she peeled the tape from the latch and closed the door as gently and quietly as she could. It clicked into place and they waited together, barely breathing, until they were certain nobody had heard them.

'Let's check on Faith,' Grace whispered, leading Pete along the hallway to one of the many rooms. She stopped and rapped her fingers gently against the door.

It opened almost immediately to reveal a mass of curly auburn hair and two large, green eyes peering out over a button nose that most girls would kill for. Not that Faith knew that of course; all she could see was the red frizz of hair and the freckles she hated so much.

Faith lurched forwards, grabbing Grace in an embrace.

'Hey, hey,' Grace said, pushing her friend back gently.

Faith's eyes were red rimmed and blackened with smudged make-up. 'Grace, are you OK? I'm so sorry, I feel so bad for leaving you.' Her chin creased and Grace pushed into the room, dragging Pete with her.

'I tried to call you,' Faith said, almost accusingly. 'You didn't answer your phone.'

Pete smacked his head and pulled a mobile from his pocket. 'I was holding it for her,' he said. 'In case she dropped it on the bridge.'

Grace took her phone and, sure enough, the screen flashed up with eleven missed calls, all from Faith. 'That's a lot of calls.'

Faith exhaled slowly and flapped at her eyes with her hands. 'I know, I know. I'm sorry. I was just so scared, Grace. He was just standing there in the bushes, watching us, so I just ran, and . . .' Faith looked at Pete. 'You saw him too, right?'

'Actually,' said Pete, 'I didn't see anyone.'

Faith's cheeks flushed red. 'But he was there.' She turned back to Grace. 'I'm telling you, there was someone standing there, as real as I'm standing in front of you right now.'

'OK,' Grace said. 'It's OK, we believe you.'

Faith turned to Pete. 'Do you believe me?' she asked, her voice quiet. Before he had the chance to answer, Faith gasped and rushed towards him, almost knocking Grace over. 'Pete, what happened to your face?' She reached out to touch his cheek, then thought better of it, instead wringing her hands as she examined the smear of blood.

Pete touched the scratch with his fingertips and glanced at Grace. 'Just caught it on a branch, it's fine.'

Grace nodded. They had agreed, for now at least, to leave out the part where the stranger had attacked them.

'But it looks sore,' Faith insisted.

'She's right,' said Grace. 'We should at least clean it. I've got some first-aid stuff in my room.'

Pete held up his hands. 'Honestly, I'm OK, I can sort it.'

Grace tutted. 'Don't be silly. If you go to bed like that

you'll wake up with some nasty infection.' She smiled and pinched his chin. 'We can't have that handsome face left with a scar now, can we?'

Pete grinned back.

'Come on then.' Faith took Pete by the hand and pulled him towards the door. 'Grace's room it is.'

Grace's room was even smaller than Faith's, just large enough for a single bed, a few pieces of bedroom furniture and a tiny sink in the corner with a mirror bolted on to the wall above. The decor was the same in all the bedrooms, a slightly grubby cream colour that Grace would never have chosen herself, along with dark blue curtains that failed miserably to block out the early morning sunlight.

With the door closed and the three of them huddled together by Grace's bed, the room had never felt so cramped.

Without a word, Pete sat on Grace's single bed and looked around at the walls, most of which were covered with photographs and posters.

On the wall beside Grace's bed were pictures of her father and her brother, Jack. Beside them was the last picture that had been taken of her mother before she died, holding Grace in the hospital just after she had been born. Grace looked a lot like her mother, everyone who saw the pictures said so. She liked that, but kind of wished she looked at least a little like her father. But Jack had got those genes, it seemed.

Jack, so much like his father in every way. The same

chiselled jawline, the same intelligence, the same career; Jack was at medical school training to be a doctor while Grace's father worked as a spinal surgeon in Singapore. There was no doubt about it; he was the golden child, the one who succeeded at everything.

Almost everything.

Forcing herself to look away from the picture, Grace found her first-aid kit and turned towards Pete with an antiseptic-soaked cotton pad.

He winced as she wiped it on his cheek. 'Ow, that stings.'

'It's disinfectant, of course it stings. Now man up.'

'Here, let me.' Faith took the pad from Grace and sat on the bed next to Pete. She reached for his chin and turned his face towards her before dabbing gently at the wound.

Grace had never seen Faith act so forward and confident with a boy. She felt suddenly awkward, like she was intruding on someone else's moment, until Pete moved back from Faith's touch.

'You know what?' he said, pushing Faith's hand away. 'I think we're done.'

'Oh, OK.' Faith stood up, folding the bloody cotton pad as she continued to stare at Pete, who seemed to be doing his best to avoid her gaze.

When the silence became unbearable, Grace cleared her throat. 'Over there,' she said, pointing to a bin beneath her sink.

'Oh, yeah. Right.' Faith placed the pad in the bin and

wiped her hands on her pyjama trousers. 'I guess we should all get some sleep,' she said, staring at Pete again.

Pete slowly rose from the bed. 'Uh, yeah. Sure.'

For a moment the three of them stood together in continued silence, until finally Pete moved towards the door. 'OK. Goodnight then.' He looked back at Grace as he walked out, his brow furrowed.

Faith followed after him. 'Night, Grace.' As she pulled the door closed, she paused, her eyes shifting as she spoke. 'I really did see someone. I promise.'

Grace nodded, though her smile felt somehow false. When the door closed, her smile faded and she sat on her bed, replaying the night's events. Faith must be telling the truth, because Grace had seen the figure herself, first walking on the bridge, then lurking in the trees before Pete had been thrown down the bank. And yet something just didn't feel quite right.

Grace reached for her mobile. She had a sudden urge to talk to her father and although she wouldn't tell him about the night's events, it might make her feel better just to hear his voice.

It was late morning in Singapore and her father would probably be at work. She hit the dial button, but a recorded female voice told her that, unfortunately, there was not enough credit to connect her call.

With a sigh, she replaced the phone on her bedside table and turned out her light.

Though she had managed to convince herself that the

hooded figure on the bridge was probably just some local nutter, she couldn't help but wonder. What if he wasn't? What if he had followed them to the bridge and hidden in the trees, just to watch?

She thought back to the way he had stood on the bridge, lighting match after match and tossing them down into the darkness. There was something about it that made her skin crawl.

Something that made her think that he was there to do more than just watch.

But what?

RETURN OF THE CLIFTON MANOR 100 SOCIETY?

Speculation has arisen that a gang of vandals known only as 'The 100 Society' is once again targeting local buildings and landmarks. Believed to have originated at the prestigious Clifton Manor School, The 100 Society was founded more than twenty years ago by the notorious graffiti artist known only as 'A'. While the anonymous artist's work now sells for millions, he has created a legacy of copycats, each hoping to 'tag' the same hundred locations. To identify the work as their own, each artist uses a different letter of the alphabet and it is believed that the current attempt is being made using the letter Q.

To date, there have been sixteen known attempts by vandals to place their own tags alongside the originals. These attempts have resulted in injury to a number of Clifton Manor students. The arrest of a prominent politician's son on a charge of vandalism seven years ago brought fresh scandal to the school, damaging the reputation of Clifton Manor and leading to a marked decline in pupil intake. As a result, five years ago the school employed a zero-tolerance policy that meant anyone caught engaging in an attempt to join The 100 Society would be immediately expelled.

The headmaster of Clifton Manor School was last night unavailable for comment.

Police are appealing for information.

'Cross is going to flip when he sees this.' Grace grabbed the paper from Ed Krazinski's hands.

'Not just Cross.' Ed looked towards the closed office door on the other side of the art studio. Inside, their elderly art teacher Miss Stone was supposed to be working, although Grace was sure she had heard the occasional snore coming from within. Miss Stone rarely interrupted their work any more, and other than occasionally popping into the studio to offer constructive criticism, left them to complete their projects undisturbed. At almost seventy years of age, she had taught at the school for most of her life and had become more a part of the furniture than a teacher.

'Then get rid of it before she comes out of her office.' Ed made an unsuccessful swipe for it.

'But I haven't finished reading it!' Grace spun away, her eyes skimming the article as Ed lunged forwards. At a couple of inches over six foot, he towered over her, his maroon school tie dangling in her face. 'I mean it, Becker, give it to me.'

His hands scrabbled at her arm, but she slipped from his grasp and darted behind a desk. 'Wait, let me finish looking at the photo.'

'Fine,' he said, holding his hands up in defeat. 'I've got more important things to do anyway.' He grabbed the huge headphones that were slung around his neck and dragged them up over his ears, then turned to the large, unfinished painting behind him.

'Morning.' Trick stood in the doorway, his shirt untucked beneath his maroon blazer. He grinned at Grace, though he looked a little sheepish behind the smile.

'What the hell happened to you last night?' She flung the newspaper at him and he ducked back into the corridor.

His face reappeared, framed by an untidy mop of black curls. 'Easy, tiger,' he said, checking she wasn't holding anything else that could be used as a missile. 'You're OK, aren't you?'

'No thanks to you,' Grace snapped, following Trick into the corridor and jabbing a finger at his chest.

'Ow!' He batted her hand away. 'Come on, if I'd have thought for a second that you couldn't look after yourself I would have stayed.'

'Yeah, right. You only ever think about one person, Patrick Turner.'

'Patrick?' Trick rubbed at his chest. 'You really are mad at me, aren't you?'

Seeing the genuine look of dismay on his face made Grace soften for a moment, but then she glanced up to see Pete walking down the corridor towards them. She grabbed Trick's sleeve and forced him around. 'Yes I am, but he's the one you should be apologising to.'

Trick stared at the scratch on Pete's face, still swollen and lined with dry blood. 'What happened?'

Pete looked at Grace. 'I'm fine.'

'No,' Grace snapped. 'It's not fine.' She glanced over her shoulder to check they couldn't be overheard by anyone in the studio. 'That guy on the bridge came back.'

'When?' Trick asked.

'Just after you left. He did that to Pete.' She gestured towards Pete's face.

'Seriously?'

'Seriously. But keep it between us, OK? I don't want to freak out the others.'

Trick looked at Pete. 'Hey, sorry.'

Pete held up a hand. 'Nothing to worry about.'

'Actually,' said Grace, 'that's not entirely true.' She led him into the studio and spread Ed's newspaper out on her desk.

Removing his blazer, Pete examined the front page over her shoulder. 'Oh man. That's not good.'

'Hey, we're famous!' Trick reached for the paper and started to examine the article.

Grace exhaled. 'It's not funny.'

'Come on,' said Trick. He shrugged off his blazer to reveal the full sleeve of tattoos on his left arm. 'It's kind of cool.'

'You're an idiot.' Grace pulled the paper from Trick's hand and stared at the photograph on the front page. It was her work all right. Hers and Trick's, to be precise. It was one of their first tags, on the gas tower just outside of town. That one had been easy. No fences, no barbed wire and a nice set of steps to take them up to the side of the tower that still bore the previous sixteen attempts made by those hoping to join The 100 Society.

'I don't know why it's of such interest, anyway,' she said, pulling the paper from Trick and flinging it into the bin.

'You really can't see it?' asked Trick. 'A bunch of privately educated kids breaking the law? It's usually the sort of thing that only riffraff like me engage in, right?'

'Oh, get over yourself,' said Grace. 'So you're from the other side of town. Who's ever made a big deal of it?'

Trick raised an eyebrow. 'Well, those two for a start.'

Grace glanced up as a tall, blonde and beautiful girl walked into the room, closely followed by a shorter boy, his face almost obscured by his long hair. The girl skipped straight over to Ed and pulled at his headphones. He turned to her and smiled before bending to kiss her tenderly on the lips.

The boy's entrance was far less dramatic. He had more of a shuffle than a walk, one designed to complement his hunched shoulders and bowed head. He moved towards the back of the room, the lenses of his glasses magnifying his eyes to almost comical proportions.

'OK, fine,' she whispered, 'but other than them.'

'What are we talking about?' The perfect face smiling the perfect smile appeared at Grace's side. She stared at Trick's tattoos, not bothering to cover her distaste.

'Shallowness,' said Trick, looking down pointedly at the girl's designer shoes.

'Oh, really?' Cassie looked at Trick with big, made-up eyes. 'So,' she asked, 'what were you saying? 'Cause, you know, it could really help with my project.'

'So ironic,' Trick muttered, turning his back on Cassie and Grace.

'Yeah, irony,' Cassie said, nodding enthusiastically. 'That's exactly what I'm going for with my project.'

Trick smirked. 'Really, Cassie? Explain the irony to me, just one more time.'

'OK,' said Cassie, skipping towards her own desk and either ignoring or not noticing the sarcasm in Trick's voice. 'You see, the whole concept of, like, beauty, is what is portrayed in the media, right? Like, everything is made beautiful with airbrushing?'

'Right,' Trick said slowly, ignoring the kick on his ankle from Grace.

'OK, so, like, what if we deconstructed beauty, but used airbrushes to do the deconstruction?' She beamed, exposing a row of flawless, brilliant white teeth.

Grace looked at Cassie's project – large photographs that depicted natural beauty; a swan, a landscape, a newborn baby. Each one airbrushed in parts to look ugly and deformed. 'You've got to admit it Trick, the girl's on to something.'

Cassie smiled at Grace and reached for the airbrush that was laid out on the desk next to her camera. She flicked her hair – long and blonde and styled to perfection.

Trick snorted. '*She* wants to talk about deconstruction of beauty? Perhaps she needs to look in the mirror and deconstruct some of the make-up that's trowelled on to her face.'

'She's harmless and you know it. Besides, she's a damn good photographer and our blog would be nothing without her pictures. Trick? Are you listening to me?'

Trick said nothing, his attention switching to the boy Cassie had walked in with.

Daniel.

He had barely looked at Grace in all the time they had worked in the studio together, let alone spoken to her. Now, he was staring at her and Trick through the thick lenses of his glasses.

'What are you looking at?' Trick stood up, the muscles in his arms clenching.

Daniel pushed the dark plastic frames up his nose. 'Don't talk about Cassie like that.'

At the mention of her name, Cassie glanced up. 'What's going on?'

'He was talking about you, Cassie,' said Daniel, his eyes still trained on Trick. His long mousy hair hung around his face in lank strands, partly obscuring his features

'Well, you know what they say,' said Cassie, turning back to her work with a shrug, 'the only thing worse than being talked about is *not* being talked about.'

Daniel's eyebrows arched. 'But Cassie—'

'Ugh, Daniel, I don't care!' she snapped, spinning to face him. 'For the last time, you don't have to stand up for me. You're not my boyfriend and you never will be.'

A deep crimson rose up Daniel's neck, creeping across his face until it looked not too dissimilar to one of the shades on his canvas. It was a bizarre painting, made up almost entirely of vivid red and orange strokes that didn't seem to take any recognisable form, though it still had some kind of hypnotic quality that meant Grace often found herself staring at it during her time in the studio.

'You heard the girl,' said Trick. 'Never will be. Now keep out of it.'

Grace laid a hand on Trick's arm. 'That's enough,' she said quietly.

'Whatever.' Trick turned to his work and reached into his pocket for his earphones, ones that were only a fraction of the size of Ed's. When Grace heard the thumping bass of some song she'd never heard of, she knew the conversation was over.

'You OK?' Pete asked as she moved to take her place at the desk next to his.

'What is the deal with that guy?' she asked quietly, jerking her head in Daniel's direction. 'You used to hang out with him.'

Pete shrugged. 'We were friends for a few years. People change, I guess. Grow apart. We don't talk any more.'

'But why the attitude?'

'Who knows? He obviously has a thing for the beauty queen over there, and a rather strong dislike for our friend Patrick.'

Grace looked at Trick, taking in the tight black trousers that barely passed for uniform, along with the bright trainers that *definitely* didn't pass for uniform and which

Pete said could blind a man at twenty paces. Not to mention the school shirt, sleeves rolled up high to expose the tattoos that would get him kicked out of school if ever discovered. It was like he dressed that way on purpose, waiting for someone to mention his appearance and how he was so different to the rest of them.

'This is looking good, Grace.'

Grace blinked. Miss Stone was peering over Grace's shoulder at her canvas. She pointed with a shaky, arthritic finger at the painting Grace had entitled 'Forever', a picture of two people entwined in an embrace, both in silhouette. 'Nice brushwork here.' She patted Grace's shoulder. 'Just like your brother.'

'Thanks.' Grace forced a smile as Miss Stone moved on to where Pete sat, struggling to re-attach what looked like an arm to the clay sculpture he had been working on after his latest attempt at a painting had failed.

'My, my,' Miss Stone said, taking the small, half-moon specs that hung around her neck. She perched them on the end of her nose and leaned in to take a closer look. 'What have we here?'

Pete placed his head in his hands and groaned. 'I don't know. I give up.'

Miss Stone laid a wrinkled hand on Pete's shoulder and tutted at him. 'No you don't, my dear. Mark my words, one of these days you are going to bring a piece of art to life.' Her eyes twinkled as she smiled. 'I can see it in you.'

'I don't know about that, but thanks anyway.'

As Miss Stone shuffled off towards Ed's canvas, there was a dull thud as Pete's clay sculpture gave up altogether and collapsed on to the table. Grace stifled a giggle. 'Sorry,' she said, reaching out to help him. 'I'm not laughing at you.'

Pete smiled and shook his head. 'It's fine, honestly. I guess it is kind of funny.' He sighed and poked at his collapsed sculpture. 'Sometimes I wonder why I took this class.'

'Why *did* you take it? It's not like you don't have enough on your plate with all the maths and science.'

Before Pete had a chance to answer, the door behind them flew open, smashing into the wall. Miss Stone clutched at the back of a chair in surprise, a hand covering her chest. Even Ed turned from his work, pulling the headphones from his ears.

Mr Cross, the headmaster of Clifton Manor, stepped into the art studio, his bulk almost filling the doorframe. His face was scarlet, his eyes huge and wild.

A tightness gripped Grace's throat.

In Cross's hand was a copy of the same newspaper she had just thrown into the bin. The same newspaper that had her artwork splashed across the front page for all the world to see.

The newspaper landed on the desk next to Grace and Pete.

'Would somebody care to explain this to me?' Cross's thick Irish accent filled the room. Then he addressed Miss Stone, his tone softening. 'Terribly sorry to interrupt you, Miss Stone.'

She nodded quickly, waving a hand for him to carry on.

Grace swallowed. If she looked away from the paper it would be obvious she was trying to hide something, but if she looked directly at him, he would see the forced expression on her face, the one she knew was doing nothing to hide her guilt. So she just stared at the front page, hoping to look like someone who had never seen the picture before.

Cross looked around the room, his wide eyes stopping

on each student as he waited for an answer. His gaze settled on Trick, who had managed to quickly roll his sleeves down to his wrists, covering all his tattoos. 'I know somebody knows who did this,' he said.

Trick laid a hand on his chest. 'Me? You're pinning this on me?' He laughed. 'Oh yeah, that sounds about right. Blame it on the scholarship kid.'

Classic Trick. Always the first to defend himself with such vehement denial, almost like a reflex he had developed over the years. To be fair, he was usually involved in most of the things he was accused of, whether he had meant to be or not. Trick was one of those guys who seemed to attract trouble; even if he just happened to stumble across someone else's misadventure, somehow he would end up in the thick of it.

Cross raised a thick eyebrow. 'Did I blame it on you, Patrick?'

Trick muttered under his breath, his curls falling across his forehead and darkening his eyes.

'What was that, Patrick?'

'Nothing, sir.' He leaned back in his seat, his biceps flexing as he crossed his arms. For a moment he made eye contact with Grace and she saw the flicker of a smile play across his lips, his face lightening as he looked at her. Feeling a sudden rush of heat to her face, Grace looked away.

Cross nodded. 'It's been seven years,' he said, addressing all of the students. 'Seven years since I've had to put up with this,' he gestured towards the newspaper, 'and I'm not planning on going through it all again.' He straightened his tie, emblazoned with the same school logo featured on the students' blazers: a two-headed eagle, wings spread wide across a golden shield.

A voice came from the back of the room. 'What makes you think it was any of us?'

The whole class turned to Daniel, his big eyes flicking in Cassie's direction, looking for her approval.

'Let me just say this,' said Cross, taking another step into the room and pointing a meaty finger at Daniel, 'and let me be very, very clear on the matter.' The tone and volume of his voice had lowered, indicating he was not a man to be messed with. 'Anybody, and I mean anybody caught defacing school property, or any other property for that matter, will be immediately excluded from Clifton.' He looked at Trick. 'Do I make myself clear?'

Trick looked away, but nodded.

'Not only that,' Cross continued, his voice gaining an altogether nastier edge, 'if I see any further evidence of this, I will cancel next Wednesday's exhibition.'

There was a collective gasp and Ed rose to his feet. 'You can't. We've spent the last year working towards that show.' The pitch of his voice rose as he spoke. 'There are supposed to be talent spotters there, from galleries, from universities. Please, don't cancel.'

Beside Ed, Cassie chewed her lip and stared at the ground. She looked like she was on the verge of tears, although Grace couldn't think of a time she had ever seen Cassie cry.

There was a flicker of triumph in Cross's smile as he took in the students' desperation. 'Well then, let's just hope whoever is responsible for this understands that.'

Ed slowly sank into his seat, his head in his hands.

'In the meantime,' Cross continued, turning towards the door, 'I've asked Mr Sylvester to be extra vigilant.'

Grace hadn't noticed the figure lurking in the doorway until he stepped into the room with a rather satisfied smile. 'That's right,' said Sylvester, his small dark eyes flicking from student to student while he pointed at them with a bony, nicotine-stained finger. 'I've got my eye on you lot.' He smiled, his teeth a similar shade to the yellow on his fingers.

Grace grimaced; the idea of Sylvester watching her was a little more than she could bear.

'I have my ways,' Sylvester said, smiling. 'I have ways of finding things out.' He leaned against the doorway, arms folded, and winked at Grace. She looked away and saw Pete trying not to laugh at her reaction.

'Thank you, Mr Sylvester.' Cross cleared his throat and placed a hand on Sylvester's shoulder, a firm indication that he was to stop talking. Then he gave a final, pointed look at the class. 'One more time,' he said. 'Any more graffiti means no art show. Am I understood?'

Only when he had received agreement from the students did he turn and walk out. Sylvester offered a quick salute to the class before following after Cross.

'Oh dear, oh dear,' Miss Stone said, shaking her head. She plucked the glasses from the end of her nose and focused on Trick. 'I suppose you're going to tell me you know nothing about this, Mr Turner?'

Trick flushed a bright red. Grace smiled. She knew of no one other than Miss Stone who could reduce Patrick Turner to a blushing mess.

Trick said nothing.

'You be careful,' Miss Stone said, wagging a finger in his direction. 'I don't want to lose my favourite student.'

His face grew redder and Miss Stone's eyes sparkled. She looked at the rest of the class, one by one. 'I don't want to lose *any* of my favourites,' she said, 'so you just make sure you take extra care with . . .' She paused and waved her hand dismissively, 'whatever it is you kids are up to.' She shuffled towards her office, yawning. 'Now, I have some work to do, so please don't come disturbing me. Understood?'

The class nodded.

Miss Stone started to close her office door behind her, then paused. 'One last thing,' she called over her shoulder. 'A dragon is a rather inspired shape for a letter Q, if you ask me. Haven't seen one that original since the class that did the letter K. Well worth looking up.' She looked at Grace and winked. 'You could ask your brother about that one.' And with that, the office door clicked shut.

'Wait,' said Ed, turning to Grace. 'Your brother is in The 100 Society?'

'Actually,' Grace said, 'he didn't make it. They got the first seventy tags and gave up.'

'Isn't he in medical school now?'

'Yep.' Grace scowled. 'He's a regular genius.'

There was a moment of silence, until Ed cleared his throat. 'So. What do we do now?' He looked at Grace. 'It's your call.'

'How's it my call?'

'Uh, because it was your idea in the first place?' said Trick.

'How does that make it my call? You each made the decision to join.' She turned to Ed. 'In fact, you and Cassie begged to be involved. I know how much this means to you, Ed.'

'I'm not saying it's not important to me, Grace.' Ed looked at Cassie. 'To both of us. I know we can't exactly write about it on our CVs but, unofficially, being a part of The 100 Society is like having a golden ticket into some of the best art colleges around.'

Cassie nodded. 'But none of that means anything if we get expelled first.'

Grace's heart sank as she looked at her friends. 'I'm not going to force any of you to carry on, but once the art show's over I'm going to finish this. There are only four more tags, I can manage them alone if I have to.'

From the other side of the studio, Daniel spoke, his

voice barely loud enough to be heard. 'You should be careful. Being out, alone at night. You never know who might be around.' He dabbed carefully at his canvas with a paintbrush, as though he hadn't said a word.

'What did you say?' Pete stood up, glaring at Daniel. 'Is that some sort of threat?'

Daniel turned, pushing the glasses up his nose. 'Nope. No threat here.'

'You don't know what you're talking about,' Pete said. 'You don't know how important this is.'

Daniel lifted his chin, this time looking Pete straight in the eye. 'All I'm saying is that it's easy to misjudge how much someone can want something.'

'You know,' Grace said, 'you can join us if you really want to, Daniel.'

Daniel laughed, though it sounded hollow. 'I'd rather die than be a part of your dumb 100 Society.'

'It's not dumb,' Cassie snapped. 'It's fun and if you can't see that, then it's your loss.'

Daniel's face darkened. 'Do you think it'll be fun when you get expelled? I could go and tell Cross right now and then I wouldn't have to look at any of you ever again.'

'You wouldn't dare,' Trick said, his voice low.

'No, he wouldn't dare,' Pete cut in, his eyes trained on Daniel. 'Because he's not the only one with information that could get someone expelled. Isn't that right, Daniel?'

Daniel glared at Pete. 'I don't know what you're talking about.'

Trick raised an eyebrow. 'Now, this sounds interesting.'

'It's got nothing to do with you, Patrick,' Daniel sneered, pushing his glasses up his nose.

Trick stood up, knocking his stool over. 'I dare you to call me that again.'

Daniel picked up his bag. 'No thanks. Besides, I've got better things to do than listen to you lot banging on about something you'll never even finish.' On his way out through the door, he turned to Grace. 'Just watch yourself,' he said.

Then he was gone.

Grace pushed what she could only imagine was some kind of casserole around her plate while Faith watched her, chewing slowly. 'I don't think you're going to make it any better by playing with it,' she said, swallowing with a grimace and laying her fork down

'I'm not hungry,' Grace replied, trying to ignore the shrill laughter of the Year Seven girls on the table beside them. She let her cutlery fall into the casserole and watched with disgust as the gravy oozed over the top of it.

'Hey guys.' Cassie placed her camera and her dinner tray on the table and sat down between Faith and the shrieking girls. There was no casserole on her plate, just a few salad leaves and tomatoes. When she saw Faith and Grace staring, she smiled. 'Got to play it safe,' she said, patting her flat stomach and grimacing at Grace's dinner. 'Besides how awful it looks, there's just no way of telling how many calories are in something like that.' She sat down and pulled out a lip gloss, pouting as she applied it in a tiny mirror.

On the other side of the hall Ed walked in, ducking, even though the large double doors had a good clearance overhead. In the crowded cafeteria he was easy to spot, towering above the other students.

Cassie raised her hand, waving to Ed. He smiled when he saw her, pushing his way through the crowds with something tucked tightly under his arm.

'Is that his laptop?' Faith asked. 'Why's he bringing that in here?'

'He spends more time with that thing than me,' Cassie said. She took a final look in her mirror, pouting as she tucked a strand of hair behind her ear, then smiled mischievously. 'Honestly, if I wasn't so fabulous I might even get a little jealous.'

Grace laughed. Though she had known her for a while, it was only when Cassie first started dating Ed that Grace began to see the girl behind the make-up. The person she had once thought of as a vacuous bimbo was actually an intelligent, talented girl who just so happened to like nice shoes. Plus, she made Ed happy, and that made Grace happy.

'Hi guys.' Ed set his computer down beside Cassie and raised the screen. 'OK, so I've updated the website—'

'Hey,' Cassie said, pouting again and pointing to her cheek.

Ed grinned. 'Sorry.' He leaned in for a quick kiss before turning back to the computer. 'OK, the website.'

Faith bit her lip. 'Ed, we can't do this in here, not when Cross is already on the warpath.' She glanced at the girls on the table beside them. 'You don't know who else is watching, either.'

'Don't forget Sylvester,' Grace said, raising a finger and pointing at Faith and Cassie. '*I'm watching you*,' she said, in her best Sylvester voice.

'Hey, heads up.' Faith lowered her eyes, but nodded towards the door of the cafeteria. Grace turned to see Daniel, his head lowered as he shuffled into the room.

'Why does he walk like that?' Cassie asked. 'He's so not doing his posture any favours.'

Daniel stopped, staring at them from behind his thick glasses and the tresses of greasy hair.

Taking a deep breath, Grace stood up. 'Daniel?'

He turned and began pushing his way back through the crowd.

'Wait a second.'

Daniel glanced around nervously. 'What?' he asked, stepping back. 'What do you want?'

'I want to talk to you.'

He didn't look at her. With his eyes fixed on his feet, he didn't make a sound.

44

'I remember a few years ago, we were in the same maths class.'

'So?'

'You were different then. You used to talk to us. I remember you used to tell jokes. You were . . .' She searched for the right word. 'I don't know. *Happy*.'

He snorted and looked away.

'Why are you so angry with us?' she asked. 'What have we done, Daniel?'

He pushed his glasses up his nose. 'I shouldn't be talking to you.'

'What? Why?'

'It doesn't matter. Just stay away from me.' He pushed his hair back behind his ear, fully exposing his face. He looked tired.

'Sure,' Grace said. 'If that's really what you want.'

Daniel started to walk away. Then he stopped and turned back. 'Watch yourself,' he said. 'Be careful what you tell people, OK?'

Grace frowned. 'Sure. OK.' She walked back to the table, where the others sat staring at her.

'What was all that about?' Faith asked.

'I . . .' She paused. 'I really don't know.'

'There's nothing *to* know,' said Ed, his fingers dancing across the keyboard. 'The guy's a weirdo, end of story. Now can we please just concentrate on this?'

Cassie sighed. 'What? What is so important that it cannot possibly wait another second?'

Ed turned the screen of his laptop to face the girls.

'That's our blog,' Grace said, frowning.

'Right. What do you notice?'

Grace pulled the computer to her side of the table and scrolled through the various posts. 'I don't know. It looks the same as it always does.'

'Exactly.'

'You're going to have to help us out here a little.'

Ed rolled his eyes and leaned across the table, his tie almost dangling in Grace's casserole. He pointed at the screen and Grace gasped. 'That's the same photograph that was in the paper! They must have taken it from the blog.'

Faith groaned. 'Oh, this is bad. This is really bad. If the papers have found it, who's to say Cross won't?'

'There's no way Cross will find this,' said Ed. 'It's buried too deep in the net and I'm pretty sure that anyone over the age of twenty-five has neither the time nor the inclination to go looking for this kind of stuff.'

'Then how did the newspapers find it?'

Ed shook his head. 'I really don't know. That's what doesn't make sense. If they had found the website wouldn't they have mentioned it? Or even published a link?'

'That's true,' Grace said. 'Someone else must have found the picture and passed it on to the press.'

'So what do we do?' Faith asked.

'We carry on as normal.' Grace turned to Cassie. 'And that includes getting pictures of last night's work, right?'

Cassie picked up her camera. 'I'm on it. In fact, I'd better get going before the sun goes down. I need some good daylight pictures of that tag on the railway bridge. Besides, I don't fancy being there in the dark, especially after your little encounter last night.'

'You want me to come with you?' Ed asked, taking Cassie's hand.

She shook her head. 'I'll be fine. Besides, if anyone tries to mess with me, they can eat lens.' Cassie wielded her camera and Ed ducked as the telescopic lens narrowly missed his head.

'That thing's huge,' Ed said, shaking his head. 'Why can't you just use a digital camera like normal people?'

Cassie lifted the camera and snapped a picture of Ed, the flash making him blink. 'Because it's art, *dah-ling*. Besides, some people happen to look great on film.' She winked at Ed and kissed him on the cheek before disappearing into the crowd.

Grace started to click through the pages of the blog, looking at all of the photographs of her work, each one taken by Cassie and uploaded by Ed. 'Is there a way of tracing who's looked at the blog?' she asked. 'Could we identify the person who stole the picture?'

'It depends,' Ed said. 'We could look at site traffic and find out the IP addresses of visitors, but that only tells us their location. No names.'

Grace nodded and clicked on the next page. As she did so, an image flashed up on the screen, making her jump.

'What the . . . ?' Clutching a hand to her chest, she stared at the picture, which took up almost the whole screen.

It was a hooded grim reaper with a scythe in one hand, the other pointing at Grace with a long, bony finger.

'What is it?' Ed asked, leaning over to look. 'Hey, what did you do?'

Grace held up her hands. 'I didn't do anything,' she said. 'It just appeared.'

'What is that?' Faith asked, pointing at a text box that had appeared beneath the reaper.

'It's a dialogue box.' Ed pulled the computer away from Grace and started typing. 'It's frozen,' he said with a groan. 'Must be some kind of virus. Nice one, Grace.'

'Hey,' she snapped. 'I told you, I didn't do anything.'

'You must have—' He stopped mid-sentence as the flashing cursor began to move across the dialogue box, leaving a trail of text behind it. '*You have been tagged. Let the games begin*,' he read out. 'What does that even mean?' He tapped at the keyboard, but nothing happened. Then, as quickly as it had appeared, the dialogue box and the grim reaper vanished.

For a moment nobody spoke.

'Was it a virus?' Faith asked.

'No. We were hacked.' Ed looked at Grace. 'Someone wanted us to see that.'

'But who?' asked Faith, her voice very small.

Grace swallowed, though her mouth suddenly felt very

dry. 'It's probably just some nut,' she said, hoping her lies sounded more convincing to the others than they did to herself. Ed was right; someone wanted them to see that message. This was personal. 'The internet's full of them.' She turned, suddenly feeling the need to check that nobody was lurking behind her.

'Just some nut?' Faith asked. 'You mean like the nut on the bridge? Or the nut who stole our picture and gave it to the papers?'

'She's right, Grace,' Ed said. 'There are a lot of coincidences here.'

'It's fine.' Grace forced a smile. 'As you said, just a few coincidences.' She looked at her watch, lowering her hand quickly when she saw it was shaking. 'Look, I've got some prep to do for tomorrow. I'll see you guys in the morning.' She rose from the table, leaving Ed and Faith staring at the computer screen. There was nothing to be gained from them seeing how shaken she was, especially when they were already on edge and questioning their involvement with The 100 Society.

Grace hurried through the dining room's large doors into the school's reception area. The front desk was unmanned, but members of staff still crisscrossed the hall, hurrying to meetings or to start supervising the younger students in their dorms.

The school's reception area was huge. Most of the timberwork had remained intact after the fire and the more damaged parts had been replaced with replica beams. The high ceilings and carved wood reminded Grace of the inside of a cathedral; beautiful in the daylight, yet somehow sinister at night when the hall was only lit by a few old lamps. A wide, wooden staircase led to the first floor of the building, one of the few original features of the hall with its carved wooden banisters and worn mahogany steps. On the wood-panelled wall above the staircase was the school crest; the two-headed eagle. Beneath the crest was the school motto, written in Latin.

Superbia et Fortitudo.

Pride and Courage.

Grace looked away, hating the way that the eagle's four beady eyes seemed to follow her as she walked across the room.

Another set of double doors took Grace into a long hall, lined with oil paintings of school alumni, all in unsmiling and austere poses. Mock lanterns hung on the walls, lighting the pictures just enough to make them appear slightly disfigured in the half-light. For a moment, Grace regretted leaving the dinner hall so quickly. When the corridors were empty like this, it made the school seem so much bigger. So much *spookier*.

She started to walk a little faster, her steps muffled by the long red carpet that lined the length of the hall. It would be quite easy, she thought, to follow someone along this corridor without being heard. And with all of the stairwells that led up to the lower school dormitories, there were plenty of places to hide.

At the next set of doors, Grace reached out to grab the handle, suddenly desperate to be in her own room. As she started to push, the handle was torn from her hand and she cried out in surprise.

'Sorry, didn't mean to scare you.' Sylvester stepped to one side, holding the door open for Grace to pass through.

Trying not to grimace at the stench of tobacco on his khaki uniform, Grace just about managed a smile of thanks as she stepped through the door.

'Night,' he said, as she continued down to her room. 'Don't let the bed-bugs bite.' He disappeared through the doorway, allowing it to slam closed behind him. The noise echoed along the stone hallway.

'Night,' Grace muttered, quickly pulling her key out of her pocket. She pushed it into the lock of her bedroom door, but it wouldn't turn. Frowning, she tried the handle and the door swung open.

It was already unlocked.

She stepped in and flicked on the light switch.

Immediately, she could tell that something was wrong. There was nothing massively obvious, no emptying of drawers or ransacking of cupboards, but it wasn't right.

The laptop that she always closed before leaving the room was open, displaying the photograph of her and her friends that she had set as her background wallpaper. Next to the laptop, her printer was blinking.

Perhaps she had forgotten to turn everything off, she

thought, although she couldn't remember the last time she had printed anything.

Yes, that must be it, because the alternative was something she didn't want to think about, even though she knew the alternative must be true.

Someone had been in her room.

6

Although it was well after midnight and Sylvester was somewhere close by on his nightly rounds, Grace knew Trick would be waiting for her.

Sure enough, as she turned the corner, she saw him lying at the foot of one of the dorm stairwells, stretched out on the stone floor with his forearm draped across his eyes.

'Sylvester's just done his rounds,' he said without looking up. 'We've probably got another hour before he comes back this way.'

Grace nodded and pulled her dressing gown a little tighter around her body before sitting on the bottom step of the spiral staircase. The cold stone immediately sent a chill through her and for a moment she questioned her sanity, coming out here this late at night.

'Did you hear about the hacker?' she asked.

'Yep. I don't think Ed was too pleased with the way you just upped and left though.'

'I didn't want to make a big deal of it.'

He peered out at her from behind his forearm. 'Isn't it a big deal?'

Grace shrugged. 'I don't know. I mean, it could all just be coincidence, right?' She remembered her unlocked bedroom door and immediately pushed away the thought.

'It could be. Or, maybe you want to finish The 100 Society badly enough to ignore the fact that someone's messing with you.'

Grace tutted, irritated at how well Trick could read her.

Trick yawned and stretched, his muscles flexing beneath his inked skin. Grace looked away, grateful for the shadows that hid the redness in her face.

The first time Grace had found him in the dorm corridors was at the beginning of the previous year, not long after he had started his scholarship at Clifton. Unable to sleep, she had decided to go and make some toast in the shared kitchen. She liked the way her feet padded almost silently along the corridors, like she was a spirit floating through the building. With its Gothic architecture, she could imagine that if ghosts really did exist, Clifton would almost be guaranteed to have a few spectres lurking in the nooks and crannies of the old brickwork or up in the beams that crisscrossed the high, arched ceilings.

On that first night over a year ago, Grace had found him sitting in the shadows at the foot of the spiral staircase leading up to the attic space that was used for luggage storage. She had frozen, staring at the unmoving silhouette who hadn't yet noticed her.

He had been sitting cross-legged on the flagstones, wearing only a pair of baggy pyjama trousers. His head was bowed, the dark curls of his hair covering his eyes and most of his face. But she could see his mouth, the bee-stung lips that she would soon find to be capable of delivering such cutting remarks. Back then, he only had a few tattoos covering his left shoulder and the top of his arm, the colours of the ink blending perfectly with his olive skin. It was the first time she had seen them and she had stared for a while, examining the intricate designs and pictures.

Then he had looked up. 'Hey,' he'd said, like he wasn't surprised to see someone else up and about in the middle of the night.

'Hi.' She'd shifted awkwardly.

'You're in my art class.'

'Yeah. I'm Grace.' She had stepped forwards, closer towards him and his dark eyes.

'Trick.'

'Excuse me?'

'My name's Trick.'

'Your name is Trick?'

'Short for Patrick.'

She'd paused. 'I thought Pat was short for Patrick.'

'Oh. Well, sorry about that.' He had raised an eyebrow,

then held out a hand as though inviting her to walk past him, but the hunger that had driven her out of her bed had vanished.

'I was just . . .' She'd faltered, unsure of what to say to this boy who was now staring at her, the smallest smile playing across his lips.

'I was actually just heading back to bed myself,' he'd said, finally breaking the silence. He stood up and, in a matter of seconds, he was gone.

The next night she had set her alarm, just to see. Sure enough, there was the new boy at the foot of the stairwell and although he looked surprised to see her, he had shuffled over a little to make a space and she'd lowered herself on the cold stone floor next to him.

Almost in the exact same position in which they now sat, side by side.

Suddenly unsure of why she had come here tonight, Grace yawned. 'I'm tired, I think I'm going to go back to bed.'

'Wait.' Trick pulled out a familiar looking sheet of paper. 'Is that what I think it is?'

'Depends on what you think it is.'

Grace snatched the paper from Trick's hand. 'The 100 Society list? Where did you get this anyway? We agreed to only have one copy of it, on my computer.' She waved it at him. 'I thought we were trying to keep evidence to a minimum?'

Trick shrugged. 'I found it in the art room.'

'Why would I leave it in the art room?'

'Who knows why you do anything? That reminds me,' he said, reaching into his pocket and pulling out a mobile. 'You left this in the studio, too. Numbskull.'

'My phone?' She took her mobile from Trick, quickly checking for any missed calls. When the screen came up blank, she sighed.

'Were you expecting a call?'

'Just my dad. I haven't heard from him in a while.'

Trick shuffled closer and Grace was able to feel his warmth through the material of her dressing gown. 'Think about something else, then.' When Grace looked at him blankly, he laughed and pointed to the sheet of paper in her hand.

'Oh. Are we really going to do this now?'

'Yes, Grace. You're the one who keeps banging on about finishing it.'

With a sigh, she unfolded the paper to reveal The 100 Society list.

'Wow, we really didn't do ourselves any favours by doing the easy ones first, did we?'

'You didn't seem to think the railway bridge was easy.'

'It would have been easier if you hadn't been such a jerk.'

'So where next?' Trick asked, deliberately ignoring her comment.

'We follow the order,' she said firmly.

Trick leaned in to get a closer look and grimaced. 'Lost

Souls Bridge? I think I might sit that one out.'

'Oh, really? I thought bridges didn't bother—'

Trick grabbed her wrist, stopping Grace mid-sentence as he raised a finger to his lips. 'What was that?' he whispered.

'What was what?'

'Shh, listen.'

Then Grace heard it. Approaching footsteps from one of the other corridors.

Trick took her hand and, without a word, began to lead her up the stone steps until the curve of the spiral had hidden them from view.

Grace peered over the top of the stone banister, hoping the shadows would be enough to keep them hidden.

'Is it Sylvester?' she whispered, turning back to Trick.

It didn't sound like Sylvester; his boots were heavy and these footsteps sounded too quiet.

Then there was a click and the night lights went out, plunging Grace and Trick into darkness.

7

'What the hell is going on?' Trick whispered. He still had Grace's hand firmly in his own.

The footsteps drew closer and Grace shivered, though she was unsure if it was through cold or fear. Trick pulled her close and she could feel his breath, warm against her face. She thought how close his lips must be to her skin and shivered again at the thought. After a few seconds, the footsteps were replaced by the sound of a zip being pulled, followed by a dull clattering. Then there was a moment's silence before a familiar rattling sound pierced the darkness.

'Is that—?'

Grace's question was answered by the rush of an aerosol.

'That's spray paint,' Trick muttered. He stood up. 'I'm going to check it out. Wait here, OK?'

'No way,' whispered Grace. She followed Trick as he crept down the stairs, the smell of aerosol clogging the air around them.

As Trick took the final step down, one of the flagstones shifted beneath his foot and clunked heavily back into place.

They froze.

For a moment there was nothing, then came the sound of an empty can being tossed into a bag, followed by a zipper being pulled.

'Hey,' Trick called out suddenly, rushing forwards into the darkness. 'Who's there?'

Grace reached for the wall, her fingers fumbling for the light switch that she knew was close by. 'Trick?'

There was no answer, only the sound of footsteps running along the corridor.

'Trick?' Grace's fingers touched plastic and she flicked the switch. The lights flickered to life and at the far end of the corridor stood Trick, shaking his head. 'Where did he go?'

'I don't know.' Grace looked at the doors and walls near where she stood, but there was no graffiti, no sign of any tag. 'What was he doing? I don't see anything.'

'I think it was a little further down this way,' Trick said, examining the doors and walls around him.

Grace's heart fluttered. 'My room's down there.'

Trick began to stride ahead. Then, just as Grace's instinct had told her he would, he came to a stop outside her bedroom. He looked at her, a mixture of concern and confusion.

'What is it?' She walked up to join him and gasped at what had been painted on her door.

It was a hooded grim reaper, pointing at Grace and Trick with one hand and holding a scythe with the other.

Grace's mouth suddenly felt very dry. 'You have been tagged,' she muttered. 'Let the games begin.'

'What?'

'That's what the hacker said. He used the same reaper picture and left that message.' Grace looked at Trick. 'What do you think it means?'

'I think it means someone isn't happy with us,' he said, continuing along the corridor. 'Maybe it really is time to stand down, Grace. Call time on The 100 Society?'

'No way,' she snapped, a little too forcefully. 'I mean,' she tried to soften her voice a little, 'we can't let a little intimidation stand in our way. It doesn't bother me.' Grace lifted her chin, determined to add a little weight to what she knew was an obvious lie.

Trick stopped outside Faith's door. 'Does it bother you that your friends are being threatened too?'

'Really?' she asked with a groan, joining him to look at the reaper on her friend's door. 'Faith's going to freak when she sees this.'

Trick looked up. 'Where's Cassie's room?'

'Back that way.' She led Trick down the hallway

to Cassie's bedroom where, sure enough, there was a third reaper.

'What a psycho.' Trick scratched at the paint with his fingernail. 'Looks like it comes away easily enough,' he said. 'I say we get these doors cleaned up before anyone sees. We don't want to draw any more attention to ourselves, not when Cross already thinks we're involved with tagging.'

The door handle turned and Cassie appeared on the other side, her eyes puffy from sleep. 'What are you two doing?' she groaned. 'It's the middle of the night.'

'Sorry,' whispered Grace. 'We didn't mean to wake you.' She glanced at Trick. 'But now you're up I guess there's something you should see.' Yawning, Cassie craned her head around the door to see what Grace was pointing at. She gasped. 'Where did that come from?' Now fully awake, she stepped out into the corridor, eyes wide.

'There's one on my door too,' said Grace. 'And Faith's.'

'And I wouldn't be surprised if a few of the boys have been paid a visit too,' said Trick.

Cassie groaned, her shoulders sagging. 'There's more, I'm afraid. I was going to wait until the morning to tell you . . .'

Trick frowned. 'Tell us what?'

'After dinner I went back to the bridge to get another picture of the tag you guys did. It wasn't there any more.'

Grace stared. 'What? How could it not be there any more?'

'Well, I suppose technically it was. But it had been covered with one of those.' Cassie pointed at the reaper before disappearing back into her room. 'I got a picture of it,' she said as Trick and Grace followed her inside. 'It's all on my camera.'

Grace looked around Cassie's bedroom. It was as over the top as the girl who decorated it. Fairy lights hung from every available surface and almost everything inside was pink, including the curtains that Cassie had hung herself. Grace stood at the window and pulled back one of the curtains. Peering out at the dark playing fields, she searched for any sign of Sylvester, hoping it might give her an indication of how much time they had before he reappeared in their dormitory. She leaned closer to the glass, catching sight of something moving in the distance.

'I don't get it,' Trick said. 'Someone's gone over our tag? And now they're tagging our doors too? Who would do that?'

'Someone who wants to get our attention?' Grace asked, her breath misting against the window pane as she strained to get a better look at what, or *who*, was moving outside.

'It wasn't just the tag I got a picture of.' Cassie picked up the camera that was lying on her desk, a large telescopic lens still attached to the front. 'I can't guarantee it was the same person who did this,' she said, pointing towards the reaper on her door, 'but I definitely got someone on film – someone who decided to make a hasty exit from the bridge when they saw me taking pictures.'

Grace glanced at Cassie. 'You think it was the same person who left the tag?'

Cassie shrugged. 'There's only one way to find out,' she said. 'I've got the darkroom booked for Sunday afternoon. Meet me there at five? We can develop the film together.'

'Sure,' Grace said. She turned back to the window, just in time to see a small flame blossom to life in the distance. It could easily have been Sylvester, lighting a cigarette as he walked his nightly route around the school, though she couldn't see the telltale red glow of a cigarette burning.

For a moment the flame burned dimly in the distance, though Grace could see neither the source nor the person holding it.

'Grace? What is it?'

She turned to see Trick, his brow furrowed with concern.

Letting the curtain fall back across the window, she shook her head, though her heart was beating double-time.

'Nothing. It's nothing.'

Having spent an hour or so scrubbing the reaper tags off doors with Trick and Cassie, Grace had only managed a couple of hours' sleep when there was a short, sharp knock on her door.

She pulled it open to see Faith, already dressed, her hair neatly arranged into its trademark set of curls.

Faith smiled. 'Morning.' She stepped into Grace's room and closed the door behind her.

Grace looked down at her own tatty pyjama bottoms, suddenly feeling very underdressed. 'Morning,' she replied, glancing at the clock. 'Faith, it's not even eight yet. How do you look so good?'

Faith's made-up cheeks reddened slightly and she shrugged a shoulder. 'I don't know. I just fancied getting dressed for breakfast today.'

'It's Saturday. We never dress for breakfast on a Saturday.'

'OK, well, sometimes it's good to mix things up a bit, don't you think?'

Faith walked further into Grace's bedroom, stopping by the photographs of Grace's father and brother. 'Have you heard from your dad yet?'

'No.' Grace sat on her unmade bed and picked at the curling corner of the photograph, held on the wall with four blobs of Blu-tac. 'He said he'd call this week but I didn't hear anything.'

'Oh. Well, I guess the time difference makes it difficult.'

'He's had five years to get used to the time difference.' Grace picked up the mobile phone on her bedside table and pressed a button to check for missed calls, but there were none. 'He's just too busy.'

'He'll call.' Faith smiled, but there was sympathy in her eyes and that made Grace want to cry. She didn't want sympathy, she wanted a phone call from her father.

'What about Jack?'

'What *about* Jack?'

'Have you heard from him?'

Grace lay back against her pillow. 'I always hear from Jack, but that's because he's always got so much to say.' She rolled her eyes. 'He got a first on his last assignment, you know. And the wedding plans are going just *swimmingly*.' She wrinkled her nose. 'Ugh, even his fiancée's perfect. *Emily*,' she said, like the name left a bitter taste in her mouth. 'The daughter my father never had.'

Faith laid a hand on Grace's knee. 'Jack loves you. So does your dad.'

Grace shrugged. Actually, she hadn't heard from her brother either, but she didn't want any more sympathy from Faith.

'Looks like it's going to be another nice day,' Faith said, standing up and moving towards the window.

Grateful for the change in subject, Grace nodded. 'Hopefully it'll hold for a couple more weeks. I want to get the last few tags done before the weather starts to get bad. I really don't fancy tagging in the rain.'

'You mean you still want to finish?'

'Why wouldn't I?'

'Because of what happened on the bridge? Because of the papers? Or the blog getting hacked?' Faith's head jerked as she caught sight of something outside.

Grace looked at the clock. It was just after eight, the time that Pete normally started his morning run. Grace moved to where Faith stood by the window. Her room overlooked the school playing field, a huge expanse of green that was framed by a few football nets and a set of rugby posts at either end. At the back of the school field, St Nicholas' bell tower rose up from behind the tree line, the only visible part of the disused sixteenth century church that stood in the overgrown grounds neighbouring Clifton's perimeter.

In the shadow of the bell tower, a familiar figure was

jogging around the running track.

'You can't see him from your room, huh?' Grace smiled as Faith pulled back from the window, her cheeks glowing bright red.

'I – I don't know what you mean.'

'It's OK.' Grace looked out of the window again as Pete reached the bend in the track and began heading back towards the dorm building. His muscular legs flexed as he ran, engrossed in whatever music was playing through his headphones. 'I can understand. He does look pretty good out there.'

Faith frowned. 'I just came to see if you wanted to get breakfast.'

'Come on, Faith,' Grace said, laughing. 'I'm only teasing.'

'Yeah, well don't.' Faith moved towards the door. Turning the handle, she looked back at Grace, though her expression was hard. 'Are you coming or not?'

By the time Pete arrived, Grace and Faith had almost finished their cereal. He walked straight up to the counter and took a glass from the draining board, filled it with water and downed the lot in three big gulps. Then he turned to the girls, his usually pale skin flushed and glistening with sweat.

'Morning.' His unstyled blond hair stuck up in various directions, his cowlick even more obvious without the wax to hold it in place.

'Morning,' Grace replied. She looked at Faith, but her

friend just stood up from the table and reached for the kettle, her cheeks almost as red as Pete's.

'Good run?'

'Not bad.' Pete patted his stomach, far flatter and more toned than when she had met him in their first year at Clifton. 'It's gotta be done, right?'

Grace nodded and yawned.

Pete smiled as he bit into a piece of toast. 'Late night?' He poured a cup of juice and sat at the table beside Grace.

'Just a bit.'

'Oh really? What were you up to?'

'Nothing.' Grace watched as Faith turned to fill the kettle. 'I'll tell you later,' she mouthed silently to Pete, jerking her head in Faith's direction. She hated keeping things from her friend, but over the years she had learned that it was best not to worry Faith unless absolutely necessary. Once, in their third year, there had been a brief but ridiculous rumour that the water supply had been poisoned by a leaking sewer pipe and even when Grace proved it false by swallowing a large glass of it in front of her friend, Faith had still refused anything other than bottled drinks for six weeks.

Pete sipped his juice. The redness in his face was subsiding, the freckles he had gained over the summer slowly reappearing. 'So, any plans for today?'

'Yep,' said Grace. 'We've got some reconnaissance work to do.'

He groaned. 'Really? I thought we'd agreed that The 100

Society was on hold until after the art show?'

'It is, but there's no harm in doing a bit of planning, is there?'

'Fine.' Pete stood up and began clearing the table. 'Where are we going?'

'Lost Souls Bridge,' Grace said, hoping her voice didn't give away her own feelings about the location.

'Lost Souls?' Faith shook her head and waved her hands. 'No way.' She paused. 'Besides, I've got some prep to do.'

'It's just a quick look, Faith. No tagging today, I promise.'

'It's OK,' said Pete. 'I'll come with you, I'm sure we can manage alone. See you in an hour, OK?'

Once he had left, Faith passed Grace a mug of tea. 'So, what happened last night?'

Grace frowned. 'What do you mean?'

'You were with Trick, weren't you?'

'Yes, but . . .'

'You should have just told Pete when he asked. He probably knows it anyway.'

'I don't get it. Why would it matter?'

'You really don't know? Why do you think Pete was so keen to find out who you were with? He knows that you meet up with Trick in the middle of the night. You don't think it bothers him?'

'Why would it?'

Faith pushed a slice of bread into the toaster. 'He likes

you, Grace. Like, he *really* likes you.' She paused. 'And I think you know it.'

'Don't be silly. He's a friend, that's all.'

Leaning back against the kitchen counter, Faith chewed her lip thoughtfully. 'Remember the night on the railway bridge?'

'Yeah.'

'He was the one who told me to run back to Clifton after I saw that weirdo in the bushes. It was like he couldn't wait to be alone with you.'

'Faith, he was probably worried about you. He just wanted you to be safe. Besides, he couldn't have known that we'd be alone because Trick was with me. To start with, anyway.'

Faith shrugged. 'Maybe. But when I asked him what he would do if you got into trouble, do you know what he said?'

Grace shook her head.

'He said he would do whatever he had to do. Whatever it took to make sure you were OK.' She looked away, but not before Grace saw the hurt in her friend's eyes.

'Faith . . .'

'I just thought you should know, that's all. Pete's a good guy. He deserves to be happy.' Her face flushed pink as she lifted the mug to sip her tea. 'I just don't want anyone to get hurt.'

'Faith, you can tell me if you like Pete, you know.'

'Me? Don't be ridiculous.'

71

'OK.' Deciding not to push it, Grace took her empty bowl to the sink. 'You sure you don't want to come into the city with us today?'

'No, it's fine. I really do have some prep to get on with.'

'Prep? Isn't that word illegal on Saturdays?'

Grace looked up to see Trick standing in the doorway, wearing only a faded pair of pyjama trousers. Leaning against the door frame he yawned and scratched at his bare shoulder.

Faith wrinkled her nose. 'No, it's not illegal. And neither are shirts.'

Unlike Pete, Trick never worked out, yet his body was athletic and muscular. Grace's stomach flipped as she took in his tanned skin, the outline of the muscles visible in his chest and stomach. She bit her lip and turned away, but not before she got a good look at some of the tattoos spilling from his shoulder. Among them, she was able to make out a skull, a cross and what looked like a cluster of red roses.

'Hey, I sleep like this,' Trick said, looking down at his torso. 'Why is it OK for you girls to walk around in your pyjamas but not me?'

'I don't know. Perhaps because you're going to be expelled as soon as someone sees those tattoos you insist on covering yourself with?'

'You sound like my mother.' He grinned, turning to Grace. 'Besides, some people happen to like them.'

Grace frowned, trying to will away the warmth from her cheeks.

'Was someone making toast?' Trick peered into the toaster.

'Yes,' said Faith. 'And it's mine.'

'All right, all right.' Trick raised his hands. 'Sheesh, what does a guy have to do to get fed around here?'

Grace tossed him the bread. 'I don't know. Make it yourself?'

He caught the bread, holding it against his bare chest like a rugby ball. 'Fine.' He flashed her a grin. 'How about a cup of tea then?'

She rolled her eyes and reached for the kettle.

'You're not seriously doing it for him?' Faith asked, incredulous. 'Tell him to make it himself.'

'Hey, hey, hey,' Trick said, walking up behind Grace and snaking an arm around her waist. 'Don't listen to her, she doesn't know what she's talking about.'

Grace tutted. She would have said something, but with Trick's hand on her hip and his body – his *half-naked* body – so close to her, she couldn't seem to find the words.

'I wanted another cup of tea anyway,' she said finally. She levelled her eyes with Trick's so she didn't have to look at the tattoos that spilled from his broad shoulders on to his smooth chest. 'Besides, who said I was actually going to make you one?'

'How about if I say please?' His grin widened.

'Oh, fine. I'll make you a cup of tea.'

He leaned in and planted a kiss on her cheek. 'Thanks, princess.' Then his hand fell away from her side and he positioned himself in front of the toaster with the bread.

On the other side of the kitchen, Faith chewed on her own toast. 'OK,' she said slowly, looking from Trick to Grace. 'I think I'm just going to go and get started on my prep.' She waved her toast as a farewell to Grace, shaking her head as she left the kitchen.

'So what are you doing for your day release?' Trick asked, turning to Grace.

'I hate it when you call it that,' said Grace. 'This place feels enough like a prison as it is. Can't you just call it a weekend, like everyone else?'

Trick laughed. 'Ok, fine. So I heard Faith say the P word. I know I'm not doing that and I'm pretty sure that you're not planning on spending your weekend working on prep either.'

Grace nodded. 'Damn straight.' Behind her the kettle started to boil. 'Pass me a mug.'

Trick lifted a spare cup from the draining board and handed it to Grace. 'So?'

'So, I thought I'd go down to Lost Souls Bridge for a quick look. Find the right spot to tag, check safety. You know, the usual stuff.'

'So you're really going ahead with this? Despite everything?'

'Despite everything,' Grace confirmed.

'OK, sweet. When do we leave?'

She turned back to the kettle. 'Actually, I was going to go with Pete.'

74

There was a pause. 'Just the two of you?'

'Well, yeah.'

'OK.' The toast popped up behind him, but Trick didn't move. 'That's cool. I might just get some more work done for the show.'

'I thought you said you weren't going to do any work today?'

He shrugged a shoulder. 'So, did you say anything to Faith about our midnight visitor?'

'Nope.' Grace pointed a spoon at Trick. 'And make sure you don't either.'

Trick smiled as he took a steaming mug of tea from Grace. 'As if I would.'

'I mean it, Trick. She doesn't handle that kind of stuff well.'

'Really? She doesn't? Because, you know, personally, I just love having psychos scrawling metaphorical death threats on my door in the middle of the night.'

Grace poked his shoulder with her spoon. 'Hey, less of the sarcasm.'

'Don't pretend you don't love me for it.'

'So you've decided on your final piece for the show?'

'Nice subject change. But a good one because it means I can talk about myself.' He laughed when Grace stuck out her tongue in disgust. 'Actually,' he said, stepping back, spreading his arms and turning slowly, 'I thought I'd just exhibit myself. A work of art, don't you think?'

'Ugh, you really are an idiot.' Grace started to walk

towards the door. 'And Faith was right – if you're planning on staying at Clifton, you should probably get yourself covered up.' She gestured towards his tattoos, taking the opportunity to get a good look at some of the more recent ones. She didn't understand what half of them meant. They were just a mixture of pictures and words, fragments of information that made no sense to her.

'I'm only getting started, baby. Plenty more room on this canvas.' He rubbed his right forearm, bare of any tattoos.

'You're not serious?'

He shrugged. 'Only partly.'

'You'll regret them in the future you know. When you're all old and wrinkly and none of them look like anything any more.'

'Yeah, but I'll remember why I got them and I'll remember the reasons behind them all.' He smiled at her. 'There are some things I don't want to forget. And some things I *shouldn't* forget, even if I wanted to.'

'Most people use photographs, you know.'

'Less personal. And pictures fade.'

'So do tattoos.'

'I thought you liked them. You sure do look at them a lot.'

Trick grinned as the heat returned to Grace's face and she turned away, scowling.

'I'd better get ready,' she mumbled, turning towards the door. 'I'll catch you later.'

'OK,' he called after her, raising his mug of tea in mock salute. 'But don't wear green. It'll clash with that red face of yours.'

'Shut up, Trick.'

9

'OK, so this is pretty high.'

Grace peered over the concrete wall that ran the length of the bridge and groaned. 'It doesn't look that bad when you drive over it.'

Pete nodded solemnly. 'I imagine it'll look far worse when you're standing on the other side. That ledge is pretty narrow.'

He joined Grace, leaning his elbows across the top of the wall and pushing himself up on his toes to get a view down to the river. The water was a murky grey against the brilliant sky. 'What do you think?' he asked. 'About sixty metres?'

'I don't want to think about it.'

They stood in silence, both staring out at the river that separated the city from the surrounding areas, mostly made up of fields and farms. It amazed Grace how quickly the tower blocks and high rises seemed to appear out of the dense greenery that surrounded the outskirts of the city, like someone had scooped up some buildings and dumped them in the middle of the countryside.

'Do you think it would kill you?' Grace asked. 'Falling that far, I mean.'

'Probably.'

'Even though you'd be falling into water?'

'You do know why it's called Lost Souls Bridge, right?'

Grace shook her head.

'Its real name is All Saints Bridge, but they started calling it Lost Souls when people started . . .' He pointed down at the water and whistled. 'You know, jumping off it.'

Grace leaned over the wall. 'That's awful. How long do you think it takes to fall that far?'

Pete closed his eyes, his lips moving silently in the way they did when he was working out some theory or formula that Grace would never understand. He did that a lot, even when they were just sitting drinking tea. His eyes would go blank, like his mind was wandering to some unknown place, and Grace knew he would be thinking about things she could never understand. 'Three seconds before you hit the water,' he said finally. 'Four at the most.'

'Really?' She peered down. 'That's not long.'

'Nope. You'd be falling at about eighty miles an hour and given that water is actually quite a dense substance, it would be a pretty hard impact. Even if the fall didn't kill you, you'd have broken bones, probably be unconscious. There'd be a good chance of drowning before anyone got to you.'

Grace grimaced. Then she smiled and bumped her hip against Pete's. 'Simple matter of physics, right?'

He returned her grin. 'Isn't it always?'

'Totally.' She tapped the side of his head with her knuckles. 'One day I'd love to see what actually goes on in that big brain of yours, although it's probably all a bit science-y for me.'

He laughed and grabbed her hand. 'Well try not to knock it all out, OK? I've spent years filling it up – I'd rather not have you concuss it out of me.'

Grace looked down at their intertwined hands, barely able to tell his fingers from her own. It was so comfortable, but still she pulled away and turned back to look out over the water. She could feel Pete staring, his gaze almost burning the back of her neck.

'Want to talk about it?' he asked.

She exhaled, her breath freezing as it hit the air. 'I don't even know myself. Just the pressure of being in our final year, I guess. You know, the art show, exams . . .'

Pete glanced at her. 'You don't ever have to worry about telling me something, you know.' Wrapped up in his immaculate black winter coat and striped scarf, he looked almost perfect against the spotless autumn sky. 'And it's not even about trust, although you know you can trust me. There's never any need for you to tell me anything. I'm never going to be mad at you for having secrets, I hope you know that.'

Grace shook her head. 'How did I end up with a friend like you?' She looked at him again and was struck by the blueness of his eyes, the smattering of freckles across the bridge of his nose and his hair like spun gold under the bright sunshine. He was so perfect, so reliable. She could do a lot worse than end up with a guy like Pete.

So what was stopping her?

Leaning back against the bridge wall, Grace kicked at the ground with the toe of her trainer. 'I think I'm just mad at the moment,' she said finally.

'About your dad?'

She looked at him. 'How did you know?'

He turned to face her, his elbow resting on the wall. 'It doesn't take a genius to work it out.'

'He said he'd call.'

'I know.'

'He calls Jack.'

'He calls you too.'

'Not this week.'

'Hey.' He reached out and took her hand. When she failed to look at him he gave it a little shake. 'Hey,' he said again.

She turned to him.

'Listen to me,' he said. 'Your dad loves you just as much as he loves Jack. So what if Jack is going to be a doctor? Who cares? You're going to do something amazing with your life, Grace Becker.'

'What am I going to do? Get a qualification in art then end up flipping burgers somewhere? It's OK for you, Pete, you're a genius, you can be whatever you want to be.' She sighed. 'My dad would love someone like you in the family.'

He smiled. 'You're going to be all right.'

Grace paused. 'Someone broke into my room yesterday.' The words were out before she had a chance to think it through, before she had a chance to talk herself out of it.

Pete stared. 'Someone was in your room?'

'I think so. I mean, it was unlocked when I got back after dinner and I never leave my computer open . . .' She stopped, realizing how much more tenuous it sounded out loud. She braced herself for Pete's reaction.

'Have you told anyone? Sylvester? Cross?'

'No, I . . .' She looked at him, at the way his eyes had changed. What was that? Anger? Fear? 'You mean you believe me?'

'Why wouldn't I believe you?'

'I don't know, I mean, I just thought maybe I was imagining things, especially after everything that's been going on. Like, maybe I forgot to lock my door or something.'

'Maybe you did. But what does your gut tell you?'

She paused. 'I think someone was in my room.'

'Then someone was in your room.' He sliced his hand decisively through the air, drawing a line under Grace's conclusion. It was a simple gesture, but one that meant so much.

'So what do I do?'

Pete shrugged. 'I have no idea. I guess you need to tell someone though.'

'There's more. Someone tagged our doors last night.'

'What? Whose doors? What tag?'

Grace sighed. 'I was with Trick last night, we were on the stairwell—'

'What were you doing on the stairwell?'

'Just talking.'

'About what?'

'Does it matter?'

Pete sniffed, but said nothing.

'Anyway, we were just sitting there when the lights went out. Someone came into the corridor and we heard them spraying paint, but we didn't get to see who it was.'

'What was the tag?'

'A grim reaper.' She shuddered at the memory. 'Who would do something like that? You can't get a much clearer threat than that, right?'

Grace looked at Pete, but he was staring out across the river, his expression almost as dark as the water. 'What?' she asked.

He shook his head a little. 'I don't know. Maybe I shouldn't say.'

'You're scaring me, Pete.'

After a moment's silence that seemed to last forever, he

faced her. 'It's just that it wouldn't be the first time that someone I know has made threats.'

'What? Who are you talking about?'

'Daniel.'

A chill ran the length of Grace's spine and for a moment it felt like her whole body had been immersed in icy water. 'You think it was Daniel?'

'I don't know. But when I think back to what happened . . .' Pete turned to look at Grace. 'He was always so angry. He never wanted to come to Clifton, he hated boarding school, but his father was in the army and they were always being shipped from country to country, so his parents decided it was best for him to stay in one place.'

Grace laughed bitterly. 'I know what that's like.'

Pete offered her a conciliatory smile before continuing. 'He used to talk about ways of getting out of the school. He was desperate, Grace.'

'So what did he do?'

'You have to promise me you won't say anything. It could put you in a bad position.'

'Of course, if that's what you want.'

'I mean it, Grace. You mustn't tell anyone.' He paused. 'Not even Trick.'

'I . . .' She was about to protest, to argue that she wasn't any more likely to tell Trick than anyone else, but she could see in Pete's eyes that he knew otherwise. 'I promise,' she said finally.

Pete nodded. 'It was just over a year ago. Daniel had just

received a letter from his parents. That always set him off, you know.'

'OK.'

'Well, he just lost it. He was in his dorm room, pulling down the photographs from his wall, kicking things over. Anyway, he got this lighter out of his pocket and set the letter on fire.'

'He set it on fire?' She stared, a horrible realization washing over her.

'Yep. Threw it in a bin and watched it burn. But then the flames got bigger, the bin started to burn and the plastic started to melt and drip on the carpet. There was this horrible black smoke, but he didn't move, didn't say anything. He just sat there. If I hadn't stamped it out, I think he'd have let the whole place go up there and then. I still remember the way the flames reflected in his glasses. It freaked me out, Grace, seriously.'

'His painting,' Grace whispered. She could picture almost every stroke, every splash of red, yellow and orange. What she had once thought of as an abstract image had taken on a new form and she could now see it for what it really was. 'His painting is fire.'

'He was obsessed, carried that lighter with him everywhere. That was when I stopped hanging out with him. He scared me, Grace.'

'You think he did something bad, don't you?'

Pete nodded. 'I think it was Daniel that set Clifton on fire. And now I think he's the one who's been following us, the one who's threatening us.' He looked at her. 'I think it's time to stop The 100 Society.'

Grace swallowed, though her throat felt suddenly tight. 'But I have to finish. I'm so close.'

'Is it worth it? I mean, if Daniel really is crazy enough to try and burn the school down, who knows what else he's capable of? I don't know. Maybe it's time for me to say something to the teachers.'

'No!' Grace cried out, more forcefully than she'd anticipated. 'No,' she repeated, deliberately lowering the tone of her voice. 'They'll ask questions. It will draw too much attention to us and it won't take long before they work out what we've been doing. We'll never get a chance to finish.'

'I'm just worried about you, Grace. You saw what he did to me by the railway bridge. What if it's you next time?'

'We can't even be sure it was him,' Grace snapped. 'He was wearing a hood.' She exhaled. 'Can we at least just sleep on it? Let's not say anything to the others, OK? Not until we're absolutely sure.'

Pete paused for a moment, then nodded. 'If that's what you really want.'

'It is,' Grace said, pulling the collar of her coat up against the bitter wind. Without another word, she turned away from the water and began walking back towards Clifton.

10

Grace and Pete heard the screaming from the school driveway.

They glanced at one another and, without saying a word, broke into a sprint. With their feet clattering in time across the shingle, they rounded the corner of the main school building to see Cassie and Daniel on the field beneath one of the rugby posts, wrestling over a small, padded envelope. They were surrounded by a group of students, some cheering while others looked on, bewildered.

'Give it to me,' screamed Cassie. She grabbed at his shirt, reaching for the packet that Daniel was now holding tightly above his head. The old brick building of the school dormitory towered over them, the banks of leaded windows like hundreds of dead eyes, watching on.

'You don't understand,' he snapped. 'I'm taking it, so let go of me.'

'You're a pig,' Cassie cried, her face streaked with tears and mascara. 'Why are you doing this?' She reached for the package again but Daniel grabbed her wrist with his free hand, twisting it until she yelped.

'Let go of her,' Grace shouted as she started to push through the crowd. 'I said let go!'

'Wait!' Pete grabbed her coat, pulling her back just as the dormitory doors crashed open and Trick barrelled out on to the field, his fists clenched and his face contorted with rage. He launched himself at Daniel and they landed together on the turf, a tangled mess of limbs as they each fought to gain control. The growing crowd drew closer and louder, some students encouraging the fight while others yelled at them to stop.

'This is what you do to girls?' Trick roared, pinning Daniel to the ground by his shoulders and straddling his torso with his knees. Cassie darted forwards and scooped up the envelope that had fallen from Daniel's hand.

'Stop it,' Grace shouted again, pulling against Pete's grip.

Trick twisted towards the sound of her voice, his eyes meeting hers as he saw her for the first time through the crowd. The distraction was just enough for Daniel to free an arm from where it had been clamped against his side by Trick's knee and he reached up, grabbing Trick by his T-shirt with both hands and hurling him on to the grass.

As Trick raised himself up on to his hands and knees, Daniel staggered to his feet, then ran forwards like a footballer preparing to take a penalty. There was a dull thud as his foot connected with Trick's ribs and the crowd drew a collective gasp.

Trick let out a hollow moan and collapsed on to his front, curling himself into a ball as he gasped, his breath ragged. There was a moment of silence as Daniel paused to straighten his glasses. Standing in the huge shadow of Clifton's dormitories, he pushed the lank strands of hair back from his face, then flashed Grace and Pete a smile that clashed against the coldness in his eyes.

Like the smile of a skull.

Then he took another step back, drawing his foot behind him as he prepared to land another kick against Trick's body.

'I said, stop it!' Grace screamed, her heart beating so fast and so hard she thought it might burst out of her chest at any moment. With a final heave, she pulled herself from Pete's grip and ran towards Trick.

'That's enough,' Pete said, his voice firm but calm. He stepped from the crowd towards Daniel, his movements as decisive as his words.

'Is it now?' Daniel asked, laughing bitterly. 'Enough? You don't know the meaning—' The words were knocked from his mouth as Trick tackled him from behind and brought him crashing to the ground.

'You're a psycho,' Trick spat breathlessly. 'This is how

you get your kicks? Beating up girls who don't like you stalking them?'

'Get off me,' Daniel shouted, his forearms shielding his face from the blows Trick was attempting to land.

Pete ran forwards, grabbed Trick by the remains of his shirt and pulled him away from Daniel. 'Trick, get off him before you give Cross a reason to kick you out of here.'

Breathing heavily, Trick raised a hand to touch his lip, then stared at his fingers, red with his own blood. He wiped them on his trousers, then wiped his mouth again, harder, before sitting heavily on the ground. His T-shirt had ripped all the way up one side and it flapped around him like a cape as his chest rose and fell sharply. He glared at Daniel, his breath coming in ragged bursts. 'It's over, buddy. You hear me? Time to leave the girl alone.'

Daniel stood up and searched the ground before picking up the glasses that had been knocked from his face. He wiped them on his shirt and pushed them over his nose before turning calmly to Trick.

'You'll pay for this.'

Trick laughed. 'Oh, really?' He stood up, his torn shirt billowing around his stomach. 'You want to go again, big guy?'

Daniel laughed, but the sound was as hollow and as empty as his eyes. He looked back to where Cassie stood, clutching the envelope against her chest. She recoiled slightly, her fingers tightening around the package.

'And you,' Daniel spat. 'Perhaps people would like you

more if you spent less time worrying about what you look like.' He turned to look at Grace. For a moment he stared at her from behind thick strands of matted hair. 'Why are you looking at me like that?'

Grace shook her head, realizing she was gawping at Daniel with her mouth agape, her eyes wide. 'I – I wasn't.'

'You're afraid of me, aren't you?'

Grace stepped back.

Daniel laughed. 'You'll be sorry too, I hope you know that,' he said. 'Especially you. You don't know what you're messing with.'

Trick took another step towards Daniel, fists clenching at his sides. 'I said, it's over.'

'You be careful with that envelope,' Daniel called back, now surrounded by the students who had given up hope of seeing any more punches and who were also making their way back to the main building. 'And don't say I didn't warn you.'

Cassie stared after him, her eyes wide and red with tears.

Trick didn't move until Daniel had disappeared into the dormitories. Then he looked at Cassie and pointed at the package in her hands. 'What is that?'

'It's just film,' she said through her tears. 'Just film rolls from my camera.' She sunk to her knees, clutching the envelope tightly to her chest.

Grace crouched down beside Cassie and placed a hand on her shoulder. 'What happened?'

Cassie squeezed her eyes shut, forcing out more tears. 'He said . . .' She choked on her words and shook her head, pulling away from Grace. 'You wouldn't believe me anyway.'

Grace glanced at Pete, though he was still staring at where Daniel had disappeared into the crowd. 'Oh, I think we'd believe you.'

'Thank you for helping me,' Cassie said to Trick, through fresh tears. 'Thank you so much.'

'You were screaming loudly enough,' he said. He licked at the cut on his lip, already swelling beneath the drying blood. 'It's not like I had much choice.' He coughed and winced, clutching a hand to his side. 'I just hope whatever you've got on that film is worth it.'

'You OK there, pal?' Pete reached out to steady him but Trick pulled away, his face contorting in pain.

'I'm fine.'

Grace frowned. 'You're not fine.' She took Trick's hand and pulled him towards the dormitories.

'Where are we going?' he asked.

'To get you fixed up.' Looking up, Grace noticed a figure looking on from behind one of the leaded windows. 'Looks like someone's been watching the show,' she murmured to Trick.

Trick glanced up. 'Sylvester?' He coughed and winced again. 'Does that guy ever sleep?'

'Do you think he's been there the whole time? Why didn't he do anything?'

'Who knows? Either way, I'm done here if he tells Cross.'

'He won't tell,' Grace said. She didn't know what made her say that, but something told her it was true. She glanced back to where Pete was helping Cassie to her feet, though his eyes were trained on Grace and Trick.

'I always knew Daniel was a freak,' Trick muttered. 'It's about time they kicked him out of here.'

Grace said nothing. As they neared the entrance to the dorms, Grace glanced up again.

This time, the window was empty.

'Come on then,' Grace said, pushing the door closed behind her. 'Get the shirt off.'

Trick raised an eyebrow. 'You're not even going to light some candles first? A little music to set the mood?'

'Can't you quit the joking for just a second?'

'Who says I'm joking?'

'Fine.' Grace stepped forwards, reaching out to grab the bottom of Trick's T-shirt. He pulled back, sucking in a deep breath.

'Careful,' he snapped. 'That hurts.'

She frowned and reached out again, taking the torn hem of his shirt gently between her fingers. 'Can you lift your arms?'

Trick raised his right arm, but his left stayed close to his ribs, cocked up across his chest. 'Not this one,' he murmured. 'Hurts.'

'OK.' Grace began to ease his shirt up over his stomach, moving slowly to ensure she didn't pull too roughly or knock against him. When her fingers brushed his bare skin, the muscles in his stomach contracted, pulling away from her touch. She glanced up to meet his gaze and for a moment the air seemed to thicken between them.

'OK,' she repeated, the words sticking in her throat. 'Just pull this arm through.' She helped guide his arm through the sleeve of his shirt, a task that was made easier by the fact that it was almost completely ripped through. When his arm was out, what was left of the shirt hung from his left shoulder, exposing his torso and the ink patterns that swirled up from his bicep and across his chest, letters and numbers etched on the pieces of skin between. Grace tried not to follow the lines that snaked down towards his un-inked stomach, the flesh of which seemed somehow more naked against the rest of his tattooed body.

'There,' she said, focusing on the material she was easing down his left arm. 'Simple when you know how.'

Trick said nothing, but Grace could feel his eyes trained on her as she worked. 'You really need to be careful around that guy,' she said, trying to focus on something other than the warmth of his skin against hers. 'I think he's dangerous.'

'Daniel?' Trick snorted. 'He's a freak, but he's not dangerous. What makes you say that anyway?'

Grace paused. 'Just be careful, that's all I'm saying.'

As she revealed more of his bare skin, his left side

covered in just as much ink as the right, Grace grew more aware of him watching her but she couldn't bring herself to make eye contact. With the way his breathing had slowed despite the pain he was in, she knew he was as aware of their proximity as she was. It was only when he took the smallest of steps towards her, the warmth of his body immediately heating the small space between them, that she finally looked up.

His eyes. The way the brown of his irises seemed to have deepened; it was almost the exact same expression he wore when he was lost in one of his paintings.

'Grace.' His fingers grazed her cheek and although he was barely touching her, it was enough to drive the air from her lungs. As his fingers moved lower to trace her jawline, Grace closed her eyes, willing the beating of her heart to slow down before he felt the pulsing in her throat.

Her fingers tightened around the fabric of his T-shirt and he stepped closer, the movement just enough to make his torn shirt come away in Grace's hands, exposing his chest.

She gasped, all the distractions of his touch forgotten.

'What?' Trick's hand fell away from her face and he looked down, gingerly raising his arm to get a better view. 'Oh, man.' He winced at the deep purple bruise that covered most of the left side of his rib cage. 'If that jerk-off's broken my ribs, I swear . . .'

He fell silent when Grace placed her fingers lightly against his skin, moving them slowly across the lines of his ribcage. He gritted his teeth against her touch, but he said nothing and Grace remained silent herself, even when a rash of goosebumps broke out beneath her fingers.

'Does that hurt?' she asked softly, increasing the pressure as she continued to trace the outlines of his ribs.

'Not so much.' His voice cracked and he cleared his throat. 'I mean, not as much as it did.'

Grace stepped back. 'Badly bruised, I think. If any ribs were broken I don't think you'd have been able to stand me touching you.'

Trick gave her a half smile. 'I don't know.'

'Let me just check online,' Grace said. The tension she had felt when his hand had been against her cheek had started to fade into awkwardness, the heat in the air now replaced with a silence that needed to be filled. 'You know, I can just look at one of those medical sites. They're normally pretty helpful.'

'Grace—'

'Yeah, because you can never be too careful, right?'

Trick paused. 'Right.'

She lifted the lid of her laptop to reveal the desktop photograph she loved so much. The picture had been taken the previous summer in the overgrown grounds of St Nicholas' churchyard. The class had gone to sketch the bell tower as part of an assignment and Trick had even gone on to create his final piece from one of his sketches.

Cassie had taken the picture on the same camera that she now used to photograph The 100 Society tags. There had been no forethought, no preparation and no posing. Crouching down amongst the long grass to snap a picture of an orchid, Cassie had glanced up to a scene that was too perfect to ignore. Under the same sycamore tree they had positioned themselves under every day for a week, Grace, Trick, Ed, Pete and Faith were sitting together. From behind them, a gust of summer wind had shaken loose a cloud of dandelion seeds and carried it across the churchyard, each seed picking up the early evening sun until it looked like a thousand droplets of golden light were falling around them.

Grace clicked the internet icon and her email homepage flashed up on the screen. A new email appeared at the top of her inbox, highlighted against the other messages.

'Look at this.' Frowning, she pointed at the name of the sender.

'*A Friend*,' he read. 'Well, that sounds legit.' He snorted. 'There's not even a subject heading. Probably a virus – I'd delete it if I were you.'

Grace moved the mouse, hovering the cursor over the delete button. 'I don't know.' She moved the mouse again and clicked to open the email.

'You're going to regret that,' Trick muttered.

Grace stared at the message. There was one sentence, only five words, but it was enough to send a shiver down the length of Grace's spine.

Trick let out a low whistle. 'Seriously. Someone's messing with you.'

Grace nodded, but there was something about it, perhaps something in its frankness, that made Grace believe it was real. She clicked on the cross at the top of the message and it disappeared from her screen, but she knew she wouldn't be able to forget the words as quickly as she could delete them.

You are being lied to.

12.

Grace gathered the neck of her jacket as she walked, barricading herself against the permanently bitter draught that breezed through the north building's hallway regardless of the time of year. Her footsteps echoed around her in the otherwise empty corridor and for a moment she paused, suddenly unsure that only the echo was following her.

Grace turned, but the hall was empty. Somewhere, in another part of the building, a door slammed shut. She watched for a few more seconds and when she was sure there was nobody behind her she continued on her way, the echo always one step behind.

She knew she was more jumpy than usual, but who could blame her? Whether she wanted to admit it or not, someone had taken a little too much interest in her movements and in The 100 Society. She could downplay it as much as she liked, she could explain the previous night's email away as spam or as a silly joke, but the surge of adrenaline that was making her walk just a little bit faster told the truth about how she really felt.

The security office was the first room Grace passed. The door was closed and a large window revealed it was empty. A khaki jacket was draped across a black chair, in front of an old desk piled precariously high with monitors that flickered constantly, the images on each one changing every four or five seconds to a different location around the school.

'Afternoon, Miss Becker.'

Grace jumped and spun to see Sylvester walking towards her. The huge bunch of keys he kept chained to his belt swung rhythmically, bouncing against his thigh with every step. She hadn't even heard him approaching.

'Good afternoon,' she muttered, stepping back from the security office window.

Sylvester stopped beside her and peered in through the window. He let out a low whistle. 'All those monitors, eh?' he said with a tut. 'It's a sad world we live in when you need all those.'

Grace forced a smile. 'Uh. Yeah.' She continued towards the darkroom as Sylvester fumbled with his keys. There was a clunk as one of them turned in the lock of the office door.

'Kids just need to be kids,' he said and Grace looked back, but the corridor was empty and the office door was closed once more.

Just how much he saw on those monitors, she didn't know. He had been standing at the window when Trick had fought Daniel, but had done nothing. Why? Grace shuddered and reached out for the handle of the darkroom door. Instinctively she glanced up to where a large red lightbulb was positioned above the doorframe. It was unlit, a sign that whoever was inside was not handling unprocessed and unprotected film. Regardless of the dormant bulb, she still knocked loudly to inform anyone inside the lab that she was about to enter, a courtesy they had been taught to follow by Miss Stone. When there was no answer, Grace turned the handle and entered what was known as the airlock, a tiny room that separated the darkroom from the corridor. It was a precautionary measure, one taken to ensure that no light was able to get in should anyone dare to commit the sin of opening the door without knocking.

With the door behind her closed, Grace was plunged momentarily into absolute darkness, unable to even see a glint of the steel door handle her hand was now resting on. Taking a deep breath, she tried to compose herself, determined to leave her worries outside.

'I'm coming in,' she called. Opening the door, she was immediately greeted with the sharp tang of chemical fumes, even stronger than usual.

'Hey,' Cassie called back. She didn't look up from the container she was holding, a three-litre bottle that looked like a cross between a milk jug and a petrol can. A thick liquid glooped out into a tray on the bench in front of her.

'Hey,' Grace replied. 'It stinks in here.'

Cassie sniffed the air, her button nose twitching beneath her heavily made-up eyes. 'I think I must be used to it, I can hardly smell it these days.' She placed the half-empty chemical bottle on the bench and turned to face Grace, her high heels clacking on the tiled floor.

'Really, Cassie? Designer shoes for developing pictures?'

Cassie looked down and laughed. 'Sweetie, there is *never* a bad time for designer shoes.'

'Honestly, if I didn't know you better . . .'

'I know, I know. I think we're just about ready. Can you get the lights?'

'Sure.' Grace reached for the first in a series of switches next to the door and the room was plunged into darkness. A flick of the next switch illuminated the safe-light, a lamp that cast a dim red glow across the room and filled it with long, black shadows.

'The film's over there,' Cassie said, pointing to a canister on the desk near the door. There was a snap as she pulled off one of the latex gloves she'd been wearing to pour the chemicals.

'So you think we'll actually be able to see the person on the bridge?'

'It depends on how sharp the image is,' Cassie replied, 'and we won't know that until we get the film out.'

Grace picked up the canister. 'Daniel sure seemed keen to get his hands on this.'

There was a moment of silence, then Cassie reached out to take the film from Grace. 'If it really is him,' she said, her voice unusually firm, 'if I really see his face on here, Ed and I will be sending these pictures to the police.'

'No,' Grace said, shaking her head. 'We can't, Cassie. We'd only incriminate ourselves.'

'But he's dangerous,' Cassie whispered, clutching the canister tighter. 'You should have seen Ed's face when I told him what Daniel did. I've had enough, Grace. I think he's even been through my locker.'

'Your locker?' A chill prickled Grace's skin. 'How do you know?'

'I just know.'

Grace nodded. Now wasn't the time to argue. If they really did find Daniel in the pictures, if they really did have proof that he was the one spraying the grim reaper over their tags, they could talk it through as a group. Right now, the important thing to do was to get the film developed, to find out just who had been on that bridge.

'OK,' Cassie said, taking a deep breath. 'Chemicals are ready. Shall we do this?'

'I'm ready if you are.'

Cassie positioned herself in front of the various trays of chemicals. 'Lights off then, if you'd be so kind?'

'Sure.' Grace reached out and flicked off the safe light, plunging the room into pitch darkness. 'OK?'

'Yep,' Cassie's voice called out from across the room. 'I'm just getting the lid off the canister. Not always easy when you can't see your hand in front of your face.' She laughed.

'OK, just let me know when—'

Click.

Grace paused, trying to work out where the sound had come from. 'Did you hear that?'

'Hear what? Damn it, these things are impossible.'

'I'm not sure. It sounded like a door handle. Maybe the airlock?'

Click. Slightly louder this time.

Cassie tutted. 'Busy in here,' she called out. 'The red light is on for a reason.'

Click. Definitely a door handle.

'I said BUSY,' Cassie snapped. 'Do not come in, I'm about to expose a film in here.'

The next sound was so loud, so unexpected, it was like a firecracker going off next to Grace's head. The door leading from the airlock to the darkroom slammed shut with such ferocity, it felt like the whole room shook with the force.

'What the—' Cassie began, then there was another almighty crash.

A piercing scream filled the room.

'Cassie? Cassie, what's happened?' Grace turned back to where she knew the light switches were located, fumbling in the darkness as she called Cassie's name over and over.

The screaming seemed to go on and on until finally, Grace's fingers brushed against the row of switches. She

105

flicked them all on, flooding the room with light.

When she turned, Cassie was no longer standing and the chemical trays were scattered across the floor.

Grace darted towards where her friend lay, curled into a shrieking ball with her hands covering her face. She was still screaming when Grace knelt beside her. 'What happened?' she repeated, her heart thumping in her chest as she tried to pull Cassie's hands away from her face. 'Cassie, talk to me, tell me what happened.' She could hear the panic in her own voice, but was unable to control it.

Cassie was moaning, a terrifying gurgling sound emanating from her throat as she drew in a deep, ragged breath.

'You have to let me see,' Grace cried. She looked back towards the door. 'HELP,' she screamed, her voice sounding somehow detached from her body. 'HELP!'

Somewhere in the distance she heard a door slam, followed by the heavy sound of running footsteps.

'Let me see,' she said again to Cassie, pulling gently at her wrists. She lowered her voice, forcing herself to calm down. 'Let me see,' she repeated.

Cassie's hands relaxed just enough for Grace to guide them away from her face. 'Help me,' Cassie whispered, her hands shaking violently in Grace's grip. She started to cough and gag, a terrible choking sound that terrified Grace.

'It's OK, you're going to be OK,' Grace said, her voice cracking as she finally got to see what lay beneath. She swallowed and looked away, trying to will away the scream that was rising in her throat.

While the left side remained intact, strands of skin that had once been attached to the right side of Cassie's perfectly made-up face had started to come away with her hands, hanging from her fingers in grotesque ribbons. Her once smooth complexion had given way to red-raw flesh that bubbled and blistered even as Grace watched, but the worst part, the thing that Grace could barely bring herself to look at, were Cassie's once-blue eyes. There was no blue any more, only a deep and terrifying red, visible beneath swollen and blistered eyelids.

Behind her, the door to the darkroom burst open. One of Clifton's security team stumbled into the room, his eyes widening as he took in the scene.

'Good god,' he choked, stepping back. 'OK, just – just stay there, I'll go and get help.' He ran, the door clicking shut behind him.

'Help me,' Cassie said again. She sounded weak, her voice barely audible.

'It's going to be OK,' Grace soothed. 'You're going to be OK.'

Cassie whimpered, shaking her head while her breath came in rasping bursts.

'Don't try to talk,' Grace said, her own breath coming hot and fast, almost matching pace with Cassie.

Seconds later, the corridor outside was filled with noise, more running footsteps and loud voices.

Cassie gasped and turned to Grace, her head moving from side to side as she tried to place her friend. 'The film,' she cried. 'Get the film.'

'Don't worry about the—'

'Please,' Cassie begged, strength returning to her voice. 'I didn't open it, it's still good. Find it, quickly.'

Grace scanned the tiles around them, but there was no sign of the film canister, not on the floor, nor on the desk where Cassie had been working.

'Can you see it?'

'No, I . . .' She paused, turning sharply towards the door that had slammed so loudly before Cassie's accident. 'Cassie, how did this happen?'

'I don't know, I tripped, or something fell against me. I don't know. Please Grace, can you see it?'

'Yes,' Grace lied. 'It's all fine. Nothing to worry about.'

Cassie sank back as the door swung open once more, the room filling with people and noise. Someone grabbed a bottle that was attached to the wall and pulled off the lid before dousing Cassie's face with the liquid.

Cursing herself for not thinking about the eyewash, Grace was pulled aside without a word as members of staff swarmed Cassie, plying her with words of reassurance and promises of ambulances and hospitals.

Grace reached up to wipe her face, slick with tears and sweat, as she searched the room. The canister was nowhere to be seen. It may have rolled into a corner somewhere, or it may have been tucked under a piece of fallen equipment, but Grace was sure that when she came back later she would be unable to find it.

Just as she sure was that this had been no accident.

Faith carried a mug of tea to where Grace sat, shivering.

'Are you cold?'

Grace shook her head. 'No. I don't know what I am.'

'You're in shock,' Faith said, taking the mug and adding another two spoons of sugar. She offered it back to Grace. 'Drink this, it'll help.'

'Thanks.' Grace forced a smile, but felt an instant stab of guilt. How could she smile when Cassie had been so horribly injured? She felt like she should never be allowed to smile again.

'Do you know what happened?'

Grace looked up. It wasn't the first time she had been asked the question since Cassie had been taken away in the ambulance, the lights flashing in the half-light of the early evening. Despite attempts by the teachers to usher them away, crowds of students had lined the driveway, watching on as the ambulance departed.

'I don't know,' Grace said. She frowned. 'I feel like I should. I mean, I was there, but I just can't get my head around it.'

'So you didn't see anything? Hear anything?'

'It was dark, we had the lights off. And all I heard was a door slam.'

'That was it?'

'Yes.' Grace closed her eyes. 'Until the screaming.'

The screaming. She could hear it now, every time she closed her eyes. She blinked under the glare of the kitchen's halogen strip light. 'So much screaming.'

Faith laid a hand across Grace's. 'Do you think she fell? Maybe the door slamming made her jump and she knocked the chemicals as she tripped over?'

Grace shrugged. 'Maybe. I don't know.' She shifted in her seat, unable to get comfortable. 'I don't think I want to talk about it any more.'

'OK. Of course.' Faith squeezed her hand. 'I'm here for you. If you want to talk about it, or if you don't, I'm here.'

'Thank you. And ditto.'

Faith paused. 'Actually, there was something I wanted to talk to you about, although I'm not sure if this is the right time.'

'Faith, anything you can say to take my mind off all this would be welcome.'

Faith took a breath. 'I like Pete.'

111

The words were out so fast, Grace barely had time to register. 'You like Pete?'

Biting her lip, Faith nodded. 'I do, Grace. I'm sorry, I should have told you before.'

'No, it's fine.' Grace knew it had been coming, so why did she feel like she'd just taken a punch to the stomach? 'You're allowed to like whoever you want.'

'I know, but you know. It's Pete. Your Pete.'

'He's not my Pete, Faith.'

'So you don't mind?'

'Why would I?'

Faith exhaled. 'Thank god. I've been so nervous about telling you. I thought you'd be mad.'

'Look, he's a friend. I promise you, that's all there is to it.'

'OK, great.'

Grace forced a smile. 'Great.'

Returning the smile, Faith took Grace's hand. 'I've missed this.'

'You've missed what?'

'Us. Just spending time together like this, alone. We used to be so close and, I don't know, I guess you've been spending more and more time with the others recently.'

'So?'

'So, it's nice to talk about stuff.'

'You mean it's nice talking about what happened to Cassie?' Grace knew she was being unfair, but she couldn't stop herself.

112

'No.' Faith was fumbling for the right words. 'We just don't do this any more.'

'What?' Grace frowned. 'This is horrible, Faith. We've never done "this", whatever "this" is.'

Faith pulled her hand away, her face falling. 'I didn't mean . . .' She shook her head, suddenly looking horrified. 'I'm sorry, Grace, that's not what I meant.' She closed her eyes. 'You must think I'm awful for saying that.'

'I don't think you're awful.' Grace sighed. 'I think this whole situation is awful.' She shook her head, gritting her teeth as she tried to hold back the tears that had sprung from nowhere. 'Poor Cassie. Poor, poor Cassie.'

Faith nodded and returned her hand to Grace's.

'Poor Cassie,' she agreed.

Grace used to like the rain.

The way the gentle, arrhythmic tapping on the window would help soothe her to sleep while she lay warm and safe in her bed, the duvet pulled up tight beneath her chin.

But knowing that Cassie was lying in a hospital bed, her eyes and face ruined by what must have been more than just a terrible accident, knowing that someone had been through Cassie's locker, had been in Grace's *room*, made it impossible to feel safe. Now, the rain drumming on the window sounded more like a thousand fingers tapping on the glass, probing the frames to find a way inside.

Grace picked up her phone and searched the missed calls list. How had she still not heard from her father? It would be at least a week before he sent her the funds to top it up again, so calling him was out of the question.

She scrolled through her address book until she came to Jack's number. Her finger hovered above the dial button for a moment before she replaced the phone on her night table.

She slid out of bed and pulled back the curtain. She knew full well that the window was tightly closed and she had already checked the lock at least three times before turning out the light, but once more couldn't hurt. She leaned in close to the glass in an attempt to view the playing fields, but between the rain running down her window and the darkness beyond, she couldn't see anything.

But that didn't mean *she* couldn't be seen.

Her breath seemed to stick in her throat and she jumped back from the window, pulling the curtains tightly closed.

Although she had seen nothing, she knew he was out there somewhere.

Watching.

Unfortunately, none of her friends were willing to believe that Cassie's accident was anything more than that; an accident. Perhaps it was just too terrible to contemplate. To admit that somebody had deliberately targeted Cassie would be to admit that they had underestimated the threat of the reaper. Maybe it was easier to say it was an accident because that way, nobody was to blame.

But now, Grace knew otherwise.

Shortly after her conversation with Faith, Trick, Ed and Pete had joined them in the kitchen and Grace's memories of what had happened had turned from a confused blur into a certainty that somebody had been in the darkroom with them.

'I'm telling you guys, there was someone at the door, I heard the door handle. We both heard it, then the door to the airlock slammed shut. Right before Cassie fell.'

Faith had been the first to offer an explanation. 'Someone probably just didn't see the light outside. I'm sure as soon as they heard you and Cassie inside, they decided to leave. The door probably slammed closed behind them.'

'That door never slams,' Grace said.

'Perhaps a gust of wind blew it closed,' Faith offered, her voice hopeful.

Grace scowled into her mug of tea. 'It wasn't the wind.' She looked up at Faith and immediately felt bad for snapping at her friend. 'Sorry.'

'It's OK. You've had a terrible shock.' She looked around the table. Pete had barely spoken, had spent most of the evening staring thoughtfully out of the window. Trick kept getting up from his seat to pace around the room, still limping slightly from his fight with Daniel. Ed, who had barely moved, sat red-eyed with his head resting in his hands. 'We've all had a shock,' Faith added.

'So how do you explain the missing film?' Grace asked, turning this time to Pete. He shifted his gaze. 'Daniel was so intent on getting his hands on it yesterday, who's to say . . .' She trailed off, unable to bring herself to make the accusation.

Trick was a little more willing. 'You think Daniel might

have done it?' He shook his head. 'I can't see it, Grace, sorry. The guy's a freak, like I said yesterday, but to deliberately blind someone?'

Ed's fist slammed into the table. 'She's not blind,' he snapped, focusing his bloodshot eyes on Trick. 'Don't say that. We haven't heard anything yet, don't go saying awful things that you don't know are true.' He glared at Grace. 'Just stop talking about it, OK?'

Trick's eyes flashed and he opened his mouth, ready to argue, but stopped when he saw Grace's expression. 'OK. Sorry.'

The rest of the evening had been spent almost entirely in silence. They had eventually decided to try and get some sleep when, at lights-out, there had still been no news on Cassie's condition. Grace had returned to her room, alone with her thoughts.

Now, finally satisfied that the window was locked and that the curtains were pulled tightly enough to stop anyone from looking in, Grace began to walk back to her bed, the path illuminated by the soft green glow of her computer's power light.

She stopped at her desk and trailed her fingers thoughtfully across the closed laptop. Then she pulled out her desk chair and sat down to lift the screen. When it flashed to life she opened her email, then clicked on the trash folder. There, at the top of the pile, was the email that had made her feel so uncomfortable earlier.

You are being lied to.

She opened the message and typed a reply.

Who's lying to me?

Grace clicked the send button, then reached up to close the laptop. Before she had even started to lower the screen, a familiar chime rang out.

She paused, then clicked to open the message.

Can't say. The truth is too dangerous.

Grace stared at the message, her eyes flicking back and forth over the words as she tried to make sense of what she had just read. The truth was dangerous? Had it been dangerous for Cassie? She placed her fingers back to the keys.

Why are you telling me these things?

She hit send and waited. As she sat staring at the computer, she noticed the printer icon flashing at the bottom right hand corner of the screen. She clicked on it and a menu appeared with various tabs. After selecting 'print history' a new screen flashed up with a list of documents beside the dates they had been printed on it. At the top of the list was a document saved as *100Society.doc*.

Her own 100 Society list.

Grace swallowed. She knew she hadn't printed anything within the last few days, so that meant only one thing. Someone had accessed her computer and printed the list.

She thought back to her nocturnal meeting with Trick a couple of nights before. He'd had a copy of the list with him, had said that he'd found it in the art studio. Grace closed her eyes, desperately trying to remember. Had she *ever* printed it out? Could Trick's copy have been something she'd left lying around? Or was it the same copy that someone had taken from her computer?

Grace yawned. It was too late to try and remember what she might or might not have printed. And it was too late to wait for a response from whoever had been emailing her. There were only a few more hours until she had to be up and in the studio and, although Grace was sure there would be no sleep for her tonight, she had to at least try.

Padding back across the worn carpet to her bed, Grace paused to look at the bottom of her door. Usually a thin strip of light from the corridor was visible but now that strip had been broken by a shadow. Tilting her head, Grace watched, trying to work out what could possibly be blocking the light. When the shadow moved, Grace felt her stomach lurch. Her mouth dry, she licked her lips, unable to decide what to do next. Her mobile phone was on the table next to her bed, but who could she call? What would she say?

Stepping closer, her heart began to pound. She pressed her ear against the door, barely daring to breathe. There was not a single sound from the other side, nothing to give away who or what might be outside.

With her fingers resting on the cool metal of the door handle, Grace steeled herself. Then, with as much resolve as she could muster, she pushed the handle down and yanked the door open.

'Good evening, Miss Becker.'

On the other side of the door, Sylvester stood leaning against the far wall. From his hand hung the long chain that connected a huge bunch of keys to his worn leather belt.

Keeping her fingers curled tightly around the handle, Grace stepped back, hiding as much of her pyjama-clad body behind the door as she could.

'Hi,' she said, scanning the corridor that she was dismayed, but unsurprised, to see was otherwise empty. She returned her focus to Sylvester, who had made no attempt to move away from his position reclining against the wall. 'I, um, saw there was someone outside,' she muttered, pushing the door another centimetre or two further closed. 'I saw the shadow.'

'Just me,' Sylvester replied breezily, swinging his keys and whistling as they turned a full circle. He smiled. 'Got to make sure everyone's getting a good night's sleep.'

Grace nodded. 'OK, well . . .'

'Sounded like you were awake in there.' The grin remained, the lines around his mouth deepening.

'Uh, yeah. I was just working. On my computer.'

Sylvester nodded and whistled again as he continued to swing his keys. 'I see. A bit late for work, but I guess that's what you kids are like these days. Always up, always on the computers, eh?' His eyes shifted slightly, his gaze moving up and over her shoulder to where the laptop sat on her desk.

'It's off now,' she said, unsure of whether she really

needed to be justifying herself.

'Well,' Sylvester said, peeling himself away from the wall. 'As long as everything's OK.' He took a step closer and Grace's grip tightened on the handle.

'It is.'

'Night then.' He touched his forehead in a mini salute.

'Night.'

He continued along the corridor, whistling quietly to himself as he walked. When he had finally disappeared around the corner, Grace closed her door and spun the internal lock. Then, remembering the keys he had been swinging back and forth, she pulled her night table away from the bed and pushed it up against the door, wedging it beneath the door handle.

Only when she had checked the locks on the window and door once more did she finally climb into bed.

15

It was only when the sun had risen that Grace finally decided sleep was not going to come.

She ate a quiet, thoughtful breakfast alone in the dorm kitchen, then showered. Where the kitchen had been empty, the bathroom was filled with girls, chatting while they washed and showered.

'I heard her eyes were melted away.'

'No way? That's so *gross*.'

Grace froze, the water beating against her skin as she listened to the conversation unfold.

'Yeah, it was like acid or something. She'll be scarred for life, like she's been in a fire.'

'Oh my god, I'd rather *die* than look like that.'

An intense heat started to simmer in Grace's chest. She wanted to tear the door open, to scream at the stupid girls

122

and tell them to shut up, that they didn't have a clue what they were talking about.

'Can you imagine?' one of them said as the main bathroom door opened, the girl's voice now a low whisper, 'You'd never find someone to love you if you looked like that.'

Not caring that she was naked, Grace reached for the lock on her shower door, ready to let rip. But by the time she pulled it open the bathroom was empty.

Ed was already in the studio when Grace arrived. He was standing in front of Trick's canvas, frowning deeply.

'You're here,' she said. It was a statement rather than a question.

Ed nodded.

'How did you sleep?'

He answered without turning around. 'I didn't.' He pointed at Trick's canvas. It was a painting of the bell tower, but the perspective was different to most pictures of such buildings. Trick had first sketched the picture while lying on the ground with the tower stretching up into the sky above him. 'How does he do it?'

'Do what?'

'Paint these pictures. He's barely in the studio, hardly seems to put any effort in, yet he still manages to produce work I couldn't even dream of.'

Grace paused, unsure of what to say. Obviously Ed didn't want to talk about Cassie, but Grace couldn't think of anything else.

'You have different styles, that's all.'

He shook his head. 'No, it's more than that.' Ed turned to his own painting. He had been so excited by this piece and had drawn sketch upon sketch before starting the final version, determined to make it absolutely perfect. It was a dark picture, one that Grace found disturbing.

The painting was supposed to mimic a child's drawing. It was a gallows, crudely drawn to look like the 'hangman' word game they all played as kids. But the man hanging from the gallows wasn't the simple stickman they used to construct; it was a detailed and vivid painting of a man in a three-piece suit, his dead eyes staring at nothing while his head tilted at a crooked angle above a tightened noose. In the man's hand was a briefcase, falling open to spill bank notes across the bottom of the canvas.

Ed called it 'Hangman'. It was supposed to represent the loss of childhood innocence that takes place once a person leaves school and finds themselves in a corporate world, a place where money talks and where simple games are forgotten.

Now, Ed stared at the canvas he had once been so excited about. He sighed. It was obvious how much he wanted to succeed with his art and what was equally obvious was just how painful it was for him to see Trick saunter in every day before lunch, spend a few hours working, then be the first to leave while still managing to outshine every other person in the room.

It was one of the reasons why he was determined to have his name added to The 100 Society. While Trick got involved simply because he couldn't turn down a chance to break the rules, Ed wanted to be someone. And he wasn't going to let anyone stand in the way of his success.

'Don't torture yourself over it,' Grace said. 'You can't compare yourself to Trick when you're so different.'

He turned to face her. 'But I don't get it. He pays no attention in the theory classes, he never finishes projects on time.' Ed picked up one of Trick's brushes from the paint-covered jam-jar on the table next to his easel. 'And he doesn't even wash his brushes out properly. Seriously Grace, it's enough to drive anyone insane.'

'Ed, you're just as talented as he is.'

Ed snorted. 'I appreciate the sentiment, but if you're going to lie to make me feel better at least make it believable. How am I ever going to make it into an art college like St Peter's when there's this kind of competition on my own doorstep?'

'Ed, do you really think this is the time—'

Ed spun to face her. 'Yes, Grace, I do think it's the time. My girlfriend's lying in the hospital, her face is a mess and we don't know if she'll ever see again. I think this is absolutely the time to talk about anything except that.'

'OK.'

Ed turned back to the canvas. 'This is one of the only things I care about besides Cassie. It means the world to me, Grace.'

'I know. And you'll get there. St Peter's would be lucky to have someone like you. You just need to have a little more faith.'

'Someone mention me?' Faith placed her bag on the desk as Trick and Pete followed into the studio behind her. 'Any news on Cassie?'

Grace shook her head and looked to Ed, but he had already pulled his headphones up over his ears and blocked out everything else but his work.

Faith studied her friend. 'You look awful, Grace.'

'Thanks.'

Shrugging a rucksack from his back, Pete nodded in agreement. 'She's right Grace, you look shattered.'

'I didn't get much sleep last night.'

'I'm not surprised,' Trick said, holding one of his brushes up to the light. He examined it as he addressed Grace. 'You had a pretty bad shock yesterday.' He nodded towards where Ed was applying bold brush strokes to his canvas. 'I'm surprised he's here.'

'I think it's taking his mind off things a bit. He can't visit Cassie yet, so what else can he do?'

Trick shrugged. 'I don't know, it just seems weird to me. I know painting would be the last thing on my mind if . . .' He stopped and looked away.

'If what?'

Trick turned back to her and frowned at the brush he was holding. 'Who's been messing with these?'

Grace stared. There were times, like now, when she

126

saw a different side to Trick. A softer side that made her feel like maybe she could tell him anything, trust him with anything.

'Good morning!' Miss Stone breezed into the room, a bright orange scarf trailing behind her before she came to a sudden stop. 'Oh. Of course,' she said, her voice lowering. 'There's no news on Cassie yet I'm afraid, but we'll let you know as soon as we hear anything.' She positioned her glasses on the tip of her nose and peered around the room. 'In the meantime, the show must go on. Everyone ready for the show tomorrow night?' The question was met with silence.

'Does it look like we're ready for the show?' Trick asked.

'Trick!' Grace turned back to Miss Stone. 'I'm sorry about him.'

'It's OK,' Miss Stone said with a sympathetic smile. 'You've all got the right to be out of sorts today.' She looked pointedly at Trick over the top of her glasses. 'Although that doesn't give you the excuse to slack off. Do you hear me, Mr Turner?'

'I hear you,' he muttered, though a smile played across his lips. 'I'm here, aren't I? Early in fact.'

'He's right,' Pete said, pointing at the clock. 'It's not even ten and Trick's in the studio? If that doesn't say people are panicking about the show, I don't know what does.'

Trick glared, aiming his brush at Pete like a dart.

'You'll all be fine,' Miss Stone called behind her as she disappeared into her office.

When the door closed, Trick launched his brush across the room. It collided with the side of Pete's head before bouncing off and clattering to the floor.

'Hey,' Pete cried, reaching up to rub his temple. 'That hurt. Besides, you said you didn't like your brushes being messed with.'

'Yeah, but someone's already messed with that one,' Trick said. He bent to pick up the brush and winced, clutching a hand to his side.

'Easy there,' Pete said. 'You need help?'

'Let me,' Grace said. She reached down and scooped the brush from the floor. Holding it out to Trick, she lowered her voice. 'How're the ribs?'

'Better. Thank you.' He took the brush, smiling as he slid it from her fingers. Something sparked in his eyes and his smile widened. 'But if you wanted to examine me again . . .'

'In your dreams, Turner.'

He reached out to gently tug at a strand of her unkempt hair. 'Don't you have to sleep to have dreams?' He sighed. 'I was awake last night too, couldn't stop thinking about what happened. I waited up for you; I thought you might want to talk.'

'I was done with talking.' She lowered her voice. 'Besides, you weren't the only one wandering the halls last night.'

'I didn't see anyone else. Except for Sylvester, that is.'

'Exactly.'

Trick frowned. 'You had a run-in with Sylvester?'

128

'Well, not so much a run-in as . . .'

'As what?'

She looked up at him. 'He was kind of standing outside my room last night.'

'What do you mean, standing outside your room?'

'He was just there. I saw his shadow and when I opened the door, he was just standing there. For like, a really long time.' Aware of how stupid it sounded, Grace shook her head. 'I'm sure it was nothing.'

'He's a security guard,' Trick said. 'It's his job to be wandering the halls at night.' He turned back to his canvas and plucked a paint-covered brush from his jam-jar. He pointed it at Grace. 'But you just call me if you get freaked out, OK? Doesn't matter what time it is. And I know you can look after yourself,' he added hurriedly, holding up his hands to stem whatever tirade he might have been expecting in reply, 'but you can. OK?'

Trying not to laugh, Grace smiled. 'OK, Trick. Thank you.' She started towards her own canvas, then turned back to face him. 'You really waited up for me last night?'

Trick shrugged, his focus now on the picture he was dabbing at with his brush. 'Just thought you might have liked to talk. No biggie.'

'OK.'

'Oh my!' Faith's voice rang out from the other side of the studio, high and panic filled.

Grace spun to see her friend sitting behind the screen of her laptop, hand over her mouth. Ed was already behind

129

her, peering over her shoulder at the screen.

'Oh man,' he said, reaching over her to tap furiously at the keyboard. 'This is bad. This is really bad.'

'What's going on?'

'You should probably all see this,' Ed said, stepping back. 'It's the blog.'

Grace didn't like the way Ed's face had contorted with concern. She rose slowly to join the others, now huddled behind Faith and her laptop. 'Has it been hacked again?' The computer screen was filled with images of all of the locations they had previously tagged, their own dragon now covered with a grinning reaper. 'Is this real?' She leaned in to get a closer look. 'Surely it's Photoshopped? There's no way someone could have covered that many tags in such a short space of time.'

Ed exhaled. 'Who knows? If someone was dedicated enough, why not?'

'What should we do?' Faith asked. 'Should we tell someone?'

'Don't be ridiculous,' Trick snapped. 'We'll all get expelled.'

'Hey,' Grace said, 'that's enough. She was only asking.' She turned back to the computer. 'So why have they plastered it all over our blog?' she asked. 'Why rub it in our faces like this?'

'Maybe someone just wants to be noticed,' Pete said. 'Get your attention.'

'Oh, they've got my attention, all right.'

130

'We can go back,' Trick said. 'It didn't take all that long – we can do it again. Besides, we've got the pictures, we've got the proof that you did it, Grace. You'll still be in The 100 Society.'

Grace shook her head, fighting back tears of anger; tears of guilt that this was upsetting her so much when Cassie had so much more to worry about.

'Did someone post these up on the site?' Faith asked.

'Nope,' Ed replied. 'The pictures are part of the content of the web page. Someone's accessed the site and embedded the photographs.'

'Why would they do that?'

'Because they can. Because they want to show us how clever they are by covering every tag we've done and by hacking our site. Whatever we can do, they can do it too.' He looked up. 'The tagging thing I can just about understand, but this is taking it a step further. This is personal.'

'How can you be so sure?'

Ed scrolled through the website. 'There's more.'

Familiar photographs began to appear. All of the photos were pictures that Cassie had taken during their tagging sessions. Pictures intended to be a record of the fun they'd had and certainly never taken to be published on a website for anyone to see. There was a picture of Grace, her Balaclava pulled up to expose her face as she held up two paint cans, grinning at the camera while Trick looked on from behind, laughing. In another, Faith and Ed stood together, high-fiving beside a tagged brick wall. Then there was one of Pete pulling a face at the camera, a torch held beneath his chin to illuminate his distorted features.

Trick lunged forwards, pulling the laptop towards him. He scrolled through the site, picture after picture of the group staring back at him. 'Who did this?' He turned to Ed. 'You're the computer whizz, you tell us how the hell someone managed to hack into this supposedly secure site and post our pictures all over it.'

Ed raised his hands. 'I have no idea. Probably the same way we were hacked before.'

'Well, delete them!' Trick shouted, shoving the laptop back at him. 'You're the one who set it up in the first place.'

'Hey, don't yell at me. I didn't put them there.'

'Well, someone did,' Trick snapped back. 'And if they aren't deleted right now, we're all going to be kicked out of here.' He ran his fingers through his hair, then turned to kick the chair beside him. It skittered across the floor before colliding with Cassie's easel.

'Hey, careful,' Ed shouted.

Trick turned to Ed, his eyes flashing. 'Careful? Don't tell me to be careful. You're the one who's leaked these pictures.'

'I told you, it wasn't me.'

'Oh, this is bad,' Faith moaned.

'It'll be OK,' Pete said, placing a hand on her shoulder. 'Ed can delete them.' He looked at Ed. 'You can delete them, right?'

'Let's see.' Ed started typing furiously while the others watched on.

'How did this happen?' Faith asked. 'How could these pictures have possibly ended up on the internet?'

'I have no idea,' Ed said, shaking his head. 'They're all Cassie's pictures, she keeps them all on her hard drive. The only copies are the negatives which she keeps shut away in her locker.'

Trick folded his arms. 'Then it must have been Cassie.'

Ed pulled back from the keyboard, drawing himself up to his full height. He jabbed a finger at Trick's chest. 'Say that again,' he dared, pushing harder with his finger.

Trick glared back at Ed. 'Take your hands off me, man.'

'Wait,' Grace cried, darting between the two boys. 'Remember what I told you last night, that Cassie thought someone had been in her locker?'

Ed's focus shifted from Trick to Grace. 'You're right.' He turned back to the screen. 'You really think this is all connected? The person graffiti-ing over our tags is the same person who broke into Cassie's locker?' Swallowing hard, he looked back to Grace. 'You really think someone attacked her?' He paused. 'You think *Daniel* attacked her?'

Grace looked towards where Daniel's easel stood, holding that fiery canvas. 'I don't know,' she whispered.

'Look,' Pete interjected, pointing at the laptop. 'We can talk this through later, but right now I think there's a job that needs doing.'

Ed glared at Trick. 'I'll do it when he apologises.'

Trick lunged forwards and Grace shot out a hand to hold his arm. 'Just do it,' she said, her voice firm.

'Fine.' Trick pulled away from her grip. 'I'm sorry,' he spat.

Ed turned back to the keys and typed while the others looked on. Finally, he nodded. 'There. All gone.'

Grace looked over his shoulder at the restored web page. 'Is there any way of tracing who did it?' she asked.

'Not with my skills,' Ed said. 'You'd need a hacking genius to uncover that kind of information.'

Pete nodded. 'You'd need to be a hacking genius to get into that site in the first place.' He leaned forwards, reaching for the laptop. 'Here, let me have a go, there must be a way of . . .'

Ed pulled the laptop away. 'Seriously, Pete? You're pulling the genius card now?'

'What?' Pete looked from Ed to Grace. 'What did I do?'

'Just use a little tact, Pete,' Grace said.

'I'm only trying to help.'

'No,' snapped Trick. 'You're trying, yet again, to show us all how much smarter you are.'

Pete pulled himself up, face to face with Trick. 'You think I need to prove that? You think you could do better?'

Trick stepped forwards, until his nose was almost touching Pete's. 'You're not the genius you think you are, buddy.'

'More than you'll ever be, *buddy*.' Pete placed a hand flat against Trick's chest and pushed.

'OK, enough.' Grace stepped between the boys, forcing them in opposite directions. 'I think we're all quite happy for Ed to be the one to handle this.'

'Fine.' Pete folded his arms and stepped back.

'Let's just hope they were taken off in time,' Trick said. 'If any of those pictures get leaked, it's all over.'

'Well, there's nothing that we can do about it now, is there?' Pete slapped Trick on the back. 'Just a waiting game, I guess.'

'It's easy for you to say,' Trick muttered. 'I'll be the first one to get expelled. Cross is looking for any excuse to get rid of me.'

'That's because you do things like get into fights,' Faith said. 'I heard what happened with Daniel.'

'Talking of Daniel,' Grace said, eyeing the empty space by his easel, 'has anyone seen him recently?'

'Probably keeping a low profile,' Pete said. 'Trying to avoid another beat-down from Trick.'

Trick winced, rubbing a hand over his ribs. 'I think I was the one who got the beat-down.'

Grace smiled, but her expression froze when Cross walked through the studio door.

Faith hurriedly lowered her laptop screen and it clicked shut, loud in the suddenly silent room.

Cross closed the door behind him and turned to face the students. 'Good morning.'

'Good morning, Mr Cross,' they chorused.

'We've just heard from Cassie's parents,' Cross said,

perching on one of the tables at the front of the room. 'She's had surgery, but it's still too early to tell if it's been successful.' He crossed his meaty arms. 'I'll need to have a chat with you at some point, Grace, to find out exactly what happened. OK?'

Grace nodded, swallowing hard against the lump that had appeared in her throat.

'OK.' He stood up again, looking around the studio. 'We've decided to go ahead with the show on Wednesday, seeing how hard you've all worked on your pieces, so long as you're all happy with that decision.'

He waited, but the room stayed silent.

'He can't have seen the photos on the website,' Trick whispered in Grace's ear. 'I think we're clear.'

'OK then,' Cross boomed. He clapped his hands once, the sound echoing around the studio like a crack of thunder. 'I'll leave you all to get on with your work and I'll see you on Wednesday.'

When Cross had gone and closed the door behind him, Faith clutched a hand to her chest. 'I thought I was going to have a heart attack,' she groaned.

Pete laughed nervously. 'Me too. I guess that means we're in the clear.' He prodded at his clay sculpture and sighed. 'There's no way this is going to be ready for Wednesday.'

'You'll get it done,' Grace said. 'Just keep going. It's looking great, I promise.'

'I know you're just saying that,' he said, 'but it's

still nice to hear.'

'Just try not to worry about it. The more you stress about it the harder it'll be.'

'You're right. Maybe I'll take a break and come back to it later.' He turned to Grace with a wry smile. 'You know, one day I'll do something that'll blow your socks off.'

Grace looked at the lumpy mess of clay, then reached out and grabbed one of Pete's hands. 'You don't need to try and impress me, Pete. You already do that every day, just by being you.'

'Thanks,' he mumbled. 'I need some more clay.'

When Pete had disappeared into the supply cupboard, Faith shook her head. 'I can't believe you.'

'What?'

'You're leading him on.'

'I'm not leading him on.' Grace glanced to where Trick stood, pretending not to listen. 'Don't say stuff like that.'

'He deserves better, that's all I'm saying.' She lifted the screen of her laptop and disappeared behind it. Soon, the room was filled with the sound of her fingers tapping a little too hard against the keyboard.

Grace turned to Trick. 'I think the whole world's gone mad today.'

Trick looked up from his painting, the sky around his bell tower almost complete.

'You know what? I've got a feeling the madness has only just begun.'

Grace stood at the window, her nose pressed against the cold glass.

A small patch of condensation appeared as she exhaled and she moved back, running a finger through the foggy patch to clear her vision to the night sky. The art studio's position on the first floor gave an excellent view across the courtyard to the main school building. At this time of night it was lit up, the leaded windows glowing softly from the lights within and occasionally allowing a glimpse of a silhouette walking along the corridors.

Grace watched as yet another figure walked the length of the hall in the opposite building and she wondered if perhaps that was the person who had sent her the emails. Perhaps that was the person who had sprayed the reapers on their doors and hacked their blog.

Maybe it was the person who had thrown chemicals in Cassie's face.

Opposite where Grace stood, a bank of tall windows revealed the inside of the Great Hall, the empty room on the first floor that, in two days' time, would be the location of the art show.

'You OK?'

Grace turned to Trick, poised behind his easel with a paint palette and brush. He was watching her carefully, his brow furrowed in concern.

'Yeah. I just can't stop thinking about Cassie.'

'I know,' he said, tossing his brush on to the table behind him and wiping his hands on his T-shirt. Smears of paint covered his clothes, but he didn't seem to care. 'But you know you can't blame yourself, right? You did everything you could to help her.'

Grace stepped back from the window, pausing at Ed's easel. 'He'll regret not finishing that tonight,' she said, leaning in closer to look at some of his more recent brush strokes. 'He was so close, too.'

'He's barely touched it since Cassie got hurt.'

'I would never have placed them together,' Grace replied with a small smile. 'But he obviously cares about her.'

'I guess you can't always predict who's going to end up with who.'

Grace took one of Ed's brushes and picked thoughtfully at the bristles. 'You do know I'm not trying to lead Pete on?'

Trick paused. 'Where did that come from?'

'Come on, Trick.' She raised an eyebrow.

'Yeah, OK. Look, I know you and Pete have this thing.'

'What do you mean, "thing"?'

'Like, you've been friends forever. And that means something. Even though at times I think he can be a bit up himself.'

'Yeah, I kind of figured he rubbed you up the wrong way sometimes. You don't exactly hold back.'

'I don't know. He just makes me feel stupid sometimes.'

'That's exactly what he's trying to do. And that's wrong, but you wind him up too.'

'I know. I guess I just want to prove to him . . .' he paused, 'to *you*, that there's more to me. That I can do more than just be that idiot who says stupid things.'

'I know that already.'

'See, then you say stuff like that and . . .' Trick scratched his head, his fingers tangling in the mop of dark curls. 'I just don't want to get in the way of anything you might have with Pete.'

'You wouldn't get in the way of anything I didn't want you to get in the way of.'

'What does that even mean?' he laughed and Grace threw one of her own paintbrushes at him.

'Hey,' he cried. 'That's my move!' He picked up the brush and tucked it behind his ear.

'OK, give it back.' She moved towards him. 'Come on, I need it to finish.'

'You shouldn't have thrown it at me, then.' Trick

stood up and darted across the room.

'Come on, Trick,' Grace said with a groan. She followed after him, hand outstretched. 'Come on, please.'

He plucked the brush from behind his ear and held it out, his back against the window. 'Here, come and get it.'

'Fine.' She stepped towards him but he dodged to one side before throwing the paintbrush across the room. It struck Grace's canvas, leaving a dark blue smudge of paint on one of the silhouettes.

'Trick!'

'Oops.' Trick turned to run but Grace reached out and grabbed his shirt, yanking him back towards her. The sharp sound of ripping material filled the room and she gasped, covering her mouth with her hands.

'Oh, you are *kidding* me.' Trick held his arms up, looking with dismay at his torn shirt.

'I'm so, so, sorry,' Grace said through her fingers.

'Two shirts in one week? And this was one of my favourites.'

Grace pushed her fingers tighter against her mouth, trying to stifle the giggle that had come from nowhere.

'You think this is funny?' His face was dark, but his eyes shone.

Grace nodded.

He beckoned her. 'Come here, Becker.'

She shook her head and squealed as he lunged towards her, grabbing her from behind. His arms snaked around her waist and he picked her up, her legs pedalling in the air. 'I'm sorry,' she repeated between bursts of laughter.

There was a sharp intake of breath from behind her and Trick released his grip, dropping her back to the ground. Grace turned to see him bent double, clutching at his ribs.

'Are you OK?' she asked, the laughter quickly disappearing.

'Yeah,' he said. He looked at her and smiled. 'Honestly, Becker, I'm OK.'

'OK.' She nodded. 'I just don't like seeing you in pain.'

'But ripping my shirt is all fun and games?'

'Oh Trick, I am sorry. It's not been a great week, has it?'

He shrugged. 'It's not been all bad. I kind of liked what happened the last time my shirt got torn.' He lifted the torn material to look at the bruise. It had darkened since the last time Grace saw it and was now a sickly purple-green.

'You mean this?' Grace asked, reaching out to touch the bruise. His skin was warm and she could feel the rhythm of his heart beneath her fingers.

Trick nodded and stepped towards her. Their bodies were close, almost the exact same positions they had been in after Trick's fight with Daniel.

'There was just one thing missing,' he said, his fingers touching her cheek. He leaned forwards, his breath warm on her lips, but the moment was cut short when Grace's phone beeped loudly, the sound shattering the silence that had fallen between them.

142

'Ignore it,' she whispered. 'It's just a text.'

Then came another beep, this one from Trick's trouser pocket.

Trick groaned, resting his forehead against Grace's. 'I think the world is conspiring against this ever happening.'

Grace smiled, reaching for her phone.

If you want to know the truth about the reaper, come to Lost Souls Bridge. Twenty minutes. Tell no one. Trust no one. Yours, A Friend.

Lost Souls Bridge.

The next tag on The 100 Society list.

When Grace looked up, Trick was frowning at his own phone. 'Let me guess. A message from a friend?'

He nodded. 'It says *tell no one*, but we've got the same message?'

Grace stared. 'What's going on?'

'Looks like someone's intent on finishing The 100 Society before we do.' Trick pointed his phone at Grace. 'I think it's time to end this. Whoever it is playing these games, and I'm pretty sure we know who, needs to be told to stop.' He grabbed his coat.

'Wait.'

Trick turned to Grace. 'What?'

She frowned. 'I know you don't believe me, but what if . . .' She paused. 'What if it really *was* Daniel who hurt Cassie?'

'I just don't see it, Grace. The 100 Society thing I get; he gains something by beating us to it. But hurting Cassie?

143

Why would he have done that? What would he have to gain?'

'Just humour me,' Grace said. 'Just for a moment. Let's say he did attack Cassie and now he's luring us down to the bridge. What if this is a trap?'

Trick zipped his coat up. 'Then we take back-up.'

'OK.' Grace nodded, but before she had the chance to dial a number, the phone rang in her hand. Almost immediately after, Trick's phone began to ring.

'Hello?'

'Grace? Is that you?'

'Yeah, hi Faith.' Grace watched as Trick answered his own phone. 'What's up? I was just about to call you.'

Faith's voice shook. 'I've just had the weirdest text message.'

'Us too.'

'It's Ed,' Trick whispered, covering the mouthpiece. 'He got the message too.'

Faith's voice rang out from Grace's phone. 'What's going on, Grace?'

'I don't know,' Grace replied. 'But I think it's time to go and find out.'

17

Grace shivered. A light drizzle had started to fall, soaking through her jacket and dampening her skin.

She clapped her gloved hands together as she searched the empty road behind her, the darkness punctuated with pools of light from the streetlamps. There was still no sign of the others.

'Cold?'

Grace nodded and exhaled slowly, her breath misting in front of her face.

'Here.' Trick threw an arm around her shoulders, rubbing her arm to try and coax a little heat back into her body. 'Better?'

Grace nodded. 'Do you think the others will be here soon?'

'They should be,' replied Trick. 'Let's give them a few

more minutes.'

The road they were on led to Lost Souls Bridge, only a few hundred metres from where they stood. While they waited, the drizzle quickly turned into something heavier. The rain sparkled as it fell through the light of the streetlamps, illuminating the pavements and concrete walls on either side of the bridge with glittering orange light. 'I can't see anyone up there,' she said, squinting into the distance. 'Do you really think we're going to find anything?'

Grace could feel his breath, warm against her face. 'I'm still sure this whole thing is just a big wind-up.'

'Hey!'

Grace turned to see two figures moving towards them, their forms taking shape as they stepped beneath each streetlight before almost disappearing into the darkness between. The shapes were familiar, a tall figure striding alongside someone much smaller, who was almost running to keep up. 'Ed? Faith? Is that you?'

A torch beam tilted upwards to illuminate the carrier's face. It was Faith. 'I'm telling you,' she said, 'I've got a bad feeling about this.'

Ed's face was barely visible, but Grace was still able to make out the tension in his jawline. 'Do we think it's Daniel?' he asked.

'We don't know,' Grace said. 'Are you sure you should be here?' she added gently.

'I'm sure. If he had anything,' he said, his voice deepening almost to a growl, 'and I mean *anything* to do with what

146

happened to Cassie . . .' He started forward, his shoulder colliding with Trick's.

'Whoa, hang on just a second there, buddy.' Trick grabbed at Ed's jacket, pulling him back. 'We don't know what we're dealing with yet.'

'Does it matter?' Ed pulled himself from Trick's grip.

'Wait a second,' Grace said, turning back to Faith. 'Where's Pete?'

'I thought you were going to call him. He's not with you?'

'No, I thought you were calling him.'

'So did anyone call him?' Trick asked. He was met with silence. 'Oh, great. Do we even know if he got the text message?'

Grace pulled her phone out of her pocket. 'I'll call him now, he's probably back at the school wondering where we all are.'

'OK, just make sure—'

A shrill cry cut through the night air.

For a moment there was nothing, just a hollow silence as everybody turned, holding their breath, towards the bridge.

Then came the shouting, sudden and panic-filled. It sounded like a fight had broken out, although Grace couldn't see anyone standing on the bridge.

Without a word, Ed started sprinting towards the voices. A moment later, Trick gave chase but Ed's legs were far longer and he easily pulled ahead.

Grace looked at Faith. Without a word, they began to run after the boys.

Ed reached the bridge well ahead of the others. He came to an abrupt halt underneath one of the streetlamps and paused, his head moving as he searched for the source of the commotion. Then he turned, running towards the side of the bridge. His body hit the wall and he placed his hands flat on the top before pulling himself up and over, disappearing into the darkness on the other side.

Moments later, Trick followed, hurling himself over the wall without a moment's hesitation.

'Trick!' Grace screamed, a burst of energy propelling her forwards. She sprinted towards the bridge wall, her breath coming in ragged bursts. As she drew nearer, the raised voices grew louder, clearer.

'Get off me,' someone cried out, muffled.

It was Daniel. He was on that ledge, fighting with someone.

'Get him! Have you got him?'

The voice was unmistakable. Daniel was fighting with Pete. He *had* got the message, but he had come here alone and Grace knew why. It was because of her, because he didn't want to put her in any danger.

'Pull him back, just—'

'No, get off me, listen, just listen—'

Grace reached the wall first and turned to see Faith still running towards her. 'They're on the ledge,' she yelled. 'Pete's there too. Quick, get your torch over here before they all go over.'

Feet scuffled against concrete on the other side of the wall and someone started shouting, almost hysterical. 'Pull him up, pull him up!'

'Faith, quick!' Grace shouted again, her own voice filled with terror.

'Please,' a voice sobbed from the darkness, 'don't let me go, please. I'm sorry, I'm sorry.'

Grace wanted to cover her ears, to cut out the cries. She couldn't work out whose voice belonged to whom any more. 'The torch,' Grace screamed at Faith, now only a few steps away. 'For god's sake, Faith, please!' She pulled the torch from Faith's hands and leaned over the wall, the beam flashing along the length of the ledge as a terrible silence fell around them.

Barely daring to look, Grace angled the torch towards the figures kneeling at the edge. A loud thumping filled her ears and she realized it was her own racing heart. With the torch beam shaking, she moved it up and down the ledge, counting one, two, three people, but that couldn't be right so she shone it again, more slowly, again counting only three figures.

In the torchlight, Ed, Pete and Trick stared back at her, their own chests heaving. Pete's arms dangled at his sides, his mouth hanging open. Next to him, Trick crouched down low to the ground, staring at his hand which was still outstretched over the side of the ledge, empty. Ed was leaning back against the wall, his hands pressed against the sides of his head, his eyes squeezed closed.

'Where is he?' Grace asked. When there was no answer, she shook her head. 'No. No, no, no.' Then she was moaning, crying, and she felt the ground, hard beneath her knees. The torch fell from her hand and rolled along the pavement, lighting a scene around her that she knew would be imprinted on her memory forever.

Faith, tears spilling from her eyes and running over fingers that covered her silent mouth.

And Ed, Pete and Trick on the other side of the wall.

Three people where there should have been four.

18

For a long while, nobody said anything. Nobody moved.

Grace had never been so aware of a silence before and she couldn't bear it, but at the same time she couldn't speak because that would mean she would have to say something about what had just happened, and that would make it all real. It would mean that Daniel was no longer on the ledge with Ed, Pete and Trick; it would mean that he was now somewhere beneath them, in the river that had looked so calm when she had stood there, in that exact same spot, with Pete. Now, in the cold and the dark, she couldn't imagine a worse place to be.

Behind them, a lorry rumbled across the bridge, the rain sparkling in its headlights. The lorry didn't stop or slow; the driver either oblivious or unconcerned by their presence on the bridge in the middle of the night.

'What happened?' Faith was the first to speak and Grace blinked as if she had just been woken from a deep sleep. 'Did he fall? What happened?' Her voice rose, filling with panic.

'I had him.' Trick's voice, from somewhere behind the wall. Still on the ledge, perhaps with his empty hand still stretched out into the darkness. 'I don't know what happened. I had him.' Then he appeared from the shadows, pulling himself over the wall before grabbing the torch that was on the ground next to where Grace was kneeling, still unable to speak. He jumped back on to the ledge and angled the torch into the blackness below. The light was swallowed up by the darkness, only the rain visible in its beam.

'DANIEL!'

Silence.

'DANIEL!' Trick shouted again, more like a scream, reacting to the panic and adrenaline that must have only just kicked in to his system. He turned back to Grace, eyes wide, a hand clutching at his ribs. 'We have to call someone, call the police, the coastguard, anyone.'

Grace was sobbing, shaking her head.

'No one can survive a fall like that.' Pete now, still on the other side, leaning against the wall, his head in his hands. 'He's gone.'

'No, he's not. We can get him, we can pull him out.' Trick started to clamber back over the wall. 'We'll find him.'

Pete grabbed his arm and yanked him roughly back on to the ledge. 'He's gone, Trick, we have to think about this.'

'There's nothing to think about.'

'I'm telling you—'

'Shut up, Pete, just shut up. You can't smart your way out of everything.'

'Maybe *you* can't—'

Trick lunged at Pete, then stopped himself. 'We have to call someone,' he repeated. He scrambled back over the wall on to the pavement before pulling his phone out of his pocket. He was breathing rapidly, his fingers shaking as he tried to dial a number. The rain had increased in intensity once more, now falling in sheets as the wind also began to pick up, and Trick had to wipe the phone with his sleeve before he was able to use the touchscreen effectively.

Pete followed after Trick, grabbing at him again. 'I said, he's gone,' he shouted over the noise of the rain. 'Why aren't you listening?'

Trick tried to shrug Pete away, but Pete held on tightly to the back of Trick's jacket, his other hand reaching for the phone. They struggled for a moment until Trick turned suddenly, throwing a fist in Pete's direction. It failed to connect with his jaw, but landed heavily on his shoulder and Pete stumbled back, releasing his grip. Trick started to dial again.

'Wait,' Ed called. 'Pete's right, we need to think.'

Trick lowered his phone. 'You're kidding?'

'He's gone.' Ed shouted through the rain. 'Nobody would have survived that fall. We would have heard him shouting.'

'So he might have been knocked unconscious. He still needs help.'

'Think about it,' Pete said, his voice firm. 'If he knocked himself out, how would he be able to keep afloat?'

'We can't just leave him there,' Faith sobbed. 'Trick's right, we have to call someone.'

'Call who?' asked Ed. 'The police? And tell them what exactly?'

'We'll tell them he fell,' said Faith. 'It was an accident.' She looked from Trick to Pete, her wet hair sticking to her face and her eyes pleading. 'It was an accident,' she repeated.

'We were fighting,' Pete said suddenly.

Ed turned to him. 'What do you mean, you were fighting?'

'He was tagging the bridge,' Pete said, his voice trembling. 'With the reaper. I found him here, and . . .' His voice cracked and he lifted his fists to his head, eyes squeezed tightly shut. 'This wasn't supposed to happen.'

'Somebody, tell me what to do,' Trick yelled, waving his phone furiously in Grace's direction. 'Do I call the police or not?'

Grace stared at Trick, his outline blurred through her tears. She didn't know what to say. Less than an hour ago he had tried to kiss her and now he was shouting at her, his lips pulled tight, his face wet with tears and rain.

'I don't know,' she whispered. Her voice sounded strange, disjointed. 'I don't know.'

With a roar, Trick turned, hurling his phone against the pavement and smashing it into pieces. Then his arm fell to his side and his whole body sagged in defeat. 'We've killed him.' There was no emotion left in his voice and he looked exhausted, dazed. He looked at Pete. 'We killed him.'

'No.' Pete jabbed a finger at Trick. 'Stop that. Don't say that. It was an accident, he fell.'

Trick said nothing.

There would be a police investigation. They would all be questioned, they would all be implicated. There was fresh graffiti on the bridge, a crime they were all already suspected of by their headmaster.

This could only end badly and Grace was sure they would all end up expelled from Clifton. Probably even worse.

She squeezed her eyes closed, the rain falling against her face as she waited for something to happen, for someone to say something or do something, but everyone else was just as incapable of rational thought as she was. It should be her, she thought, she should be the one to start talking, to come up with a logical next step, but right now she couldn't seem to make her brain work properly.

'We should go.'

Grace opened her eyes. Faith was on her feet, standing

with her chin lifted and her shoulders square in a posture that was as decisive as the words she had just spoken.

Grace stared at her friend and when Faith met her gaze there was a tiny flicker of self-doubt, but she quickly looked away. 'If we're not going to call someone, we need to get out of here.'

Nobody spoke.

Faith took a step away from the wall. 'Now,' she said. 'We go now.'

Ed moved after her. 'She's right,' he said. 'We have to get out of here. Right now.'

They started to walk away from the bridge.

Pete turned to Grace and, although he said nothing, she could see the fear in his eyes. Without a word, he followed after Faith and Ed.

None of them looked back.

'I can't get up.' Grace's legs felt almost numb, like they didn't belong to her. Her jeans were soaked and clung to her skin, but she didn't care.

'Here.' Trick reached out a hand. 'We should go with them,' he said flatly.

She nodded. 'It's late,' she said, her voice hollow. 'We can call someone tomorrow.'

Trick didn't reply. They both knew they weren't going to call anyone. Not that night, not in the morning.

Not ever.

'We should get his stuff,' she said, shining Faith's torch over the wall and illuminating the backpack that was sitting on the ledge, its owner now somewhere in the darkness below. Grace was shivering and she hugged herself, her teeth chattering violently.

'I'll get it.' Trick climbed over the wall and even in the dim light from the distant streetlamp, Grace could see he was shaking just as much as she was.

'What about the graffiti?' she said eventually.

'What about it?'

'It links us to here. To Daniel.'

'Nobody even knows he was here. Besides, it's not our tag.'

Grace closed her eyes. They were talking about evidence. How had it come to this? How had it come to be that somebody was dead and now they were removing his things, objects that could link them to the scene?

The crime scene.

Nausea twisted her stomach and she realized she was going to vomit. She pulled herself up, leaned over the wall and retched.

'Hey,' Trick was beside her, one hand on her back, the other supporting her as she heaved. 'It's OK. It's OK.'

'No,' Grace sobbed. 'It's not OK. It's never going to be OK again and you know it.'

She buried her face against his chest, the wet cotton of his shirt tight against his skin. She could hear his heart racing, his breath coming in ragged heaves as she realized he was crying too.

Standing alone together on the bridge with the rain

falling around them, Grace was reminded of the words Trick had spoken to her earlier.

I've got a feeling the madness has only just begun.

Grace and Trick were the last back to Clifton. The tape that held back the lock of the fire door was still in place and together they peeled it away, checking carefully for any remnants.

'I'll get rid of it,' Trick said, slipping the tape into his pocket.

Grace nodded, trying not to think about the fact that this was yet more evidence they were disposing of, just like Daniel's bag and the paint cans they had thrown into a dumpster on the way back from the bridge.

'We should get some sleep.' His voice wavering, Trick spoke to the floor, still wet with the footprints of their friends.

Grace nodded, unable to make a sound past the lump in her throat. When she started to walk towards her room,

Trick took her hand, pulling her back.

'It's going to be OK,' he said, although Grace could see he was only saying it because he thought he should. His eyes said something different.

Grace's nod was just as much of a lie as Trick's words, but it was all she could manage. She buried herself against him.

'Don't leave me,' she whispered. 'Not tonight.'

Trick nodded.

Grace led him towards her room, not letting his hand leave hers. Her bedside lamp was still on from earlier, the gentle glow casting light across a room that looked exactly the same as it had done only a few hours earlier, except somehow, somehow everything was different.

She shrugged her jacket from her shoulders and kicked off her trainers, then lay on her bed. Trick took his own jacket off and stripped off his wet shirt, then lay down beside her. He took a strand of hair that had fallen across her tear-streaked face and tucked it behind her ear.

'We should try and get some sleep,' he whispered.

She caught his hand as he reached for the light. 'No. Leave it on. I don't want it to be dark.'

If it was dark, it would mean there would be nothing to see except for the pictures in her head, the same images she saw every time she closed her eyes: Ed, Trick and Pete standing alone on the side of the bridge.

Trick's hand fell on to her side and he pulled her closer to him, his body warm against hers.

Grace closed her eyes, but she was sure there would be no sleep. How could anyone sleep when their head was filled with the cries of someone begging for their life?

But when she next blinked her eyes open, the orange glow of the rising sun was visible through the gap in her curtains.

There were a few blissful seconds before the explosion of memories from the previous night, and for a moment she struggled to breathe as thoughts of Daniel's floating body made an unexpected and most unwelcome appearance. She looked down at the hand that lay across her body. In the dim glow of her bedside lamp it looked like the white, bloated arm of a corpse; one that might have crawled out of the water in the middle of the night, intent on revenge.

She screamed and pushed the arm away, scuttling across the bed before tumbling with the sheet into a tangled mess on the floor.

'What the . . . ?'

Grace looked up to see Trick, leaning over the side of her bed and blinking at her with sleepy, bloodshot eyes, the red rims a sign that he'd also had a bad night's sleep.

'I'm sorry.' She pulled herself up to kneel in front of him. 'Bad dream.'

'Yeah, had a few of those myself.' He sat up and reached for his shirt.

'Wait,' she said, climbing back on to the bed beside him.

She reached out to touch one of the inked patterns that ran from his bicep up to his shoulder and across his chest. He shuddered and smiled wryly as goosebumps broke out across his skin. 'You see what you do to me?'

'Tell me what they're for,' she said, tracing a finger over the ink. 'I need to think about something else.' She closed her eyes. 'Anything else.'

He paused for a moment, uncertain. 'OK,' he said, looking down. 'These ones,' he said, pointing at a set of numbers, 'are the dates of birth of my parents.'

'What's this?' Grace asked, pointing towards the skull and roses.

Trick looked away. 'I lost a friend,' he said. 'It was my way of paying my respects.'

Grace nodded. 'And this?' Her finger came to rest on the word CHILTERN, written beneath a swirl of ink on the muscle of his chest.

'This's where I grew up. Chiltern Court. It's a council estate on the other side of town.'

Grace nodded. She knew of Chiltern Court, but only because her parents had warned her against going there. It was a notorious estate, one that was often featured in the local paper underneath dramatic headlines that screamed of drugs and gang violence. 'I didn't know you came from there,' she said. 'You've never mentioned it.'

'Why would I?' Trick yawned and ran a hand through his matted curls. 'People here think I'm scum anyway, why add fuel to their fire?'

162

Grace touched the CHILTERN tattoo. 'Not everyone thinks you're scum.'

'No. I know.'

'Why did you get it tattooed? If you didn't want anyone to know?'

'Because it's for me. And besides,' he said with a forced half-smile that betrayed his bloodshot eyes, 'not many people ever really get close enough to take much notice of what it says.'

'I'm glad I got the chance.' Grace lay back on the pillow and trailed a finger down his inked arm. 'But that still doesn't answer my question.'

He sighed. 'OK. Well, all of the tattoos mean something to me. They're inspired by things that have affected me, positively or negatively. Things I'm proud of, things I'm not so proud of but that have shaped me into the person I am. They're there so I don't forget where I came from. That stuff is important to me.' He grabbed his shirt from the end of the bed and pulled it over his head. Then he turned to Grace. 'You're important to me too. I hope you know that.'

She nodded and closed her eyes against the familiar sting of tears.

'Hey,' he said.

Grace looked at him.

'We have to be strong,' Trick said, his voice firm. 'We made our decision and we have to live with it. There's no going back.' Although his decisiveness was familiar, there was now a hard edge to his voice that Grace had never heard before.

'I . . .' she started, unable to find the words that might soften the look in his eyes, a severity that made something inside her run cold. Eventually she just nodded.

'We'll talk later,' he said, pulling his shirt down to meet his jeans. 'I should get back up to my room before anyone notices I'm missing.' He glanced at his watch. 'There's a couple of hours before we need to get to the studio. Try and get some more sleep, OK?' He leaned down to kiss her forehead and was out of the door before she had the chance to answer.

'Bye,' she whispered to the empty room. She lay back, but this time sleep was less forthcoming. Without Trick's warmth beside her, the memories of what had happened were all too real.

They had killed him. It didn't matter that Grace wasn't the one who had fought with him on the ledge, it didn't matter that Ed and Faith didn't want to be there. They *had* all been there, they had all been part of what led to the death of a person, someone who might have deserved *something*, but not that.

Grace turned to the wall by her bed and was met by the face of her father, smiling at her from the photographs. She closed her eyes, imagining the shame he would feel when he found out his daughter had been involved in something so horrific.

His own daughter, a killer.

She thought of Daniel's parents, unaware that their son was even missing, unaware of the pain they would feel when they found out that his body had been in that river, cold and dark and alone.

Then there were the thoughts of her friends, their lives and futures now hanging by the threads that she had spun, the whole thing a product of her own needs and desires.

The 100 Society had been her idea after all, and what for? To prove some stupid point, to prove that she was just as good as Jack, her brother who was so perfect and who made their father so proud. The one who had succeeded in everything.

Almost everything.

Jack was the one who had told Grace about The 100 Society. He had read about it online and decided that he and his friends would be the ones to recreate it a few years previously, but it had been too much for Jack, too ambitious, so he had given up.

But Grace wouldn't give up. It was the one thing she could do to prove, in her own mind, that there was something she could do that her brother couldn't. It may have been stupid and she knew it wouldn't make her father move home or call her any more often, but it was hers. It was something she could be proud of.

And look at what it had led to.

Cassie was in the hospital, Daniel was most likely dead and she had ruined the lives of her best friends.

If all of this had been because of The 100 Society, if it had all been because of her . . .

She closed her eyes tightly, trying to will away the terrible thoughts.

For the next hour, sleep came in broken segments, punctuated with nightmares of Daniel, his white skin tight around his water-bloated body as he crawled out of the river with only one thing on his otherwise-empty mind.

Revenge.

20

The first thing Grace saw when she opened her curtains was Pete, running his usual morning circuit. A thin veil of mist carpeted the field and his breath condensed in rhythmic bursts as he ran. The sky had cleared from the previous evening, but grey clouds were rolling in from the west, the brilliant white rugby posts clashing against the darkness as it moved towards the school.

Grace watched Pete until he stopped on the far side of the field. He stood panting, hands on his hips while he looked up into the sky, before suddenly crouching to the ground with his head in his hands.

Closing her curtains once more, Grace reached for her clothes. She knew it was unlikely that Pete would be able to see her changing from such a distance, but with the curtains

167

closed, at least she didn't have to watch him crumble.

There would be plenty of time for that later.

By the time Grace reached the kitchen, Pete was already sitting at the table, his back towards the door and his chin resting in his hand. He was still in his running gear, the sweat glistening on his bare shoulders. At first, Grace thought he might be asleep but he moved suddenly, leaning back in his seat and running both hands through his hair.

'Morning.'

He jumped and turned to face her. 'Grace? You scared me.'

'Sorry.' She hovered in the doorway, unsure of what to do. What was the etiquette in these situations? How were you supposed to talk to someone the morning after something so horrible?

She took in the dark shadows beneath his eyes. 'Have you slept?'

'Not really. I gave up in the end and went for a run to try and clear my head. Did you get any sleep?'

'On and off. More than I deserved.' On the table in front of Pete was a mug with just a splash of coffee left in the bottom. 'Do you want a fresh one of those?' she asked, reaching out to take the cup.

Pete smiled gratefully.

Grace filled the kettle in silence. Outside, the corridors started to fill with the sounds of other students as they moved from their rooms to the various bathrooms and kitchens. Doors slammed, voices rang out in greeting and there was the familiar rattle of pipes as showers started to run.

While Grace waited for the water to boil, Pete picked at the edge of the wooden kitchen table. He looked broken, like his entire world had shattered overnight. She had never seen him like this; he had always been the positive one in their friendship, the one who could always be relied upon to pick up the pieces.

Once, when Grace had failed miserably in a science exam, he had been the one to sweep her away from it all. She closed her eyes at the memory, almost feeling the warmth of that summer's day when he had taken her from the school grounds into the land surrounding the school. The meadows had been bursting with colour and they had walked together for what felt like hours through the fields, the air alive with dandelion seeds, before finding a patch of grass way out of Clifton's sight.

They had lain together, heads almost touching, as the clouds moved across an impossibly blue sky.

'You know,' Pete had told her, 'there's nothing you can't do.'

Grace had snorted in response. 'I think Mr McKenna might disagree with you, given the grade I just got in his test.'

Pete had raised himself up on an elbow. 'You don't care about science, you never have. You'll never be good at something you don't care about.'

'I do care,' Grace had replied sulkily.

Laughing, Pete had plucked a daisy from the ground and twirled it between his fingers. 'You care about a lot of things. You care about your friends, you care about your art.' He had slipped the daisy into Grace's hair. 'You do *not* care about science.'

Grace had smiled and closed her eyes. 'How do you always know how to make me feel better?'

'Because, although I actually *do* care about science, I care about other stuff too. I care about you.'

The kettle whistled.

Grace poured water into the two mugs and carried them to the table. Pete took his without a word. The strength he had carried for both of them over the last few years had disappeared and now he just looked so empty.

'I wish I knew what to say,' Grace said. 'You always knew what to say to make me feel better and I wish I could do that for you.' She reached out and took his hand. He looked away, his chin creasing. 'Tell me what to say, Pete.'

He shook his head, but his fingers tightened around hers.

There was a quiet knocking from behind and Grace turned to see Faith standing awkwardly at the kitchen door.

'Faith.' Grace pulled her hand from Pete's. 'How are you?'

Faith was paler than Grace had ever seen her. The skin beneath her freckles was almost white and her eyes were pink and puffy. She shrugged. 'I don't know how I am. How are you?' She stared at Grace, her voice carrying an almost accusatory tone.

At the table, Pete sniffed deeply. 'This isn't right,' he said. 'We shouldn't just be acting like nothing's happened. Maybe Trick was right, maybe we should call someone.'

'No.' Faith took the chair on Pete's other side and rubbed his shoulder. 'We can't, it's too late.'

'She's right, Pete.' Grace shifted in her chair, suddenly uncomfortable. Faith had brought a new tension into the room, one that Grace was unable to work out. Was Faith mad with her? Did she blame Grace for what had happened? Grace stood up. 'There's tea,' she said, feeling the need to do something. 'Or coffee. Do you want a coffee?'

'No. I don't want anything.'

'OK.' Grace nodded. She lifted her own mug and sipped, but the tea was hot and scalded her mouth. She swallowed it anyway, welcoming the momentary distraction of the burning liquid. 'Has anyone seen Ed?' she asked, unable to take any more silence.

'No,' Pete answered.

'Not since last night,' added Faith. 'He got back to the dorm at the same time as me and Pete, but I've not seen him since.' Her eyes shifted to Grace. 'What about Trick? I assume you two came back to the dorm together?'

'You know we did. You walked off before we had the

171

chance to decide whether to leave.'

Faith's hand fell from Pete's shoulder. 'You had just as much of an opportunity to come as Pete and Ed. It's not my fault you decided to stay with Trick.'

Grace felt a stir of anger, a rising heat that flushed her neck and cheeks red. 'We made sure there was nothing left,' she snapped. 'Daniel's things were on the bridge – at least we had the sense to pick it all up.'

'Yeah, funny how you couldn't have mentioned that while the rest of us were still there. Only something the two of you could do, I suppose? Like your little night-time meetings?'

Pete stood up. 'Hey, hey.' He raised his hands to the two girls. 'What are you two doing?' He looked at Faith. 'Why does it matter to you so much anyway? Why are you making such a big deal over who she was there with?'

Faith's mouth opened and closed, her eyes brimming with tears. 'I'm not making a big deal of it.' She looked away. 'It's obviously none of my business.'

'No,' snapped Grace. 'It's none of your business. It never was, Faith.'

Pete took Grace's arm. 'Hey,' he said again, softer this time.

Faith nodded, tears spilling from her already-bloodshot eyes. 'Yeah, don't worry, I get it.' She laughed bitterly. 'I always got it.'

'Faith,' Pete started, reaching out to take her hand too. She pulled away.

172

'No, it's OK. It doesn't matter what I do, does it? Just like it doesn't matter what she does. It doesn't matter how she treats you, does it, Pete? In your eyes, she's the only one who matters. You may be a genius, but when it comes to Grace I think you're the dumbest person I've ever met.'

Pete shook his head. 'I don't understand . . .'

'Then you're blind, Pete. Open your eyes, for god's sake.' She looked to Grace. 'Tell him,' she cried, 'just tell him what you told me. That you don't want him. Because he doesn't get it and it's just not fair. He doesn't deserve it.' And with that she turned, walking quickly from the kitchen and slamming the door closed behind her.

Grace blinked. 'Where did all that come from?'

Pete sank back into his seat. 'She's in shock. She doesn't know what she's talking about.' He frowned and took a drink from his coffee mug.

'I think we're all in shock, but still . . .'

'Let it go, Grace.' Pete rubbed his forehead, his eyes tightly shut.

'What she said, about you. About Trick—'

'Enough about Trick!' Pete slammed his mug on to the table, the hot coffee spilling on to his hand. 'Damn it!' He stood up, almost knocking his chair over as he rushed to the sink to thrust his hand under the cold tap. 'I don't care what she said about Trick.' He fell silent for a moment, then he exhaled, his shoulders slumping in defeat. 'The rest of it's true though, isn't it?'

'What's true?'

'That you don't want me.' He glanced at her. 'I think I get it now.'

'Pete, she didn't know what she was saying.'

'She did.'

Grace couldn't see his face. She didn't want to, because she could tell he was crying and it terrified her. 'I'm an idiot,' he said. 'All these years, I've believed in something that never existed. How could I have been so stupid?'

'Don't say that.'

'No, it's time to be honest. Last night changed everything, can't you see that?' He turned off the tap and without the sound of the running water the room was filled with an unbearable silence.

'Pete? Are you OK?'

He turned to face her. She realized she had never seen him cry before, not once, and it broke her heart.

'Are you seriously asking me that? After everything that's happened?'

Grace eyed the door, suddenly wishing to be anywhere else. Her own face was wet with tears. 'I don't know what I'm supposed to say.'

'There's nothing you can say. Can't you see that? Stop trying to make it all better. This is something that can't be fixed. We have to move on. From last night, from everything we can't control. Everything.'

'But—'

'No.' Pete moved towards the door. 'Some things are

just too damaged to make right. You have to walk away from them, it's all you can do.'

'Don't say that.'

'I have to. You have to let me go, Grace. I can't go on being just a friend when you know I want more. Not at the moment. Not after what's happened. I'm not strong enough.'

'Pete, wait.' There had to be something she could do, something to make him stay in there with her, because she knew that the moment he walked out of the kitchen he would be walking out of her life.

'I'm sorry, Grace. I can't pretend any more. It hurts too much.'

Grace's sadness melted away as panic gripped her and she propelled herself forwards, grabbing Pete and turning him to face her. 'You can't,' she sobbed, one hand tangling in his shirt, the other reaching up to touch his face and wipe away his tears, her fingers pushing into the blond hair she knew so well. His forehead fell against hers, his breath hot against her tear-stained cheek and it felt so good, so familiar and she could feel something inside her dying at the thought of losing him.

Then, somehow, somehow, his lips were on hers and they were kissing, stumbling back into the kitchen, his hands moving over her face, into her hair and on to her back, pulling her closer.

And then it was over.

'No,' Grace cried, trying to pull him back to her, desperate to feel his arms around her and suddenly so sure that she *could* love him, she really could.

'I'm sorry, Grace.'

'Pete, please.'

But Pete said nothing. He simply walked away, leaving her all alone.

21

'Come in.'

Grace pushed open the door to Cross's office. He was sitting behind his desk, a huge piece of carved mahogany that didn't look out of place in what must be the grandest room of the entire school. It was more than an office, really. It was a boardroom, complete with a pair of leather Chesterfield sofas and a long table surrounded by a set of antique chairs that could be used either for dining or meetings. All of the furniture had been brought in after the fire that had destroyed Cross's office, as well as the new carpet. The smell of fresh paint still lingered, clashing against the mustiness of the old furniture.

'Please, Grace, take a seat.' Cross rose to his feet and held out a hand, offering one of the large Chesterfields to Grace. She walked slowly towards it, her body stiff and awkward as cool beads of sweat began to dapple her brow. Although there could be a number of reasons, Grace didn't actually know why she had been called to Cross's office that morning.

The message had arrived only moments after Pete had walked out of the kitchen. A younger student had appeared in the doorway, already in uniform with a badge on his blazer that said 'Office Monitor'. He had been clutching a handful of notes, one of which he passed to Grace.

'Message for Grace Becker,' he had stuttered, not bothering to hide his amazement at seeing a sixth-former crying alone in one of the dorm kitchens. Even when she had taken the note from him, he continued to stand there, staring at Grace as she tried to compose herself.

'Thanks,' Grace had replied curtly. When he still failed to move, Grace simply walked past him and back to her room. Inside, she had opened the note to see a demand from Cross, expecting her in his office at 8.30 that morning. The clock on her nightstand told her it was 7.50. She had just over half an hour to get herself dressed and to compose herself before she met with him. She looked in the mirror, at her bloodshot and red-rimmed eyes, her face blotchy from crying and her hair a tangled mess. Taking a deep breath, she had gone to her sink and scrubbed at her face with cold water in an attempt to wash away the horror of the last couple of days.

Now, sitting on one of Cross's Chesterfields, she decided she should have scrubbed a bit harder. Her hands were clammy and she balled them into fists on her lap, digging her nails into the palms of her hands and hoping the pain might help her to focus and quell the rising panic.

Cross walked from his desk to the other Chesterfield in less than three large strides. His face gave nothing away.

Did he know about Daniel? Did he finally have proof that Grace was the ringleader of The 100 Society? She hadn't seen any of the others, so there was no sign that anyone else might be in trouble. She swallowed as Cross sat down opposite her and it took all of her energy to stop from screaming out that it was her, she was the one responsible for The 100 Society, that the whole thing had been her idea and it was her fault that Daniel was dead.

Cross smiled, and in that moment Grace was ready to cry again, but this time it was tears of relief that were stinging her eyes. She blinked, trying to regulate the breathing that she realized was much too fast.

'How are you, Grace?'

'I-I'm OK.'

Cross nodded. 'I asked you in here today to have a chat about Cassie.'

Cassie? Of course. Cross had said only yesterday that he wanted to talk to her about what happened, but yesterday afternoon felt like a lifetime ago. So much had happened since then, so much had changed. Grace tried to focus on Cross's mouth, because if she didn't concentrate very hard on what he was saying to her, the thoughts and memories of the last few hours would win and she would crumble.

'Yes,' she said. 'Cassie.'

Cross leaned back, managing to look far more comfortable on the hard sofa than Grace thought could be possible for someone with such a large frame. 'Firstly, we've had some news. The surgeons have managed to save the sight in one of her eyes, which is more than we had hoped for.'

Grace felt a small surge of joy. 'Really? That's great.'

'Yes, but there's still a long way to go. How much of her vision she'll get back is still unclear, but it's certainly better news than we were expecting.'

'What about her face?' Grace closed her eyes, trying to push away the unwelcome memories of the accident, of how Cassie's flesh had come away so easily in her hands.

Cross paused and, for a moment, glanced away. The look in his eyes was enough to tell Grace everything. 'She's not going to look the same as she did before,' Cross said, the deep timbre of his Irish accent adding a warmth that Grace had never heard from her headmaster before. 'But she's still the same girl and she's going to need her friends to realize that.'

'Of course.'

'She'll be well enough for visitors soon and her parents have asked that her school friends go to see her. Do you think you'd be comfortable with that?'

'Yes, of course.'

'They've also asked that a visitor – a friend,' he said with a kind smile, 'might be able to bring in a small bag of her belongings. Just to make Cassie feel a little more at home. I can give you a key to her room, I'm sure you'll know what she might like to have with her.'

'Yes. I can do that. Of course.'

'OK. Now I wanted to ask you about what happened on that day. Do you feel ready to talk about it?'

Grace nodded, but she wasn't ready. She wasn't ready at all.

'Grace, Cassie has said that someone tried to enter the darkroom just before her . . .' He paused. 'Just before she was injured.'

Why did he pause? He was going to say accident, but stopped himself. Why? What did he know?

'Do you know who it was?' he continued, watching Grace carefully as he spoke.

'No. I don't know.'

'Did you see anyone come into the room?'

'No, it was dark.'

'OK, did you hear anything?'

'Yes. I heard the door handle. Someone turned it, then the door slammed shut.'

'Was it the internal door of the airlock or the external door?'

'I don't know. It was loud though, so I think it must have been the internal door.'

'OK, you're doing really well, Grace.'

Grace didn't feel like she was doing well. She felt like she was walking a tightrope, unsure of how much information she needed to give, how much to keep to herself. She wanted to help Cassie and she wanted to tell the truth, but she also didn't want to say anything that might later connect her and her friends to Daniel.

'Cassie said she had been having trouble with a member of the art class recently. Do you know anything about that?'

'Yes.' The room suddenly seemed very bright. And hot. 'Daniel.' Her voice sounded weak.

'And has Daniel ever said anything in front of you? Anything threatening?'

'I-I don't know. I don't remember.'

'This is very important, Grace.'

'I didn't see anything. It could have been anyone.'

'Do you think someone came into the darkroom?'

Yes.

'I don't know. I didn't see.'

Cross paused. He raised a hand to his mouth and tapped a finger against his lips, as though he was unsure whether to share something with Grace.

'What is it?' Grace asked.

Cross lowered his hand. 'The burns that Cassie received. They don't think they could have been caused by the chemicals in the darkroom.'

'What?'

'It's not impossible, but they're doing some tests to find out. The chemicals would have to have been very strong to do so much damage.'

'She was mixing the chemicals when I arrived.'

182

'OK, well that's useful to know.'

But Cassie had mixed the chemicals hundreds of times before. She knew what she was doing. However, the alternative, if Cassie hadn't made an awful mistake, was too terrible. Could someone have actually brought their own chemicals to attack Cassie with? Had Daniel gone so far as to throw acid into Cassie's face, just to stop her from developing that film?

'Did Cassie ever show you the emails she received?'

Grace stared. 'What emails?'

'She said she'd received many emails from Daniel over the last year. She's not sure if any are left on her computer.'

'No, I've never seen those.'

'OK.' Cross stood up. 'Thank you Grace, you've been very helpful. I'll probably need to speak to you again, if that's OK?'

'Sure. Can I go now?'

'Yes, of course.' Cross took a small envelope from the coffee table and passed it to Grace. 'That's the key to Cassie's room. If you get some things together for her later this morning, we can arrange a taxi to take you to visit her in the hospital this afternoon.'

'OK.'

'And perhaps we could squeeze someone into the taxi with you. Maybe Ed would like to go too, do you think?'

'I think he'd like that.'

Cross opened the door for Grace and stood to one side as she left. He glanced at his watch. 'You'd better get straight to class. Are you almost ready for the art show tomorrow?'

'Yes, I think so.' She tried to think of her picture, 'Forever'. It was hard to remember what it looked like now, but she was sure it was almost complete, certainly good enough for the show if she didn't do anything else to it today.

When the door to Cross's office had closed, Grace turned away from the main exit that would take her to the art studio and instead made her way down the corridor, back to the dorms.

Was it all true? Had Daniel been in the darkroom that day? She had to find out more, had to get more evidence, because if Daniel had really done that to Cassie, if he had ruined her face, her eyes and her life all because of some incriminating photographs, then she had to know. Then she would have a reason to hate Daniel and if she had a reason to hate him then maybe, just *maybe*, she could get through life with the knowledge of what had happened to him on the bridge.

Outside Cassie's room, Grace ripped open the envelope and let the key fall out into her hand. Looking quickly up and down the empty corridor, she slipped the key into the lock and turned the handle. When the door opened, Grace stepped back, crying out in surprise.

The room was a mess.

Drawers were open, their contents spilled on to the floor. Cassie's mattress had been turned over to expose the slats and her sheets lay in a crumpled pile on the floor. Her wardrobe was open, some clothes hanging askew while others were scattered below. Her designer shoes had been tossed carelessly around the room; little splashes of colour peeping out from underneath piles of papers, books and dresses.

Grace stepped inside, quickly closing the door behind her. There was no way that Cassie would leave her room like this. Her clothes and shoes were too important to her, almost as important as—

Grace gasped. Cassie's camera lay on the floor, smashed. She picked it up to get a closer look and the back flapped open, empty of any film. Looking around, Grace tried to think of where Cassie might keep her developed films. Then, seeing the small blinking light of Cassie's closed laptop, she remembered why she had wanted to come here in the first place.

Lifting the screen, Grace did a quick search before finding the mail icon. She clicked it and Cassie's email popped up. Scanning the list of senders, it didn't take long before she saw Daniel's name beside an email without a subject. She clicked on the message and it flew up on to the screen.

I know you think I'm a loser, but all I'm asking for is one chance. Just come for a walk with me, please? We can talk, you can get to know me.

Grace closed the message and found another.

Hi, me again. Just wanted to say how nice you looked today.

You probably think that's a bit creepy though, ha ha. OK, well see you tomorrow.

Another.

Hi Cassie. How are you doing? Your art project is looking great. Deconstruction of beauty is an amazing concept – you're so smart!

Grace frowned. None of the messages were threatening, none of them gave away any information that might help her and none of them looked like they had been written by the Daniel she knew. She skimmed the list of messages before another caught her eye. She didn't recognise the name of the sender, but the subject line made her stop.

RE: DAILY HERALD *ARTICLE 'THE 100 SOCIETY'*

Grace clicked on the message.

Dear Cassie,

Thanks again for the pictures. I've written the article and while it won't make tomorrow's print run, you should see it sometime this week. I'll be in touch again shortly, otherwise let me know when you get any more information.

Ben.

What pictures? What article? Grace sat down on the chair by Cassie's desk and started to search the files on Cassie's computer. It took her a few minutes, but eventually she found a folder simply called '*100*'. Grace opened it to find another set of files, all of which had dates and locations as their titles. Apart from one.

HERALD.

With a shaking hand, Grace clicked on the folder and suddenly Cassie's computer screen was filled with photographs of Grace's 100 Society tags.

And one of them was the same photograph that had been printed on the front page of the *Herald* newspaper.

22.

With a shaking hand, Grace pulled Cassie's door closed before locking it with Cross's key.

She had managed to pack a small bag of Cassie's belongings, including her MP3 player, some pyjamas and the stuffed bear that Ed had bought her for Valentine's day earlier that year. They were all items she had discovered as she had cleared up, returning as many of Cassie's things to their rightful places as she could. She had left the camera on Cassie's desk, next to the laptop she had switched off. But it still contained the pictures, the emails to the newspaper; signs that one of her best friends was a liar and had betrayed them all. Part of her, the part that was hurt and angry by what she had found on Cassie's computer, wanted to leave the room as it was but at some point Cassie's parents would arrive to collect more belongings and, if they discovered the break-in, questions would be asked. Questions that Grace and the others could do without.

Grace stopped at her own room and unlocked the door. She could keep Cassie's bag in here until later, but she had to get to the studio before her absence began to raise questions. As she opened the door, she almost expected to see her belongings ransacked in the same way that Cassie's had been, but everything was as it should be. She placed Cassie's bag on the floor beside her bed, locked up and slipped her key into her pocket beside the one Cross had given to her.

Hurrying along the corridor towards the front of the school, she chewed on her lip as she debated how much she should share with the others. Should she tell them about Cross's suspicions that Daniel was involved with Cassie's accident? What about the break-in? Somebody had been searching the room for something, but what?

When Grace reached the entrance hall, she hurried past the door to Cross's office, now slightly ajar. She had told him she was heading straight to lessons and didn't want to explain where she had been all this time. She hurried out into the courtyard, the shingle crunching underfoot. The art block stood directly opposite, rising high into a now totally grey sky that seemed to be growing darker by the second. Although it was still morning, she could see lights on inside the classrooms. On the ground floor, younger students were moving around with aprons and paint pots, smiling and laughing behind the windows. Above, on the first floor, was the studio. As she looked up, she saw Pete, watching her as she crossed the courtyard. Her heart skipping, she started to raise a hand, but before she had a chance to wave he turned away.

When Grace walked into the studio, she was met with silence.

Trick was nowhere to be seen and Pete had moved to a different desk on the opposite side of the studio. He glanced up as Grace walked in before immediately returning to his work without a word. Miss Stone was beside him, talking quietly as he manipulated his clay sculpture.

Ed hurried over to Grace. His face had a familiar hollowness, one that Grace recognized after seeing her own face in the mirror that morning.

'Where've you been?' he asked in a hurried whisper. 'And where's Trick?' Across the room, Trick's canvas stood untouched, as did Daniel's.

'I've been with Cross. And I've no idea where Trick is.'

'Cross?' Ed glanced towards where Miss Stone still sat with Pete. He lowered his voice. 'What happened? Does he know something?'

'No, he just wanted to talk to me about Cassie. He said we can visit her this afternoon.'

Ed's face brightened a little, but only for a moment. 'Really?' He shook his head. 'I don't know. I don't know if I can face her today, not after what happened.' He ran his shaking hands through his hair and exhaled an unsteady breath. 'How did this happen, Grace? How have we got into such a mess?'

'It's going to be OK,' Grace whispered. 'Nobody knows except us. We just have to get through it.'

'But how do we get through it?' He looked at Grace, his eyes pleading. 'I don't know how I'm supposed to act.'

'You carry on as normal,' Grace said, forcing the steadiness in her voice. 'Do whatever you normally do.' She picked up a brush from the table beside her and held it out to Ed. 'Paint.'

'I don't think I can.' A tear spilled down Ed's cheek and his breathing quickened. 'I don't think I can do this.'

Grace grabbed one of Ed's hands and squeezed, hard. 'You can do it. You have to.' She thrust the brush into his hand and closed his fingers over the top. 'Do you hear me?' She glanced to her right, where Miss Stone had turned to watch them, and squeezed harder. 'Do you hear me, Ed? We need you. We all need you to do this.'

'Yes.' Ed nodded furiously and wiped his face with his free hand. 'OK. I can do this.' He exhaled again, steadier this time.

'We'll meet after lunch to go and see Cassie,' Grace said. 'Because that's normal, right? That's what we would have done any other time.'

Ed nodded again.

'OK. Now go, finish your painting. When it's done, you don't have to come back to the studio, not until the art show.'

Ed turned and walked stiffly back to his canvas. He stopped in front of his hangman painting, the brush Grace had given him hanging loosely in his hand. For a moment Grace thought he might crumble, but then he reached for his paint.

She felt herself relax, but the tension quickly returned when Faith approached.

'I wanted to apologise,' Faith said, her arms folded tightly across her body. 'I was out of line this morning. I know I said some horrible things, but my head is all over the place.'

'I think we can safely assume that we're all feeling like that.'

Faith paused. 'Pete said you guys had a row.'

'He told you?'

'Yeah, but I'm not planning on taking sides, I want you to know that. I think we all need each other right now.'

Grace frowned. 'Yeah. Yeah, we do.'

'Good morning, Grace,' Miss Stone called out, waving a hand that was covered in rings.

'Morning.'

'Grace, have you seen Patrick this morning?'

'I . . .' She glanced at Trick's easel, untouched since the previous night. 'No, I really have no idea where he is.'

'And Daniel? Nobody seems to know where he could be either, although—'

'Although what?'

Miss Stone wrung her jewelled hands. 'Oh dear, oh

dear. What a mess this all is.' She leaned towards Grace, her voice dropping to a whisper. 'You don't really think he could have done something so awful, do you? Mr Cross said—' She cut herself off and shook her head. 'No, it's not my place to say.'

'I'm sure everyone will turn up,' Grace said, trying not to look at Daniel's artwork.

'Of course.' Miss Stone nodded, forcing a smile as she raised her arms theatrically, her kimono-like smock billowing around her. 'Anyway,' she said, gesturing towards Grace's own easel, 'the show must go on, must it not?' She swept away in a flurry of blue material, stopping by Ed's canvas before exclaiming what a masterpiece he had created.

Grace stared at her canvas, the blue smudge still visible from where Trick had thrown Grace's brush. She reached out to touch the smear and her fingers came away clean. The paint had dried thickly, leaving a mark, a scar on the picture that could be covered but never erased.

Grace looked at Trick's canvas. Where was he? His painting was almost finished but the show was only a day away.

'You don't think that he's gone and done anything stupid?' Faith asked, following her gaze.

'What kind of stupid?'

'I don't know,' she whispered. 'Like going to the police?'

'No.' Grace shook her head. 'No, I'm almost certain he wouldn't do that.'

'How can you be certain?'

'I can't.' She turned back to her easel. 'Forever'. It was supposed to be such a positive piece of work, full of love and promise for the future, but right now it felt like a lie.

Grace looked outside at the swollen sky as fat drops of rain began to strike the window.

'Hey, look.'

She turned to see Faith pointing at a familiar figure on the school driveway, approaching the school through the rain.

Trick.

Grace ran from the studio, her feet clattering on the steps as she hurried to the bottom of the art block. She burst through the doors just as Trick disappeared into the school building. She chased after him, up the stone steps and into the entrance hall, where a set of wet footprints led towards the dormitory corridors. Following the prints, she pushed through the door to the dorms and looked around. The corridor was empty and the footprints dried up after only a few metres.

'Trick?' Her voice bounced off the stone walls and carried up to the rafters that crisscrossed the high ceilings. There was no answer. Walking down the empty hallway, she listened intently, stopping when she heard a familiar whistling.

At the far end of the hallway, Sylvester appeared. 'Ah, Grace Becker. Why am I not surprised to see you?' He stopped, his slender frame somehow managing to fill the corridor, blocking her path.

'What do you mean?'

'You seem to make a habit of wandering these corridors when you're not supposed to,' he said, lifting his wrist to glance at his watch. 'Shouldn't you be in class right now?'

'I—' She stopped. What did he mean, 'making a habit of wandering the corridors'? 'I just had to get something from my room,' she muttered.

'Ah, yes,' he said with a wink. 'Of course.' He stepped back, holding the door open. Grace was almost at the other end of the corridor and she briefly considered returning to the art studio, but she had to know where Trick had been.

'Thank you,' she mumbled to Sylvester, passing through the door he was holding for her.

'No problem at all. Just doing my job.' He gave her a little smile, like they were sharing a secret. She shuddered, but kept walking towards her room until she heard the door close behind her. She waited a moment before turning back, checking that Sylvester really had gone before finding the stairs that led up to the boys' dormitories, the only place she could imagine Trick would have gone.

Gripping the handrail as she slowly climbed the spiral staircase, she listened intently, unsure of which direction Sylvester might have taken. Returning to her own room during school hours was one thing, but she would be in a whole different kind of trouble if he found her in the boys' dorms.

She almost lost her grip when her phone started to beep

in her pocket. Quickly pulling it out, she flicked the switch to set it to silent before opening the message.

It was from her mysterious friend, the same person who had told her to go to Lost Souls Bridge.

But that wasn't what made her breath catch in her throat.

What took her breath away was the message itself.

You're going to pay for what you did.

Grace and Ed barely spoke in the taxi, other than a brief exchange about the impending art show, a conversation Grace forced herself to participate in for appearance's sake. It was the first time she had spoken to anyone after receiving the text message.

Shaken, she had given up looking for Trick and had returned to the studio to work on 'Forever'. She had debated whether to tell anyone about the message, before deciding to keep quiet for now. Ed had gone into enough of a tailspin as it was and although Faith was doing such a good job of holding it together, Grace wasn't sure how much more she could take. That left Trick, who still hadn't turned up, and Pete.

Pete had barely even acknowledged Grace since walking out on her that morning. She could hardly look at him without a lump rising in her throat and, despite feeling like she needed him more than ever, she had to respect the fact that what *he* needed was space from her.

There was nothing she could do but paint.

Although she had started with a shaking hand, she soon found herself immersed in her work and before she knew it the painting was finally finished. She had missed lunch and had barely noticed the others leaving the studio, so washed up her brushes alone before standing back to take in the work of her classmates.

Ed's 'Hangman' was complete, as was Faith's modern take of 'The Scream'. Cassie's 'Deconstruction of Beauty' was as she had left it before the accident, although Miss Stone had declared it fit for display at the art show. Pete's clay sculpture had gone into the kiln, so Grace was yet to see the final product.

The only painting that needed to be completed was Trick's, but by the time Grace had left the studio to meet Ed, he had still not set foot in the studio.

Now, as the taxi pulled up in front of the hospital, Grace was still unable to make herself care about the art show. Ed's levels of enthusiasm were similar and, despite the paleness of his face and the slight tremor to his voice, he managed to put on a good show of normality for the taxi driver.

Standing on the pavement outside the hospital entrance with Cassie's bag at her feet, Grace waited for the taxi to pull away before she turned to Ed. 'Are you ready?'

He exhaled. 'As I'll ever be.'

Picking up the bag, Grace turned towards the entrance but Ed caught her arm.

'Wait.'

She looked at him. He looked sick, drawn, like he could easily have been a patient at the hospital himself.

Ed waited as an elderly couple passed by them. 'Are we going to tell Cassie?' he asked.

'Tell her what, exactly?'

Ed's eyes shifted. 'About what happened. You know, on the bridge. With Daniel.'

'I really don't think that's a good idea.'

He nodded. 'That's what I thought.'

Grace took in his haunted expression, the way the sweat glistened on his pale face. 'Are you sure you want to do this?' she asked. 'You don't have to come in.'

'No.' He frowned. 'I have to.' He looked at Grace with a wildness that scared her. 'Act normal, right?'

'Right.'

They walked together into the hospital building and life seemed to suddenly speed up.

Phones were ringing, people in uniform rushed past and others, visitors like Grace and Ed, hurried back and forth, looking at signs or talking into mobile phones as they gave updates on friends and relatives.

Grace examined the multi-coloured signs bolted on to a wall by the door and consulted a sheet of paper that Cross had given her. 'She's in the ICU,' she said, looking back up at the sign. 'That's two floors up.'

They shared a lift with a porter and a woman sitting in a wheelchair, wearing a hospital gown that drowned her. The woman was no older than forty, but her body was twisted, her fingers curled tight against her palms as she stared at nothing. There was a dried patch of drool on her chin and Grace wondered if the woman ever had visitors. Her unkempt hair and long nails said she probably didn't.

The lift stopped at the first floor and the porter pushed the wheelchair out into the bustling corridor before the doors slid closed again. Although it was already lit, Ed pushed the button for the second floor, tapping it impatiently until the lift started to move. He looked at Grace apologetically.

'I don't like lifts.'

Grace nodded as the lift stopped once more, the doors sliding open to reveal a sterile looking hallway with white walls and blue Lino on the floor. The corridor was empty. It stretched out in either direction and was lined with closed doors. Someone somewhere was sobbing, their muffled cries echoing along the hallway. From a different direction, Grace could hear the clacking of high-heeled shoes on a hard floor.

There was a single sign on the wall in front of them, telling them that the ICU was to their right. Above them, a too-bright light flickered. With their own footsteps echoing as they walked, Grace and Ed made their way along their corridor, glancing at each set of doors until they reached the ICU.

The ward was almost empty. A doctor bustled past as they walked in, not bothering to stop or apologise as he bumped against Grace's shoulder. With his white coat billowing behind him, he swept out, the sound of his footsteps quickly receding as the doors closed behind him.

'Can I help you?' A young nurse with an Australian accent and a light blue uniform smiled at them from behind a reception desk. She had a pen in her hand, poised over a chart.

'We're here to see our friend,' Grace said. 'Cassie Phillips?'

The nurse nodded. 'We've been expecting you,' she said. 'Cassie's parents have gone downstairs to get a coffee but they said you could go straight in.'

Beyond the nurses' station was the ward, containing only four beds. Grace could see a single pair of feet poking out from behind a curtain, but they were too old and male looking to be Cassie's.

The nurse laughed. 'No, that's not her. Cassie's got her own room. She's a lucky girl.'

Lucky? It was all Grace could do to bite her tongue and not launch into a tirade, to tell this nurse in no uncertain terms that Cassie was most definitely not lucky.

The nurse slid her pen into her breast pocket. 'This way.' Her shoes clicked on the smooth floor as she led them down yet another empty corridor. They passed one empty room after another before arriving at the only closed door. On the outside was a small whiteboard with Cassie's name written in black pen. Beneath her name, the words *Consultant – Lowe* had been scrawled in spidery handwriting. There was a small window in the door, but a thin blind had been drawn so it was impossible to see inside. The nurse rapped on the door before opening it and peering inside.

'Cassie, hun? It's Leanne. You've got a couple of visitors. Is that OK?'

Cassie's voice called from somewhere inside the room and the nurse stepped back, holding the door open with a smile. 'Twenty minutes,' she whispered. 'She still needs her rest.'

'Sure.' Ed went first, but stopped when he had taken only a few steps into the room. Grace followed and the door closed quietly behind them.

'Hello? Who's there?' Cassie turned her head towards them, huge swathes of bandages covering her eyes and the right side of her face. There was a large white patch covering her throat and too many tubes and wires for Grace to count. They seemed to be attached to every part of Cassie's body and machines all around her blinked and pulsed, while others fed bags of liquids into the tubes attached to her arms.

'It's Grace,' she said, unsure of why she was forcing herself to smile. 'And Ed.' She nudged him and his eyes widened, like she had woken him from a daydream.

'Hey,' he said softly, stepping forwards and gently taking

one of Cassie's hands. He looked down at the tubes, then cleared his throat. 'I missed you.' His voice cracked and he sank into the chair beside her bed.

'Hey yourself,' Cassie said. She squeezed Ed's hand in her own. 'I'm OK,' she whispered. 'Please don't be sad.'

Ed nodded, but tears were streaming down his face. Grace stood behind him and squeezed his shoulder. 'He's OK, Cassie. Just give him a second.'

'OK.' Cassie nodded, her head moving from side to side as she tried to place Grace. She smiled. 'It's OK for me, I guess. I don't have to see what I look like yet.'

'You look as fabulous as always,' Grace replied.

Cassie laughed. 'Yeah, I did specifically request a Gucci hospital gown.' She lowered her voice. 'But I think they screwed me over.'

Ed coughed out a laugh and leaned forwards, kissing Cassie gently on her un-bandaged cheek.

Cassie reached up, fumbling to find Ed's face. With her thumb, she wiped away his tears. 'Listen to me,' she said, her voice suddenly stern. 'These are the only tears you get to cry, do you hear me Ed Krazinski? This is your one free pass. Then you've got to be strong for me. OK?'

'OK,' Ed said, taking the hand from his face and kissing it. 'I can do that.'

Grace placed Cassie's bag on her bedside table. 'I brought some things in for you.'

'Thank you. That's really kind of you.'

'Hey, that's what friends are for, right?'

Cassie paused. 'Right.' She took a deep breath. 'There's something I need to tell you – I have to get it off my chest.'

Grace looked at the various monitors, at the pump that was slowly pushing painkillers into Cassie's body. 'You don't need to tell us anything. Not now.'

'No. It has to be now.'

Ed frowned. 'What's this about?'

'Cassie, this isn't the right time. You're on all sorts of drugs—'

'The newspaper,' Cassie started. 'It was me. I was the one who sent them the picture. I sold them the story about The 100 Society.'

The air in the room suddenly felt very still. Ed stared first at Cassie, then at Grace. 'What? I don't understand.'

'Ed, I'm sorry. I should have told you.'

He dropped Cassie's hand and pressed his fingers against his temples. 'You're telling me you sold us out to the papers?'

'Yes,' Cassie whispered. 'And I am so, *so*, sorry.'

Silence.

'Ed? Are you there?' Cassie reached out, but Ed stood up, moving away from her grasping fingers.

'You lied to me.'

'I'm sorry.'

Ed turned to Grace. 'Did you know about this?'

Grace swallowed. 'I found out today.'

Ed clenched his fists. 'Jesus, Cassie. How could you?

You could have ruined everything for me. What did you think would've happened if your little stunt got us arrested? What then?'

'Ed—'

'No,' Ed spat. He started walking towards the door. 'I can't believe this.'

'Ed . . .' Cassie started to sit up. 'Please.'

Grace reached out for his arm, but he shrugged her away. 'No. I can't. I can't do this now.' He pulled the door open and marched into the corridor. The door slowly closed behind him and when it clicked shut, Cassie began to sob.

'Grace, I'm so sorry.'

Sitting in the chair where Ed had been only moments before, Grace took her friend's hand. 'I know. He'll come around.'

Cassie shook her head. 'No, he won't. And why should he? He's right, I acted so selfishly. I had an opportunity to get my pictures noticed by the media and I took it without a single thought for the people I love. I could've ruined Ed's future.'

'But you didn't. And you've apologised. He loves you, Cassie. Just give him time.' She paused. 'He's got a lot on his mind, we all have.'

Cassie turned her face towards Grace. 'Why? What's happened?'

Grace took a deep breath. Although she had vowed not to fill Cassie in on what had happened, the opportunity to be able to talk about it with someone who wasn't there was one she couldn't pass up. So, in measured tones, she told Cassie. About the emails, the suspicions that Daniel was behind everything. About Lost Souls Bridge.

For a long while, Cassie said nothing. When she finally spoke, her voice shook. 'If Daniel really did this to me,' she whispered, 'then I'm glad.' She squeezed Grace's hand. 'Do you think he's . . .' She stopped, but Grace knew exactly what her friend was asking.

She was asking if Daniel was dead.

'I don't know.'

For a long while, neither of them spoke. Cassie's breathing finally fell into a slow, steady rhythm and Grace glanced at the clock. She had been there half an hour already and Cassie's parents would be back soon.

Then something moved behind Grace, almost too quiet to hear. She turned to see the door handle turning. Behind the thin blind, a shadow moved.

Had Ed come back? The silhouette didn't look quite tall enough.

The handle continued to turn. Slowly, quietly.

'Hello?' Grace called out. 'Is someone there?'

The handle stopped moving.

Cassie stirred, her hand twitching in Grace's as she shifted in her bed.

Grace glanced at Cassie for a moment, then turned back to the door. The handle was still and the shadow had gone.

'Grace?' Cassie yawned. 'Are you still there?'

'Yes,' Grace replied, her eyes still trained on the door. 'I'm still here.'

In her pocket, Grace's phone buzzed. She dropped Cassie's hand to open the text message.

She froze.

How does she look? As ugly on the outside as she is on the inside? Maybe you should put her out of her misery.

'Grace? Did you get a text? Who's it from?'

'I don't know,' Grace said, fury replacing any fear she had felt. 'But I'm going to find out.'

She pressed a button that allowed her to call the sender of the message and held the phone up to her ear. The line rang once before going to voicemail.

'Hi. This is Daniel. I can't take your call right now, so please leave a message.'

Grace dropped the phone as though it might burst into flames at any moment.

'Grace?'

'He's alive,' Grace said, turning to face the door. 'Daniel's alive.'

Grace burst into the crowded dinner hall, almost colliding with Cross as she ran.

'Grace?' He reached out, gently taking her by the shoulder. 'Is everything OK? Did you get to see Cassie?'

Grace nodded, peering around Cross's huge frame to search the dining hall. It didn't take her long to close in on the others.

Ed, Pete, Trick and Faith all sat together on one table, in silence.

'Everything's fine,' Grace said, taking a moment to smile at Cross. She imagined the way she must look, her eyes wild, her forced smile like that of a grinning skull. 'Cassie's doing really well. It was nice to see her.'

'OK.' Cross nodded, but there was concern etched into the lines of his face. 'You just take it easy, all right? No more running.'

'Sure.'

Grace weaved through the crowd until she reached the table. She immediately noticed the mobile phones lying on the table beside their owners.

'I think we're in trouble,' she said.

When nobody spoke, Grace sat down and produced her own phone. 'I think Daniel's alive,' she said, desperately trying to make eye contact with someone. After another moment's silence, Grace slammed her hand on the table. 'Hey,' she said, almost shouting. 'Are you listening to me? Why is nobody saying anything?'

'We know,' Ed replied. 'We've been trying to decide what to do.'

'Why did nobody call me? I've been looking all over for you guys.'

Nobody spoke. They didn't even look at her.

Grace looked back to Ed. 'What the hell is going on?'

'If Daniel's really alive,' Ed said, ignoring Grace, 'then we need to go to the police. We can show them the messages. They'll know that he was the one who did this to Cassie.'

'No.' Trick shook his head. His own phone was missing, was probably still lying on Lost Souls Bridge in pieces. 'If we go to the police, he'll take us all down with him.'

'But he's been making more threats.' Ed waved his phone. 'What are we supposed to do?'

'We sleep on it,' Pete said. He stood up and took his

own phone from the table.

'He threatened you?' Grace reached up, grabbing Pete's sleeve. 'What did he say?'

Pete pulled his arm from her grip and turned to Faith. 'Are you coming?' he asked.

Faith glanced at Grace, then nodded and stood up, following Pete into the crowd.

Grace turned back to face Trick and Ed. 'What did Daniel say? What happened?'

'He warned us to not say anything,' Ed said. 'About the tagging, about what happened on the bridge.'

'I don't understand,' Grace said. 'Why is it all such a big secret? We know he was the one tagging the reaper, so why won't he just admit it? And where is he? This whole thing gives me the creeps.'

Ed nodded. 'Look, as far as I'm concerned we need to get the police involved. But I'm happy to do what Pete said and wait until tomorrow. Hell, I'll even wait until after the art show.' He rubbed his face. 'This is such a mess.'

'Ed, it's going to be OK.'

Trick laughed. 'I don't think he was just talking about Daniel.'

Grace frowned. 'What are you talking about?'

Ed gritted his teeth. 'All the lying, all of this.' He gestured towards Pete and Faith's empty seats. 'It has to stop. It's tearing us all apart.'

Grace paused. 'You told them about Cassie? About the papers?'

210

'Of course he told us,' Trick snapped. 'It's our business, don't you think?' He glared at her. 'Or perhaps you just thought it was *your* business.'

Grace stared. Why was he looking at her like that? The last time they had spoken was in her bedroom, when they both thought Daniel was dead. He had told her everything would be OK. What had happened since then?

'Trick, what happened to you this morning?'

'I had to clear my head.' He laughed, but it was bitter. 'Looks like I've got a lot more of that to do.'

Suddenly angry, Grace snapped. 'Would someone please tell me what the hell is going on?'

Trick stood up. 'I don't want to talk about it,' he said. 'Not now.' He pushed his way into the crowd and was gone.

'Ed?' Grace was pleading now, blinking away tears.

Ed sighed. 'It's not like I don't have bigger things to worry about,' he said, frowning at his phone. 'But if you must know, I think they're mad because you kissed Pete.'

'What . . .' Grace cleared her throat and started again. She shook her head. 'How—'

'Does it matter how they know? Everyone's pissed at you, Grace.' He pocketed his phone and stood up.

'Ed, wait.'

'No. You knew what Cassie had done and you didn't tell me? I had to find out like that?'

'I'm sorry, Ed. I didn't think it was my place.' She turned

in her seat as he walked away. 'Ed? I think Cassie's in danger.'

'She's in the hospital. Nothing's going to happen to her there.'

'But—'

'I can't talk about this now. I need to go,' he called back. 'We'll figure it all out tomorrow.'

The chairs that had so quickly emptied around Grace were suddenly filled with younger students. Watching as the group talked and laughed, she had never felt so envious.

She had never felt so alone.

25

Grace checked the lock on her door again before crawling back into bed. She still couldn't sleep and, even with the light on, she felt like she was living in a waking nightmare.

Once again, she checked her phone, but there were no new messages. Nothing from any of her friends, no missed calls from her father.

Not even a message from Daniel.

Perhaps she should block his number. Would it be better to get nothing from him, or would not knowing his movements be even worse? She wasn't even sure she knew how to block a number.

She scrolled through the menu on her phone. It didn't take long for her to find the settings that would allow her to stop any incoming calls or texts from a chosen contact. She clicked on the link and frowned.

Her father's number was listed beneath a heading titled 'blocked numbers'. Beneath that was her brother's number.

Why was her father's number blocked? Her brother's?

She unchecked the numbers and within seconds her phone started to beep. Her heart beating in her throat, she raised the phone to her ear to listen to the voicemails that had started pouring in.

'Hey, princess. Just checking in. Guess you're busy. OK, well, I love you and we'll talk soon.'

Beep.

'Grace? Can you try and get to your phone, hun?'

Beep.

'Grace? It's Jack. Dad's worried about you, numbskull. Call him, OK?'

Beep.

'Hi Grace. Dad again. I wanted to tell you that I'm flying in for your exhibition next week. It was supposed to be a surprise, but obviously I don't know how I'm going to contact you. I'll try and call the school, I'm not sure if you've lost your phone or something.'

Beep.

'Hi. Did you get my message? I called the school, they said they'd get it to you.'

Beep.

'OK, the school said one of your friends received the message. A boy? Not sure of his name. OK, well I hope you get it.'

Grace lowered her phone. Why had her father's number

been barred from her mobile? And her brother's? They'd been trying to call her all this time. With a shaking hand, Grace started to dial, hoping she still had enough credit to connect her call to a UK number.

'Hello?' A groggy voice answered.

'Jack?'

Pause. 'Grace?' The voice instantly became more alert. 'Jesus, it's three in the morning.'

'I know.' Grace didn't even realize she was crying until her voice cracked.

'Are you OK? Dad's been going out of his mind with worry about you. If the school hadn't told him you were fine . . .' There was another pause as a female voice mumbled in the background. Grace heard Jack quietly talking, his voice muffled. 'Sorry.' He was back. 'What's going on with you?'

'I don't know, Jack. I think I'm in trouble.'

'What kind of trouble?'

She was sobbing now. 'The 100 Society.'

'The 100 Society? Oh man, what have you been up to? Did you get arrested? Do I need to call Dad?'

'No, that's not it.'

'So what is it? Grace? Are you there?'

'Yes.' Her voice seemed so small. 'I need you, Jack. I think something bad might be happening.'

He sighed. 'OK. Look, Dad's flying in tomorrow morning. We'll be with you in the evening for your show. Is that OK? Or do you need me sooner?'

A gust of wind blew through Grace's open window. It looked like the bad weather was set to make a return.

'I guess I can wait until tomorrow.'

'OK.' Jack's voice started to sound a little calmer. 'Damn it, Grace. You really had us freaked out. Don't do this again, you hear me?'

'I hear you.' With her brother on the end of the line, everything that had happened started to feel a little less serious.

Daniel was alive. They hadn't killed him, there was no proof they were even on the bridge so it was his word against theirs.

There was also no substantial proof that she, or any of her friends, were involved with The 100 Society.

She closed her eyes. Her father would be here tomorrow. She was safe.

'All right,' Jack said. 'Look, I'm going back to bed. I'll speak to you tomorrow, OK?'

'OK.'

'I love you, sis.'

'I love you too.'

She placed the phone on her bedside table as another gust of wind rushed into her room, her curtains billowing. She slid out from under her covers and pulled back the curtains before reaching out to close the window. Outside, the clouds parted to reveal an almost-full moon and for a moment the playing fields were bathed in a ghostly light.

Seconds later, the clouds closed in again, plunging the school grounds into darkness once more, but she was sure she had seen someone on the field.

Unmoving.

Watching.

26

Grace awoke to her phone buzzing on the night table beside her.

She reached out, grabbing the phone before her eyes were even fully open.

It was Daniel again.

I hope you're ready for the big show.

She sat up and pressed the button that allowed her to dial the sender's number, but this time it didn't ring even once. Grace listened to the answer phone message, unsure of what she was going to say until she opened her mouth.

'That's it, it's over. Time to stop. We know what you did to Cassie, we have your messages. We have proof. If you don't turn yourself in to the police, we're going to do it for you.' She hung up, her hands shaking.

A few seconds later, her phone beeped again.

Pay close attention, Grace. You tried to kill me. There is proof that puts you and your friends on that bridge. Unless you want to lose everything, say nothing.

Say nothing.

Grace lowered her phone and glanced at her bedside clock.

It was after nine. How had she managed to sleep in? Cursing loudly, she started to pull on her uniform before stumbling out of the door. The corridor was alive with students already on their way to lessons and Grace joined the throng, pulling her fingers through the knots in her hair.

By the time she reached the studio, most of her classmates were already sitting at their desks, listening to Miss Stone.

'Good morning, Grace.' Miss Stone glanced at the clock. 'I was just filling everyone in on the plan for today.' She looked at the empty seat next to Ed's easel. 'I also hope Ed joins us soon, as I would rather not have to repeat myself.'

Grace slipped into her chair, looking around at the drawn expressions on her friends' faces.

'So, just to recap,' Miss Stone said, positioning her glasses on her nose and peering at the sheet of paper on the desk in front of her. 'We're setting up the hall after lunch, so that means you can take your own pieces across.' She glanced at Pete. 'Peter, your sculpture needs glazing, so I suggest you do that this morning, then bring it across later this afternoon when it's dry.'

Pete nodded.

'OK,' Miss Stone continued. 'Patrick, did you get your piece finished last night?'

'Yep.'

Grace turned to look at Trick's painting and gasped.

It was incredible.

It had always been good, but whatever he had done last night had made the piece come alive. She almost felt a sense of vertigo as she looked at the painting of the bell tower, the way it spiralled up into a brilliant blue sky, spotted with clouds that seemed to move across the canvas.

'It's beautiful,' she whispered.

Trick glanced at her, his face flushing a deep crimson before he looked away again.

'And that leaves Grace,' said Miss Stone, 'and Faith.' She looked up, making eye contact with Grace. 'Are we happy with our work?'

Grace nodded.

'I could maybe add a couple more touches,' Faith said quietly.

'That's fine,' Miss Stone replied. 'You and Peter can use the studio this morning and bring your pieces over together.' She lay the sheet of paper on her desk. 'Doors open at seven,' she said. 'And I've heard this morning that we're expecting visitors from Deansfield College, as well as Nightingale and St Peter's.'

Grace looked up. 'St Peter's? Isn't that where Ed wants to go?'

Miss Stone smiled. 'I think it's at the top of his list. Perhaps one of you would be so kind as to fill him in? I'm sure he'll be excited to know that they've sent a talent spotter over.'

There was a muttering of agreement from the class and Miss Stone stood up, tucking her chair in behind her desk. 'On a more personal note,' she said, removing her glasses, 'I wanted to acknowledge the fact that it hasn't been an easy few days for you all. With Cassie in the hospital and Daniel . . .' She paused, her eyes shifting to where Daniel's canvas stood in the corner. 'With Daniel's whereabouts still unaccounted for, I know that you all have a lot on your minds, so it's to your credit that you've managed to produce such truly outstanding pieces of work.' She clasped her hands together and smiled. 'Right, so it's action stations, everyone. If anyone needs me, I'll be in the main hall.' She turned, her smock billowing as she swept from the room.

'I can't believe it's all still going ahead,' Faith said.

'What else are they supposed to do?' Trick asked.

'I know, but while Daniel's missing . . .' Faith paused. 'I don't know. It just doesn't feel right.'

'That's because we know the truth,' Pete said. 'Besides, we don't know how they're handling it all behind closed doors. If they really have suspicions that Daniel was involved with what happened to Cassie, you can bet that they've got the police involved.'

'I'm sure the police are involved,' said Trick, 'if only for the reason that Daniel's effectively been missing since the weekend.'

'Unless they have reason to believe that he's still around,' Grace said.

The others turned to look. 'Why would they think that?' Faith asked.

'He's been in touch with us,' Grace said. 'Who's to say he hasn't been in touch with the school?'

'So there's a chance the police haven't been called at all?' Trick shook his head. 'No, I can't believe Cross would be dealing with this by himself.'

'Why not?' Grace asked. She stood up and took her canvas gently from the easel. 'He said how sick the press attention from The 100 Society made him. Don't you think he'd go to any length to protect the school's image?'

When nobody spoke, Grace continued. 'I guess I'm just a little concerned by the lack of police presence over all this. None of it sits right with me.'

'Daniel will be back,' Pete said. He didn't look at Grace and she wasn't even sure if he was addressing her or the others. 'Then it won't matter. He's just playing games, trying to get back at us for what happened.'

'Do you really think he's going to keep quiet about that?' Trick asked. 'I mean, if it were me—'

'There's no proof we were even there,' Pete said.

Grace thought for a moment. The previous evening she had finally managed to get some sleep, sure that there was nothing linking her or the others to Lost Souls. Now, she didn't feel quite so sure.

She stood up and approached her canvas, scrutinising her painting as though it might hold a clue as to what she was missing.

Forever.

She stopped, before looking around the room at the other pieces.

The Scream.

Hangman.

The Bell Tower.

Deconstruction of Beauty.

Fire.

Something clenched inside her stomach. There was something there, something she couldn't quite place, but it was something that terrified her.

Outside, despite the clear sky, there was a distant rumble of thunder.

A storm was coming.

27

Grace was one of the last to set her work up in the Great Hall.

Accessed by the wooden staircase that swept up from the entrance hall, the room was as grand as the other original features of Clifton. Despite its name, the Great Hall was in fact decidedly small for a school with such a large pupil population. Rarely used these days, the room was left to gather dust until required for an open evening, or teacher-parent consultations. Or events like the art show. A lectern stood in the far corner of the room in front of a small stage and the walls were lined with wooden panels, interspersed with floor to ceiling leaded windows along one side of the room.

After placing her canvas on the easel that had already been set up in the middle of the room, Grace stood back to look at the other pieces. In the centre of the hall, Pete's sculpture sat atop a pedestal, although Grace felt this did little to add to the impact the piece so desperately needed. She sighed and touched the sculpture, the glazed surface cool and smooth. There was no doubt that Pete had put effort in, but it just looked so out of place, especially next to Cassie's 'Deconstruction of Beauty'.

Trick's 'Bell Tower' stood beside Ed's 'Hangman'. Trick had carried both canvases over after Ed had still failed to show up, despite numerous attempts to call his mobile. Pete had even gone to the dorms looking for him, but there had been no answer when Pete knocked on his door.

All of this Grace had overheard in conversation while she worked on finishing her piece. Although she desperately wanted to join in and offer help or advice, she knew it was too soon. People were angry at her, they refused to look at her, let alone listen to anything she might have to say.

Miss Stone had swept in and out of the studio, growing more flustered as the morning progressed. More than once she had cursed Ed and his lack of commitment, although Grace knew her teacher was just as concerned by his absence as they were.

And so Ed's painting had been moved without him, as had Daniel's. Daniel's 'Fire' picture stood at the far end of the Great Hall, beside a long table that held stacks of white china cups and saucers, alongside two large, silver tea-urns.

Grace walked over to the great bank of windows. On

225

one of the wooden panels beside her was the school's crest, the same shield she wore on her blazer. The two-headed eagle looked out in either direction; towards the school's driveway on one side of Grace and, on the other side, the blue and grey monstrosity that was the art block.

From her position behind the lead-lights, Grace could just about make out the inside of the studio. It was empty now, the members of her class having returned to their dorms to prepare for the start of the show. Grace glanced at her watch. It was five p.m. – only two hours to go.

Her stomach flipped with excitement. Her father would be here. Her brother, too. She felt a surge of shame and regret at the thought of everything that had happened, over the actions she had carried out in an attempt to gain her father's attention and to prove to herself that she could succeed where her brother had failed.

Now, looking at her artwork, she realized she had nothing to prove. Her father loved her regardless; he was flying in from Singapore especially to see her work in the show she had worked so hard for.

He was proud of her.

She closed her eyes. If Daniel was so desperate to finish The 100 Society, let him have it. Grace didn't need it any more.

Besides, the last few tags – if you didn't count Lost Souls Bridge – were the most risky. They were to be applied in the school grounds, one of them within the very room she was standing in. If Daniel wanted to take that risk, he was more than welcome.

For Grace, it was over. When the art show finished, she would let The 100 Society go.

It was time to move on.

She turned away from the windows to see Faith standing on the opposite side of the hall.

'Oh, hey,' Grace said. She looked at the door, wondering if she could make it across the hall and out before Faith had the chance to launch into one of her tirades.

Instead, Faith offered a lopsided smile. 'Hey.'

For a moment Grace said nothing, sure she was about to come under attack for something. She looked around the room, struggling to find a topic of conversation. 'So, uh, I think that's your spot over there.' She pointed to the last empty easel.

'You mean the one with my name on it?' Faith asked, although there was not even a hint of sarcasm behind her smile.

Grace laughed. 'Sorry. Yeah, I guess you knew that.'

Faith carried her canvas to the easel and positioned it on the wooden frame. She stood back and Grace joined her. 'It's great, Faith, it really is.'

'Thanks. Although it does freak me out a little.'

'I think that means you did a good job.' Grace had to admit that the picture was somewhat strange to look at. Almost a direct copy of the classic painting 'The Scream', there were a few differences that made the picture Faith's own – but the one main difference, the one that made it almost uncomfortable to look at, was the face of the screaming figure. The once abstract features had been changed to look more human, including deep green eyes, a button nose and freckles. Though the face was still contorted, the mouth widened in horror and the eyes hollow and emptied by fear, there was no mistaking Faith's own features peering out from the canvas.

'I have to say,' Grace said, 'the idea of turning a classic into a self-portrait was a stroke of genius. I actually wish I'd thought of it myself.'

Faith smiled. 'You don't have to say that.'

'It's true.'

'OK.'

There was a moment of silence while Grace tried to work out if she and Faith were friends again, or if she still needed to address what had happened between her and Pete.

She blushed at the memory, remembering the way his lips felt on hers, but the heat in her face was more from embarrassment than anything else.

Grace turned to Faith, deciding it was time for them to talk about Pete and what he actually meant to each of them, but Faith was looking at her phone with a strange frown.

'Faith?'

Faith glanced up, her face immediately flushing scarlet.

'What is it?' Grace asked. 'Another message from Daniel?'

'Uh, no.' Faith slipped her phone into her pocket. 'It's from Pete.'

'Oh.' There was something in the expression on Faith's face, the way her eyes shifted, that told Grace her friend was hiding something. 'Faith, you know I don't have any feelings for Pete, right? Kissing him was a mistake.'

There. She'd said it. It had been a mistake, perhaps one of her worst.

By kissing Pete, she'd managed to hurt some of the people who meant the most to her, including Faith.

Faith frowned. 'Yeah. Well, maybe it was a mistake for *you* . . .' Her words trailed off and she finally looked at Grace.

'You've kissed Pete?'

'He kissed me, actually.'

Grace paused. 'He did? When?'

Faith frowned again. 'He needed a friend.' She glanced at her watch. 'I have to go, he wants to talk to me in his room.'

'You're going now?'

'I have to go back to the studio first to get the rest of my portfolio, but after that, yeah.' She started towards the door. 'Can we finish talking about this later?'

Grace nodded, a little too fast. 'Sure. Sure.'

So Pete kissed Faith.

Grace wasn't sure how that made her feel. She knew she wasn't jealous, but she didn't feel comfortable for some reason. Perhaps it was because it must have happened so soon after Grace had kissed him.

Or had it?

Her mind raced. Could Pete and Faith have kissed before then? Could that be the reason why Faith had been so upset?

Her thoughts were interrupted simultaneously by the buzzing of her phone and the sound of running footsteps approaching the Great Hall. As she reached into her pocket for her mobile, Pete barrelled in through the door.

'Grace,' he panted, pointing a finger out of the window. 'Daniel's back.'

'What?'

Grace ran towards the window and looked out. Scanning the driveway, she stopped when she saw a familiar piece of graffiti on the outside of the art block. The art block was directly after Lost Souls Bridge on The 100 Society list. Number ninety-eight and the first piece of graffiti to be completed within the school grounds. Grace had saved all of Clifton's tags until the end, to give them the best chance of finishing before being caught.

'Another reaper?'

Pete stood behind her. 'He's come back to finish it.'

'Let him finish it. I don't care about that any more.'

'You don't? Should we tell someone that he's here? The school are looking for him, maybe they'll call the police if they know he's back.'

Grace chewed her lip. 'No. I don't think we want to get the police involved. Not yet.'

If it was going to happen, if Daniel was going to turn them in for what happened on the bridge that night, it could wait until after the show. Until after her father had seen her work.

Pete nodded. 'Yeah, OK.' He started towards the door.

'Wait,' Grace called. Pete turned back to face her. 'I thought you were meeting Faith?'

'What?' Pete shook his head, his brow furrowing in confusion. 'No.'

'She just had a text message from you. You said to meet her in your room.'

Pete shook his head again and reached into his pocket. 'No, look—' His face froze, his eyes widening in horror as he looked at Grace. 'My phone, I left it in the art block.'

Grace looked out again at the reaper, then up to the studio.

Anyone could have gone in.

Anyone could have picked it up.

'Wait,' Grace cried, digging in her pocket. 'Someone sent me a message just before you came in.' She pulled out her phone and brought the screen to life.

If you liked my work with Cassie, just WAIT until you see what I've done with Faith and Ed . . .

Grace dropped the phone, her hands flying up to cover her mouth.

'What is it?' Pete picked up the phone and looked at the screen. 'Oh, this is bad. This is really bad.'

'We have to find her.'

Pete nodded. 'You said Faith's gone to my room?'

'I think so.' She paused. 'No,' she cried. 'Wait, she said she had to go to the studio first.'

'Then you go up to the dorms,' Pete said, already at the door. 'I'll check the studio and meet you up there.'

'OK,' Grace said, taking her phone back from Pete. 'Do you think we should tell someone? Cross?'

Pete shook his head. 'I don't think we've got time.' He grabbed Grace's hand. 'Just be careful, OK?'

Grace nodded. 'I promise.' She squeezed his hand back. 'You too.'

She ran from the room, her feet hammering the wooden staircase as she descended into the entrance hall. Elaborate flower arrangements had appeared on the tables in the reception and an easel stood in the middle of the floor, holding a sign welcoming Clifton's visitors to this year's art show. Grace ran past, almost knocking the sign over and hitting the doors that led to the dormitories with enough speed for them to burst open and crash against the walls. The corridor was empty, most of the students having already made their way to the dinner hall. When Grace reached the staircase that led up to the boys' dormitory, she slowed down, suddenly fearing what she might find.

Forcing each step, she climbed the staircase before pushing her way through the door that led on to the boys' corridor. Her heart skipped with relief when she saw Faith at the far end, staring at her phone with confusion.

'Faith?'

Faith looked up. 'Grace? What are you doing here?' She took a few steps along the corridor towards Grace, away from the door that led into Pete's room.

'That wasn't Pete,' Grace said.

Faith stopped outside Ed's room, reaching for the handle. 'What wasn't Pete?'

'The text you got. We think Daniel sent it.'

'What? No, Pete just sent me another message.' Faith started to push open the door. 'He's found Ed, they're both in his room.'

'No!' Grace was running before she had time to think. 'Don't do it,' she shouted, her feet pounding the hallway as she reached out, desperate to stop Faith from walking in on whoever might be waiting for her.

But it was too late.

Faith stood in the doorway, her body frozen.

Grace wanted to turn, to run from whatever Faith was staring at, but she couldn't move.

And then Faith stumbled back, her mouth widening, her eyes filled with terror as she let out the most awful scream.

It was enough to unstick Grace from the carpet and again she was running, hurtling towards whatever awful thing was inside Ed's room.

As Grace pushed past where Faith stood, her hands now covering her face in an almost-exact replica of the painting she had worked so hard on, Grace finally saw what had filled her friend with so much horror.

Ed, hanging from the light fitting, a noose pulled tight around his neck.

His eyes were open, bulging with the terror of his last moments. Bloody trenches had been gouged into the skin on his neck from where he had clawed at the rope in a desperate attempt to save himself. A chair lay on the floor beneath his feet.

But in a room that was filled with evidence of a suicide, there was one thing that told Grace everything she needed to know that this was murder.

On the wall above the bed, pointing at Ed's swinging body, was another tag.

Another reaper.

Grace didn't scream.

She didn't make a sound.

She was running again, this time towards the front of school where she would find Cross, find *anyone* and tell them what had happened to Ed. She knew what was happening now; she knew exactly what Daniel was doing.

It wasn't enough for him to finish The 100 Society, it ran far deeper than that, and he had to be stopped. They were all in danger, every single one of them.

She was on the staircase, taking the steps two at a time, when her phone buzzed again.

Poor Ed. He couldn't live with the guilt of what happened on the bridge that night. Of what you all tried to do to me.

As she neared the bottom of the staircase, still clutching her phone, Grace almost ran headfirst into Sylvester.

'Hey,' he cried, grabbing her arms and almost toppling over. He steadied himself and grinned at her. 'Easy there. In a rush to finish our little "paintings", are we?' He bent his fingers in quote marks around the word 'paintings'.

Grace pulled away, her breath coming in quick bursts. 'What?' She glanced back up the stairs.

Sylvester tapped his nose. 'One hundred little secrets,' he whispered with a wink. 'I see everything, Grace. It's my job, remember?'

Looking down, Grace saw the mobile phone clipped to his belt. The screen was lit, showing it had recently been used. She took a step back up the stairs, inching away from him.

When he saw her expression, his face fell. 'Hey, don't worry. I'm not going to say anything. I remember what it's like to be young.'

'I don't—'

'Look,' he said, 'it's like this. I know what Mr Cross can be like. I just try to be fair, you know? Only fill him in on the important stuff.'

From upstairs, there was another scream. Sylvester's head snapped up and he started to push past Grace. 'What's going on up there?'

'Someone's . . .' She stopped, unable to bring herself to say the word 'dead'. 'Someone's hurt,' Grace sobbed, inching her way down the stairs, away from Sylvester.

He turned back to her, pointing with a long, thin finger. 'You wait there.'

When Sylvester had disappeared around the bend in the spiral staircase, Grace started to run again.

Maybe she should call Trick, tell him everything, tell him what had happened to Ed and warn him that he too was in danger. Maybe he would know what to do.

She pulled out her phone, blinking away tears. Her fingers shook as she prepared to dial, but something made her stop.

Grace knew what they had left behind on the bridge and it was something that belonged to Trick.

She couldn't call him, because Trick had smashed his phone on Lost Souls. It lay on the pavement, complete with the sim card that would lead back to him. It was the one piece of evidence that linked them to everything, to what had happened to Ed, to Cassie, to the reaper tags. It was the one thing that would tie in with Daniel's story should he attempt to turn them in for what had happened that night.

Attempted murder.

Daniel might have killed Ed, but they had tried to kill Daniel. Who was to say the two events wouldn't be linked?

Who was to say they wouldn't be implicated in Ed's death?

Grace continued towards the front of school, but when she reached the entrance hall she didn't head for Cross's office. Instead, she ran out through the main doors, her feet crunching the gravel of the driveway as she ran from the school. Black clouds were rolling in from the west and more than once she heard a distant rumble, growing louder as the wind picked up.

Out of the school gates and into the road, Grace didn't stop running until she was at the outskirts of the city and the rain had started to fall. Pulling the hood of her sweatshirt up against the wind and rain, she slowed to a fast walk, her chest burning and her heart racing. The sky was darkening overhead and the trees that lined the road were swaying in the wind. Occasional gusts whipped the leaves up from the gutters in mini cyclones.

The burning in Grace's chest started to recede as her breathing slowed, but it was replaced with a hollowness, a new pain that had started the moment she had seen Ed's lifeless body.

Pushing the image away, Grace pulled the drawstrings in her hood, tightening it against her tear-streaked face. Whatever uncharacteristic warmth they had been experiencing that October had now gone and goosebumps were rising on her arms, but she was almost at the bridge and in a couple of minutes she would have picked up all the pieces of Trick's phone.

Then she could get back to the nightmare that was unfolding at Clifton. She would finally be able to tell Cross everything, to turn Daniel in to the police without fear of him framing them.

When she turned the corner on to the road leading up to Lost Souls Bridge, she froze, her gasp whipped away by the wind.

Ahead, blue and white police tape stretched across the road, tied on to the lampposts either side. Beyond that, a number of police cars lined the pavements, some parked up on the curb while others blocked the middle of the road. Beside the police cars was a fire engine and on the bridge itself stood a single ambulance, the doors at the back open to reveal an empty interior.

The blue lights atop the police cars were silent but flashing in a steady pulse, bright against the darkening sky.

A small crowd had gathered near the police tape, whispering to each other as they stared at something out of Grace's view.

She wanted to turn, to leave before she also got to see what the crowd was staring at, but her feet betrayed the voice in her head telling her to run.

As she drew closer, the wind seemed to pick up yet again, this time bringing with it a more intense downpour. Nearing the back of the crowd, she was able to hear snippets of conversation before the words were picked up by the wind and carried away.

'. . . someone jumped . . .'

'. . . a young one, apparently . . .'

'. . . the parents, can you imagine?'

'. . . boy, can't be any more than seventeen . . .'

Still, Grace continued forwards, pushing her way through the crowd until she reached the front. If the police tape hadn't been there, separating her from the bridge, she was sure she would have continued forwards.

On the bridge, a number of police officers stood together. One turned towards the crowd, meeting Grace's eye. She stared back, hidden beneath her hood and the strands of wet hair that whipped across her face.

It was only when the police officer's eyes moved in the direction that the rest of the crowd were staring did Grace finally look. At the top of the steep bank stood a number of fire-crew, holding on to a set of red ropes that led down to the river. Grace followed the red lines with her eyes, down to where six firemen were working on the muddy riverbank.

They were securing the ropes to something.

After a few moments the firemen at the bottom of the bank stepped back, waving as they shouted up to the crew at the top. They started to pull and, finally, their load came into view. It was a stretcher, carrying something that had been covered with a blanket.

Another gust of wind rushed past, this one strong enough to strip away part of the blanket from the object on the stretcher. The crowd gasped collectively and hands rose to cover mouths, heads turning away from what had just been revealed. A fireman shouted, dashing forward to cover what had been uncovered, but it was too late.

Grace had seen it, a scene from her nightmares.

Daniel's face.

White, bloated, unmistakable.

Dead.

In her pocket, Grace's phone vibrated. With a hand that didn't feel like hers, she pulled it out and opened the message.

The show must go on.

By the time Grace had returned to Clifton, the storm was raging.

She raced up the gravel path, the conifers lining the driveway bending and creaking with every gust of wind. Behind Clifton's roofline, punctuated by the silhouettes of chimney stacks, a fork of lightning split the sky in two. A crack of thunder erupted moments later, rumbling on as Grace neared the school's entrance.

It was chaos.

In a scene that was all too reminiscent of the one she had just left at Lost Souls, the front of the school was filled with police cars and ambulances, but there were dozens of other cars parked along the driveway and small groups of parents stood in the rain, voices raised in the wind. As Grace neared the school she could see Cross, hands raised as he tried to hold back the crowd of parents who were demanding to see their children. She looked around, but saw no sign of her father or brother.

Ed's parents might be here, Grace thought. Perhaps they were already inside, being told that their son was dead.

She walked past a row of police cars and inside one she saw Faith, wrapped in a blanket. Her blank eyes stared forwards, unfocused, while a policewoman spoke to her, the words lost behind the glass of the car window.

Grace pushed through the crowd, unnoticed in the chaos as she neared the entrance. She looked up. Through the leaded windows of the Great Hall, her own painting was visible, alongside those of her classmates. But they would not be seen by anyone else tonight, not after everything that had happened.

Grace wondered if news of Daniel's death had reached the school yet. Perhaps some of the police cars were here because of him as well as Ed.

Another sheet of lightning lit the sky around her.

Grace ran up the stairs to the school's entrance, her wet clothes sticking to her skin as she burst in through the front doors. The hall was empty apart from that sign, standing on a small easel in the middle of the marble floor.

Welcome to Clifton Academy
Art Show in The Great Hall
➡

'Hey.'

Grace looked up to see Trick, almost smartly dressed in a shirt and tie above his usual tight black jeans. He looked calm. Did he not know what had happened?

When her eyes met his, he frowned.

'Jesus, Grace, you look awful. What happened? Where the hell have you been?'

'Where have I been?' she shouted, her breath coming in ragged bursts as she strode towards him. 'Where the hell have you been? Where were you when all this was going on?'

'What? I . . .' Trick stopped, his eyes shifting over Grace's shoulder to where the blue lights flashed outside. 'I've been getting ready for the show. What's happened?'

'Ed's dead,' she sobbed. 'And so is Daniel.'

'What are you talking about?'

There was something about the way he was talking – so cool, so calm – that wasn't right.

Grace stepped back, a coil of fear tightening in her stomach.

'Grace?'

She shook her head, her eyes darting towards the door.

'It's OK.' Trick stepped forwards slowly, his hands raised palm-out up in front of him. 'Everything's OK,' he said, bringing his hands slowly down on to her shoulders.

Grace looked up at him, into the brown eyes she knew so well. It couldn't be Trick, could it? Could he have been the one to send those messages?

'Daniel's not dead,' Trick said. 'He's been sending us texts, you know he has.'

'He is dead,' she blurted out, her vision blurring through her tears. 'I saw it. I saw his body. Someone else has been sending those messages from his phone.'

For a moment Trick said nothing. 'You're shaking,' he said, glancing at the policewoman who had just walked in through the main entrance. 'Come on, let's get you back to your room.'

His lowered his hands, his fingers closing around hers as he started towards the dormitory corridor. Grace allowed him to lead her through the doors, into the dormitory hallway that was now filled with students who were huddled into small groups. Some of them were crying.

Trick led Grace into the girls' dorms. When he reached her door, he turned to her.

'Quick,' he said, keeping his head down as another group of girls walked past. 'Get the door open.'

Grace nodded. She pulled her key from her pocket and, with a shaking hand, unlocked her door. Trick pushed his way in first, then reached out to grab her hand and pull her in. Slamming the door closed, he stepped back and looked at her.

'What happened to Ed?' he asked. 'Tell me slowly.'

'I don't know,' Grace sobbed. 'He was in his room—' She choked on her tears and Trick was there, folding her into his arms.

'You're shivering,' he said, releasing her and stepping back. 'You need to get out of those wet clothes.'

'What about Ed?' she asked. 'What about Daniel? What are we going to do?'

Trick cut her off. 'Clothes first, then we'll talk.' When Grace didn't move, he turned away. 'I won't look,' he said, sitting down on the end of the bed.

With his head in his hands, it looked like the news of Ed's death was beginning to sink in. His shoulders rose as he took a deep and unsteady breath.

Grace peeled her wet sweatshirt from her skin. She was shaking violently now and her fingers, numb from cold, fumbled with the material as she pulled it off. She threw it on to the bed behind Trick before quickly pulling her T-shirt off and tossing it on top of the sweater.

The rain beat against her window, filling the otherwise silent room with noise. It was almost fully dark outside and with her curtains open she was able to see her reflection in the glass. She could also see Trick, his eyes cast down away from the window.

'I thought you were mad at me,' she said, watching his reflection.

Trick glanced up, his eyes briefly meeting hers in the window.

'I was. But that doesn't matter right now. You need me.'

Grace pushed her wet hair from her face. 'I needed you then.' She was suddenly furious, the initial surge of adrenaline and fear beginning to recede into exhaustion and anger.

'Let's not talk about this now.'

'I have to talk about this now.'

Trick's fists clenched against his knees, but still he didn't turn around.

'Stop it, Grace.'

'No.' She clenched her own fists. 'Why did this have to happen?'

'You want to know why?' Trick jumped up, spinning to face her, his eyes locking with hers. 'This whole thing was your idea, Grace.' He spat his words like they were poison in his mouth and, for a moment, Grace recoiled. She had seen him angry before, but she had never been on the receiving end. Not like this.

He stepped towards her, his lips thinning. 'All of this happened because of you and your damned 100 Society. Don't tell me you don't know that.'

Grace opened her mouth, ready to argue, but Trick continued.

'I know, Grace. I know why you wanted to do it. It's because of your brother, because it's the one thing you could beat him at.'

'How did you—'

'How did I know?' He threw his hands up in frustration. 'Because I know *you*. Jesus, Grace, when are you going to realize? Why can't you open your eyes and see?' He was shouting now, the corners of his mouth pulled tight. 'I

247

know everything about you because, for the first time in my life, I've found someone I actually care about. It's as simple as that.'

'I don't think you're capable of caring about anyone but yourself.'

'Oh, is that right?'

'Yeah, that's right. If you cared so much, you wouldn't have left me alone on the railway bridge that night. The slightest hint of trouble and you were off, without a moment's hesitation.'

'That's where you're wrong.'

'I saw you, Trick. You jumped off the bridge on to the bank.'

'Yeah, and I stayed there until I was sure you'd made it too. I stayed there, in the dark, until Pete led you off into those woods. I stayed there while that freak stood on the bridge, chucking lit matches on to the tracks.'

Grace paused. 'You really waited for me?'

'Until I felt sure you were safe.' He looked away. 'I thought you were safe, Grace. I didn't know he was going to come back.'

'Why didn't you say anything?'

'Because it didn't matter. Pete was there. Just like he's always there.' Trick frowned.

'You can't blame Pete for that, you know.'

Trick shook his head. 'You're never going to give up on him, are you?'

'What are you talking about?'

'You don't think I can see what's going on there? He's the one your dad would approve of, which is why you've been stringing him along all this time. Like your feelings for him might change and for once you might be able to do something that might make your father happy.' He laughed. 'Because god forbid you should bring someone like me home.'

Grace shook her head, but she felt suddenly weak.

'Come on, Grace,' Trick said, jabbing a finger at the photographs on her wall, the pictures of her father and brother. 'Everything you do is because of what you think your father has done to you. But you know what? He loves you, he's paid for you to have this education, these opportunities. You're one of the luckiest girls alive and you don't even know it.'

'You don't know anything about me and my father.'

'I know enough to see that you're a prime example of a spoiled girl with daddy issues.' Trick's voice lowered. 'Case in point is you kissing Pete.'

Grace's hand struck the side of Trick's face, cracking in time with a strike of lightning outside.

For a moment the only sound came from the incessant beating of rain on glass. Trick's chest rose and fell, his breathing coming in quick bursts as he reached up to touch his lip.

Grace caught sight of herself in the window. Dressed in just her bra and jeans, she looked a mess. Her hair hung in wet, matted strands and tears streaked her face, her skin

249

flushed bright red.

Her eyes locked with Trick's. 'Get out.'

'No.'

'I said, get out.' She lunged forwards again, but he caught hold of her, his fingers encircling her wrists.

Grace tried to swallow, but she was finding it difficult to breathe with Trick so close. The anger that had darkened his eyes had gone and there was now a resignation in the way he was looking at her.

He loosened his grip on her wrists, but he didn't let go.

'Trick—'

'If you really want me to leave,' he said, his mouth centimetres from hers, 'then I'll leave. Just say the word.'

'No,' she whispered. 'I don't—'

His lips took away the rest of her sentence. He released her arms and reached up to touch her face. The kiss was slow, gentle, and as soft and as sweet as she had imagined. They stumbled back, Trick's hands moving from her face to her neck, down to her waist and she was suddenly so aware that the only thing separating his skin from hers was his shirt. She needed to feel him against her, she needed to feel his warmth, to feel safe and to know that whatever had happened, whatever was going to happen, he was hers.

She tugged at his tie, but it only seemed to grow tighter beneath her fingers.

Trick pulled at it, releasing the knot before throwing it on to Grace's bed. Then his hands were back on her waist, his fingertips pressing against her skin, the pressure just enough to make her forget, to push away the thoughts of what had happened to Ed, of what had happened to Daniel, if only for a few moments.

Grace grabbed at Trick's shirt, pulling it from his jeans and pushing it up his body. He stepped back and unfastened the top button before pulling the shirt up and over his head.

Grace's breath caught in her throat. She could see the flutter of Trick's heart, pounding behind his bruised ribcage. She trailed her fingers across the ink of his tattoos, before leaning in to kiss his skin. Breathing in deeply, she inhaled his scent and spread her hands across his back, pulling him tightly against her and squeezing her eyes closed as she tried to push away the pain of everything that had happened that day.

'I'm here,' he said, kissing the top of her head. 'And everything's going to be OK.' He placed a finger beneath her chin, lifting it to look into her eyes. 'Everything's going to be OK.'

His head dipped to kiss her once more. They stumbled together again, this time hitting the door. Trick reached out, pushing a hand back against the wall as he tried to steady himself and stop them from toppling over. His other hand slid down to her waist, his finger hooking the top of her jeans.

His lips moved to her cheek. 'Are you sure you want to do this?' he murmured against her skin, moving to kiss her jaw, her neck.

Trailing her hands across his skin, so warm, so alive, Grace nodded.

For now, she could forget about everything else.

For now, they could just exist together.

Everything else would come after.

Grace opened her eyes and watched their reflection in the window, her arms around his neck as he trailed kisses along her collarbone. Trick's shoulders flexed as he moved, his tattoos dancing as his fingers searched out the light switch.

In the moment before Trick plunged the room into darkness, Grace caught sight of a new tattoo on his back, one she had never seen before.

One that was terrifyingly familiar.

A grim reaper, poised with a scythe and pointing directly at Grace.

30

Trick lay on the floor of Grace's room, crumpled in a heap from where she had violently pushed him away. 'What the hell was that?' he asked, wincing as he clutched at his ribs.

Grace's hand seemed to be stuck to the light switch. 'Stay there,' she cried, fumbling for the alarm clock on her bedside table. 'Don't come any closer.' She lifted the clock above her head, not taking her eyes from Trick as she stumbled to where her T-shirt still lay on the bed. She grabbed it, a fistful of wet material that she clutched against her chest, trying to cover as much of herself as she could.

It all made sense.

Trick, who never felt like he belonged. He had always thought he wasn't as good as the rest of them and had always hated the way Cassie acted so superior, so he had destroyed her in the worst way possible; by taking away one of the things that mattered the most to her – her beauty.

Deconstruction of Beauty. He had tortured her with her own work because of the way she made him feel.

That was why he had taken it upon himself to complete his own version of The 100 Society, with the reaper tag that he couldn't resist having tattooed as a personal reminder of his achievement. Had he also killed Ed? Set him up as the Hangman so that when Faith found him it would also bring her painting to life?

What was he going to do with her?

With Pete?

Panic gripped her as she realized she hadn't seen Pete since he left the Great Hall. 'Where is he?' she cried. 'What have you done with Pete?'

'Grace, what's going on?' Trick started to get up, but Grace thrust a finger at him.

'Don't you move,' she said, lifting the clock higher.

'OK,' Trick said, raising his hands. 'Just calm down.'

Grace stepped back towards the door. 'I saw it, Trick. That thing on your back.' Her fingers found the door handle and she yanked it open just as Trick got to his feet. He launched himself forwards, reaching for her, but she threw the clock and it struck his head, splitting the skin above his brow.

'Jesus, Grace,' Trick yelled, his hands flying up to his bleeding face. He lunged again, but Grace slipped out of the door, pulling it closed. 'Grace,' he shouted, 'wait . . .'

She fumbled in her pocket and pulled out the key, her

other hand still on the door handle. From inside, she could hear Trick shouting, pounding on the door. She slid her key into the lock and turned it. Then, holding it in place with a shaking hand, she carefully let go of the handle. For a moment there was nothing, then the handle began to rattle furiously again, the key moving as Trick tried to unlock the door from the other side.

From inside the room came an almighty roar, followed by a crash.

Then silence.

Grace glanced up and down the corridor. It was empty and all of the doors were closed.

Grace pressed her ear against the door and listened. There was nothing. No talking, no movement, no rattling of the door handle. Quickly, she pulled her still-wet top on and, with her hand shaking, slowly pulled her key from the lock.

Then she ran.

Her feet beat against the floor as she sprinted towards the front of the school, hurling herself through the first set of doors that led out of the dormitories. Ahead, she could see the next set of doors that would lead her out into the entrance hall.

She had to find Pete. She had to make sure he was OK.

Grace barrelled through the final set of doors, almost tripping as she ran into the entrance hall, now filled with police. She looked at the clock on the wall. It was almost seven, the time the art show was supposed to start.

She should be in the Great Hall now, waiting for the crowds to arrive.

Waiting for her father, her brother. They must be here, somewhere.

Grace glanced around, but the hall was filled only with police and staff members. Across the room, Miss Stone stood wiping her tears with a lace handkerchief while a policewoman laid a hand on her shoulder. She nodded at something the policewoman said and mumbled a reply before covering her eyes, her shoulders lifting as she sobbed.

The last time Grace had seen Pete was in the Great Hall.

With her hand on the mahogany banister, she started to climb the stairs but stopped when she saw something on one of the steps in front of her.

She bent down to pick up what looked like a small piece of pottery and turned it over, frowning as she ran her fingers over the familiar looking shard.

It was from Pete's sculpture.

Searching the steps around her she saw there were no other large pieces, but small white splinters littered the staircase.

Grace slipped the broken piece into her pocket and continued to climb the stairs. When she reached the top, she stepped into the Great Hall and, for a moment, she thought her heart might stop.

It was empty.

No, that wasn't quite true.

The walls were covered with graffiti, paint dripping from where each grim reaper had been hurriedly sprayed.

The Great Hall. Number ninety-nine on the list. It was almost over, but at what cost? And what else was to come?

The easels stood empty, like rows of wooden skeletons where their paintings should have been. In the middle was the pedestal where Pete's sculpture once had pride of place.

Grace's phone buzzed.

You've made me angry now. Not a good move, but I understand. Just like you'll understand, soon enough.

Another message.

I did this all for you, Grace. You'll realize that soon. It's almost over. One final scene that will finish it all.

One final scene?

Grace looked around the room, at the empty easels and the grim reaper tags dripping on the panelled walls. The Great Hall was tag number ninety-nine. That left one more.

The bell tower.

It was the final place, the last tag.

And it was also the subject of Trick's painting.

She burst from the Great Hall, no longer caring about what might happen if she and her friends were linked to the graffiti or to Daniel's death. There was more at stake now, there was the possibility that something terrible was about to happen to someone she cared so deeply for.

She couldn't let anyone else get hurt.

'Please,' she cried, running down the great staircase into the entrance hall. 'I need help. I think someone's in trouble.'

257

A silence fell across the hall as the police officers turned to stare at Grace. From behind the banisters, Cross appeared. 'Grace?'

'Mr Cross, you have to listen to me,' she cried. 'It's not Daniel, none of this was him, he's dead.'

Cross frowned. 'Grace, I hate to be the one to tell you this, but it's not Daniel who died.'

Grace shook her head. 'No, I know. I mean, I know that Ed's dead too, but—'

A policeman was suddenly next to Grace, a hand on her arm. 'Come on love, shall we go and have a chat in the office?'

Grace pulled away. 'No, you have to listen to me. Daniel fell in the river. It was an accident, but he's dead.'

For a moment no one said anything. Then the officer beckoned his colleague over. 'You got anything on radio about an accident in the river?'

The officer nodded. 'Yeah, they found a kid in there today.' He looked at Grace. 'You know something about that?'

'Yes, but that's not what I'm trying to tell you.' She stepped back, pressing her clenched fists against the sides of her head. 'Please, just listen to me.'

'OK, now calm down . . .' He turned to Cross. 'What's her name?'

'Grace,' she screamed. 'My name is Grace and I think someone's going to get hurt, just like Cassie got hurt. Just like Ed.' She turned to Cross, her face wet with tears. 'Mr

Cross, please, I think Pete's in trouble.'

'Pete was here earlier, Grace.' Cross's voice had lowered and he spoke to her in slow, measured tones. 'He's fine.' He reached out for her arm but she pulled away, then one of the policemen was on Grace, grabbing her wrist and pulling it up behind her back.

'OK, love, time to calm down,' he said, pushing her towards Cross's office.

'Please,' Grace cried, staggering as he forced her forwards. 'You're hurting me.'

He leaned down to speak into her ear, his words calm but forceful. 'Then you need to relax.'

'OK,' Grace said, nodding. 'I'm calm.' She felt his grip loosen and she forced herself to relax, letting him lower her arm. The pain receded and quickly she spun away from him, pulling her wrist from his meaty hand.

'Hey,' he shouted, lunging towards her, but she was quick and dodged in the other direction, slipping beneath his arm as he made an attempt to grab her.

'Someone stop her!' he shouted.

The room erupted.

Hands reached for her, clutching at her clothes, but she was quick and had made her way to the front door before any of the police managed to get a good grip. Cross's voice boomed from the other side of the hall, shouting at the police to be gentle, to leave her alone.

And then she was outside, running in the pouring rain as wind whipped all around her, water splashing beneath her feet and her already wet T-shirt soaked to the skin.

She didn't know if she was being followed because she didn't look back, but she knew exactly where she was headed.

To the bell tower.

It didn't take long for Grace to reach the churchyard.

There was a gap somewhere in the rotting fence, but in the darkness she was unable to find it.

She found a space between two of the trees that ran alongside and squeezed through, placing a foot on the fence before pulling herself up, the branches groaning around her as the wind rattled past. The wood was soft beneath her fingertips and as she pushed with her foot she could feel it splintering under her weight.

Quickly, she hoisted herself up and over, jumping into a tangle of weeds on the other side. As she landed, her foot hit a tree root and for a moment she stumbled, crying out as her ankle twisted under her.

She clutched at one of the many headstones that filled the churchyard, taking deep breaths while she waited for the pain in her ankle to subside. When it had lessened to a dull throb, she carefully placed her foot on the ground.

Nothing broken.

When she started to walk again, it was with a limp, but at least she was mobile.

Ahead, she could just about see the outline of the church, the building blacker than the night sky. But there was some light, a dull orange glow that lit the small slit windows in the side of the bell tower.

Wiping the rain from her eyes, she negotiated her way through the graveyard towards the tower, occasionally stopping to flex her ankle, but when a cry rang out from somewhere within the church, a surge of adrenaline pushed her onwards. With her ankle screaming at her to stop, she propelled herself forwards, her limp growing more pronounced with each step.

The wind seemed to change direction every few seconds, sometimes whipping the air from in front of her and, at other times, carrying towards her the shouts and screams that grew louder with every step she took on the waterlogged ground.

Nauseous with fear and from the pain in her ankle, she ran until she was in front of the arched wooden door that led into the bell tower. It was slightly ajar and she was just able to make out a soft, flickering glow inside.

Now sheltered from the rain, she shivered, her wet clothes colder than ever. Slowly, she pushed the door open another centimetre or two, just enough to be able to see

262

inside. Where she had earlier heard cries and the shouting of voices that were distorted and unfamiliar in the wind, there was now silence. Barely daring to breathe, she pushed the door open a little wider.

Inside the bell tower, a row of candles had been laid out, surrounding the inside of the stone wall. A wooden staircase spiralled up, and from where Grace stood she was able to see the first few steps, also lit with the same tea lights. A gust of wind blew in through the open door and the candles flickered almost to the point of being extinguished, creating long, dancing shadows around the staircase.

A drip fell into a muddy puddle on the floor in front of her and echoed around the tower.

Grace stepped inside, pulling the heavy door closed behind her without making a sound. She checked the handle, making sure it wasn't on the latch, just in case she had to make a fast escape.

It wasn't as cold inside as Grace had been expecting, partly thanks to the shelter it provided, but also because the sheer number of candles gave just enough warmth to take the chill out of the air. There was a thick smell of damp inside the tower, mixed with the clogging scent of the candles, making the small space seem even more constricted.

The first thing Grace saw was Daniel's painting. Resting against the wall, it was surrounded by the same tea lights that lined the inside wall of the tower. In the orange glow, the subject matter of his work was unmistakable. Almost like an extension of the flames themselves, the colours of the paints blended effortlessly with the tiny licks of fire that danced in front of the canvas. Grace took another step further into the building, away from the door. She looked up at the wooden staircase, curling up into the darkness around the inside wall like a coiled snake. A slit window punctuated each level of steps, black against the dim candlelight.

Grace swallowed. Forcing herself forwards, she moved to the staircase, but the wooden rail on the outside of the steps looked as rotten as the fence had been. Instead, she placed her hand on the metal rail that was attached to the tower's stone wall.

She placed her foot on the first step, gently, in case the wood creaked underfoot and gave away her presence. The stairs were rotten too, the wood yielding slightly as she stepped up.

The steady rhythm of dripping water echoed around her and the smell of damp grew thicker as she continued her ascent. It seemed to clog the air, making it harder to breathe, although she knew it was really the adrenaline that was causing the tightness in her chest and throat.

Once she had reached the first landing in the stairway, she stopped.

There was another row of candles, these ones laid out beside Cassie's artwork, her pictures resting neatly against the tower's stone wall. But that wasn't what made Grace want to turn and run, to go back and beg the police for help once more. What terrified her was the photograph that had been taped to one corner of Cassie's canvas; a Polaroid photograph of Cassie, lying in her hospital bed with her face covered in bandages.

Instantly, Grace was taken back to the day she visited Cassie in the hospital. Someone had been outside the room, she had seen them turn the handle, but when Grace called out, they had left.

Had it been Trick? Had he come that day to take this very photograph?

Grace closed her eyes. If only she had chased after him, if only she had confronted him on that day, perhaps it wouldn't have come to this. Ed might still be alive. Pete wouldn't be in danger.

She shook her head. There was no going back for help now. Who knew what was going on in the top of the tower? Perhaps she was already too late.

Pushing the thought away, she continued forward. A few steps up the next section of staircase, Grace became aware of voices from somewhere above. Two males talking, too quiet for her to make out the subject matter or to even judge the tone. It was all she could do not to shout out, not to break into a run, but she did start to climb a little faster.

On the next landing, another set of candles had been laid out, shrine-like, in front of Ed's painting. Grace's hand flew up to cover her mouth when she saw the Polaroid, taped on in the same way that Cassie's had been. It was Ed, hanging from the light fitting, his hands frozen in time as they scrabbled at the rope around his neck. Grace choked out a sob as she tore her eyes away from the image. The photograph had been taken while he was still alive, while he was still fighting for his life.

Next to Ed's picture was Faith's scream, propped up at an angle so it was facing Ed's hangman, as though the figure on the canvas was reacting to the sight of the man swinging from the noose, just as Faith had done when she had discovered Ed's body.

Nausea twisted Grace's stomach and she looked away. The sickness started to recede and was quickly replaced with anger. A new, more powerful surge of adrenaline rushed through her.

A gust of wind and rain blew in through the slit window behind Grace, almost as if it were urging her to continue.

Grace started forwards, on to the next set of steps. She pulled herself up on the handrail as she went, using it like a crutch to keep the weight off her twisted ankle. Any time she felt the fear resurface, she pushed down hard on her bad leg, the pain keeping her focused, lucid.

She was on the final ascent now; the voices from above were becoming clearer and she was finally able to recognize who they belonged to.

It was Trick and Pete, arguing, although she was still unable to make out the content.

There was only one more flight of steps before she reached the top of the tower and the belfry. Looking around

266

her, Grace realized she had come empty-handed. She knew that whatever lay on the other side of that door was dangerous, that her life was at risk. She could have kicked herself for coming all this way without anything to protect herself.

The fear returned then, stronger than ever. As she glanced around, the adrenaline surged faster, clouding her mind. She clutched at the wooden handrail on the other side of the staircase, the handrail that was supposed to stop anyone from falling over the side, down to the bottom of the tower. Her fingernails sunk into the rotting wood as she gripped harder, trying to think of something, anything, she could use as a weapon.

She took her hands away from the rail and looked down at where her fingernails had left small half-moons in the wood. The rail was thick, perhaps two by two inches, and certainly hefty enough to do some damage if she needed it to.

Leaning back on to the stone wall, Grace placed her good foot up against the wooden handrail, wincing in pain as her twisted ankle took all of her weight. She pushed against the wood, feeling it give slightly under the pressure. When nothing happened, she drew her foot back, bending her leg at the knee before kicking out, hard. The rubber sole of her trainer slipped against the wood and she reached out to grab the metal handrail behind her, repositioning herself before kicking again. There was a splintering sound, but little movement, so she drew her foot back before kicking again. With one final strike, the wood gave way and her foot shot through the rail, almost causing her to lose balance.

With her breath coming in ragged bursts she took hold of the rail at the broken point and levered it backwards and forwards before pulling it sharply towards herself. There was another, louder crack as the rail came away in her hands. This time she did lose her balance, falling backwards on to a step, her elbow breaking through the soft wood. She pulled herself free, thankful that her arm was uninjured, and examined her prize.

The broken section of rail was almost a metre long and, despite the rot weakening its structure, was still a decent weapon. Feeling somewhat more prepared, Grace turned her attention back to the door that led into the belfry. She carefully placed a foot on the step that her elbow had gone through and it bowed significantly under her weight, but held as she moved up to the next step. She continued up the final few stairs until she found herself outside the door to the belfry. It was closed, but the latch on the outside was not in place.

Placing a trembling hand on the handle, she paused and took a deep breath.

It was only when the shaking in her fingers stopped that she finally opened the door.

The scene that greeted Grace was not what she had expected.

The inside of the belfry was filled with candles, more than twice the number that Grace had seen on her journey up the tower. It was significantly warmer than it had been on her ascent, although the slit windows surrounding the bell allowed the wind and rain to blow through, the huge bell hanging in the middle of the room resonating with each gust.

Grace's painting had been mounted on one of the stone walls and beneath it were rows upon rows of candles, burning beside vases of lilies and roses.

Like a shrine.

Beneath one of the windows was Trick's picture, his own version of the bell tower, the one that Grace had loved so much. But there were no candles there, nothing to suggest it had received the same treatment as any of the others.

Then there were Trick and Pete.

Clutching at her broken stair rail, raised up over shoulder like a baseball player preparing to bat, Grace's heart galloped as she took in the scene.

Pete was laying on the floor, his hands tied behind his back, a piece of black gaffer tape covering his mouth. A huge, egg-like lump protruded from his forehead. One of his eyes was swollen shut and a small trickle of blood escaped from his nose. He was looking at her with wide, pleading eyes, his breath coming in quick bursts through his nostrils. His whole body was writhing, his shoulders flexing as he tried to escape whatever was binding his hands together.

On the other side of the belfry, slumped against the wall, was Trick.

His face was battered, his eyes almost swollen shut. His lip was split and his hair was matted with blood. One hand was placed against his bruised ribs, his swollen face contorted in agony.

'Grace,' he said, his voice ragged.

'What the hell is going on?' Grace cried. Without taking her eyes from Trick, she inched her way towards Pete, who was moaning behind the tape that covered his mouth. He was trying to talk to her, trying to tell her something in pleading tones.

'Grace, don't,' Trick said, although there was little strength to his voice.

'You just stay there,' Grace shouted back at him, her fingers tightening around the wood in her hand.

Slowly, she bent down beside Pete. 'It's OK,' she said, watching as Trick tried to push himself up from the floor. 'We're going to be OK.' She took a corner of the tape in her fingers and pulled it sharply, tearing it from Pete's face.

He cried out, turning his face away as he stretched his mouth wide and took deep gulps of air.

'He went crazy,' Pete cried, nodding towards Trick. 'He's gone mad, Grace.'

Grace turned back to where Trick had finally managed to stumble to his feet, his hand still clutching at his side.

Grace stood up herself, brandishing her makeshift bat. 'Get back down,' she said, pointing at the floor. The boards creaked beneath her feet as she took a step towards him.

'He's lying, Grace,' Trick said. He was almost bent double and even in the shadows, Grace could see the ashen tone of his skin. 'He told me you were up here, he said you were in danger.' He slumped back against the wall, his eyes tightening in pain. 'I came looking for you.'

Grace looked back down to where Pete lay, shaking his head. 'No, no, I'm not lying.' He looked directly at her. 'You know me. We've been friends . . .' He paused. '*Best* friends for years. You know I'd never lie to you, Grace.' He choked out a sob. 'Please, just untie me. We have to get out of here.'

'OK.' Grace nodded. She knelt down beside Pete, placing her weapon on the floorboards beside her. It looked like Trick's bruised ribs had now progressed to being fully broken, so he wouldn't be moving anywhere fast.

Still, she watched him as her fingers worked the knotted rope at Pete's wrists.

'Please,' Trick said again. 'Please, Grace, don't. He'll kill us both.'

The first knot fell away in her fingers. As she continued, Grace looked around the belfry, at the various items littering the floor.

The first thing she saw was a small red canister, something that might hold a liquid of some kind, next to what looked like a pair of night-vision goggles. Then a roll of gaffer tape and a long rope, the same kind that had been used to tie Pete's hands. Beside one of the cut ends was a knife, the blade black rather than silver. Near Trick was a can of spray paint and next to that, a stencil with a familiar looking shape cut out of it. She looked up and, sure enough, there was the final tag. The grim reaper, plastered across the bell.

It was finished. The 100 Society tags were complete.

Grace looked at Trick, at the fingers clutching his side.

'Show me your hands.'

He glanced at her, but his eyes were glazed. He coughed weakly.

'Trick, I said show me your hands.'

Trick lifted his free hand. It was clean.

'And the other one.'

Wincing, Trick pulled his hand away from his side. His fingers were covered with black paint.

'That's all I needed,' Grace spat. She returned her attention to Pete's hands, now bound by a single knot.

Grace froze.

The fingertips on both of his hands were black.

'Grace? Why have you stopped?' Pete rolled over to look at her. 'Grace?'

Grace shuffled back, her eyes widening. She looked again at the items on the floor, before realizing that the blade of the knife wasn't actually black.

She rushed forwards, scooping the knife up. She turned it towards the candlelight and the steel glinted beneath the thick red coating covering it. Crying out, Grace dropped the blade, allowing it to clatter on to the floor before she rushed to where Trick lay, crumpled against the wall.

'Show me,' she said again. Turning his hand towards her, she saw that what she had thought was black paint was actually the same red liquid that covered the knife.

Trick's blood.

Pete had stabbed him.

Grace turned quickly, but Pete was already up, the rope that had been binding his hands now at his feet.

'I had to do it,' Pete said, raising his hands. 'He was going crazy, Grace. You have to believe me.'

Slowly, not taking her eyes from Pete or her hand from Trick's, she pulled her mobile out of her pocket and found

273

one of the text messages from Daniel's phone. With a shaking hand, she pressed the call-back button.

There was a moment of silence before the tinny sound of a ringtone filled the belfry. Pete's hand flew to his pocket and he pulled out a phone.

'That's Daniel's,' Grace whispered.

Pete dropped the phone and rolled his eyes. 'Oh, fine.' He tutted and shook his head. 'You could have waited, you know. I was going to tell you to come up here eventually. When I was ready.' He shrugged a shoulder, looking annoyed. 'You've kind of ruined it now.'

Grace stared as she tried to process what Pete was saying to her, to the sudden change in the way he was holding himself and speaking to her.

From behind her, Trick coughed again. This time it sounded a lot wetter and when Grace turned she saw a spatter of blood on his lips. 'You stabbed Trick?' The question was more of a statement, aimed at herself as much as Pete as she desperately searched for an explanation to all of this.

'Well, he was more than a little reluctant to go along with things,' Pete said. He touched the lump on his head. 'Just as well I got him first or he might have got away after he knocked me out.' His expression suddenly changed, his lips drawing tight across his teeth as he pointed a finger at Trick. 'Knocking someone out is NOT. FAIR. FIGHTING.' He jabbed his finger with each word before turning back to Grace. 'I guess we can still work it out,' he said, bending to pick up Grace's wooden rail and running his finger along its length.

'Stay away from me.' Grace scurried back, positioning herself closely against Trick. 'Stay away from both of us.' She held out the knife, still sticky with Trick's blood.

Pete looked at the piece of wood he was holding. He frowned. 'You think I'm going to hurt you?' He shook his head, his brow furrowing deeply. 'Why would I do that?'

'I don't know,' Grace cried, wiping the tears from her face with her sleeve. 'You hurt Trick.'

'Yeah, but that's all for a reason, isn't it?' Pete turned to the window and dropped Grace's weapon out into the darkness. He leaned out to watch it fall. 'It's pretty high, Grace. He won't feel anything.'

'What are you talking about?'

'He wants me to jump.'

Grace turned to Trick. His eyes were a little more focused now, but he coughed again and more blood appeared at the corner of his mouth. He looked at Pete. 'If I jump, will you promise me you won't hurt her?'

Pete laughed. 'Of course I won't hurt her.' He looked at Grace and rolled his eyes. 'Don't be silly.'

'No!' Grace cried. She lifted the knife higher, pointing it at Pete.

'Come on, Grace,' Pete said. 'Put the knife down and stop being so daft.'

'I swear to god,' Grace said through gritted teeth. 'If you come a step closer . . .'

'What? What are you going to do? Throw the knife?' He laughed again. 'Grace, the chances of you being able to hit me with that thing from, what – three metres? – are incredibly slim. You'd have to get the exact angle, the correct trajectory. A simple matter of physics, I'm afraid.'

Grace stared. 'Pete,' she whispered. 'What have you done?'

'What have I done?' He stepped towards her, stopping and raising his hands when she lifted the knife again. 'What I've done is art, Grace.' He frowned. 'Can't you see that?'

'Art?' Grace shook her head. 'You call this art?'

Pete shifted, looking suddenly uncomfortable. 'It's not as impressive if I have to explain it to you. Come on, I need you to work with me on this one. I know you're not quite as –' he tapped his head – 'as me, but you're not dumb.'

Grace leaned back against the wall, trying not to focus on Trick's increasingly shallow breaths. 'You mean you did this as an art project.' She sat bolt upright and pointed at the grim reaper on the bell. 'All of this, finishing The 100 Society, bringing everyone's pictures to life. You did this to impress me?'

Pete waved his hands and grinned. 'Ta-da.'

'Let me get this straight,' Grace spat, anger boiling inside her. 'You almost blinded Cassie. You killed Ed, you killed Daniel.' She turned to Pete with a sob. 'You tried to kill Trick? All to *impress* me?'

'Well, yeah. I didn't know what to do for my final project.' He bent to pick up a bag from the shadows. Grace

276

hadn't noticed it before. He started to pack away the rope and tape, then reached for the red container. As he lifted it, Grace caught a faint scent of petrol, but a gust of wind blew through the belfry, quickly taking any fumes with it. 'And when Miss Stone said that one day I'd bring a piece of art to life, well, that was what I decided to do.'

'You're sick,' Grace spat.

His face darkened. 'Jeez, it's not my fault everyone's pictures had to be so damn depressing. I mean, a hangman? Come on.'

'You killed him, Pete. You killed Ed.' She paused. 'And Daniel. That was you too, wasn't it?'

Pete held his hands up in defence. 'Hey, hey, now that one wasn't entirely my fault.'

'What?'

He shrugged. 'Well, it was, I guess, because I pushed him . . .' When Grace tried to speak, he continued over her. 'You don't understand, Grace, he was going to ruin everything.'

'What?'

Pete sighed. 'Well, I suppose you might as well know now.' He shoved the red container into his bag and zipped it up. 'Everything I told you about Daniel was true. He hated Clifton and he did say he was going to burn the school down, but it wasn't him who set the fire.'

Grace looked at Pete's bag, remembering the strong scent of petrol. 'It was you?'

'I did it for him,' Pete said. He pressed his hands against

277

the sides of his head and groaned. 'I did it for him, Grace. Just like I finished The 100 Society for you.' He stood up suddenly and kicked the huge bell, the metal humming as his foot struck against it. 'Damn it, why do I bother doing these things for people? You're all so ungrateful.' He stepped towards her again, his lips tight, his teeth bared. 'He said he wanted it to happen, but he lied. What's wrong with people? Why does everyone have to lie?' His voice started to rise as he paced back and forth, his fists clenching and unclenching at his sides.

'I don't know why people lie,' Grace said, her voice very small. There was something in the way Pete's expression had changed that told Grace she needed to be very careful with what she said.

'Don't give me that,' Pete shouted, spittle flying from his mouth. 'You're one of the worst, Grace, you've spent years . . .' He stopped, straightening his shoulders as he composed himself. 'I'm sorry, I know you've been very confused about your feelings.'

'So what happened with Daniel?' Grace asked. She looked at the door. It was open, but Trick wasn't going anywhere fast. She had to stall for time while she figured out a plan. 'It sounds like you tried to do something really big for him.'

For a moment Pete stared, his eyes narrowing. Then he smiled again, more modestly this time. 'Yeah, well. I guess I thought he'd at least get some time with his folks if the school burned down.' He laughed a little. 'It's not like I

278

expected the *whole* school to burn, of course. But I hoped it would be just enough to give him some time away with his parents.' He shrugged. 'They managed to put the fire out before enough damage was done, unfortunately. But it's the thought that counts, right?'

Grace wondered if she could take Pete on with the knife, but she wasn't sure of her chances. He was a lot bigger than her and there was a good chance he would be able to wrestle the knife away from her. 'That was very selfless of you.'

'See, now I knew you'd understand.' His eyes softened. 'It's a shame Daniel didn't feel the same way.'

'What happened?'

'I told him everything. I told him how, why, where. And you know what he said?'

Grace shook her head.

'He told me I was sick.' Pete laughed. 'He said *I* was the one who was sick. It was his idea, not mine.'

Grace glanced at Trick. His eyelids were fluttering. She had to get him out of here. 'Did he tell anyone?'

Pete shook his head. 'He threatened to. But you know what, Grace? I like to be modest, but the truth is that I am smarter than anyone I know. I know that makes me sound arrogant, but really, how can it be arrogant when it's the truth?' He waited for an answer but Grace said nothing. 'And you know, he'd already started that painting of his, the one that's at the bottom of the tower. Not to mention the lighters of his I'd taken, all with his fingerprints on. It's

279

amazing how these things can be found so long after a fire, if you just look in the right places.'

'So you threatened him? He thought you would frame him? Just like you were going to frame us?'

'No, no. I wasn't going to frame you, don't be silly. I only said that stuff to stop you from going to the police. It would have ruined everything.'

'And Daniel?'

Pete shrugged. 'He was my friend. I didn't want to, but I would have turned him in if necessary. It wouldn't have been hard. He'd already been questioned about the fire because of his painting. And when they found out he'd been lighting fires in his bin, it became pretty obvious that he was a pyro. All they needed was a little hard evidence to tie him to it. A strategically placed lighter would have been plenty.'

Grace shook her head. 'So all this time . . .'

Pete turned to pick up Trick's canvas. 'Look, I'm a reasonable person, Grace. I could have turned him in, but I chose not to.'

'There was nothing to turn him in for.' Grace rested her head in her hands. 'All this time, we thought he was a freak.' She looked up at Pete. 'But he was just scared. He tried to *warn* us. Is that why you pushed him off the bridge?'

Pete stepped back as he held up Trick's painting, searching for the perfect place to put it. 'He got cocky. He brought you all to the bridge that night to expose me. He had to go.' He finally laid the picture back against the wall, beside the window.

'So he was the one texting me, calling himself *A Friend*? Emailing me?' She gasped. 'That was him on the railway bridge that night, wasn't it?'

'Yep. He'd taken it upon himself to start following me, for some reason.'

'Because he knew you were dangerous.' Grace groaned, remembering Daniel's warnings. 'He was trying to tell us.'

Pete's eyes darkened. 'He always thought he was one step ahead of me, always trying to get me caught out. He knew I was tagging the grim reaper and he was trying to get evidence to use against me, the sneaky bastard.' He shook his head.

'That was why Daniel wanted Cassie's photos. He knew it was you. He thought he'd finally get the evidence he needed.' She thought back to the day she found Daniel wrestling with Cassie, desperately trying to prise the film from her fingers.

'Oh yeah,' Pete said, laughing. 'That was a good one. I came this close to being found out.' He held his thumb and forefinger apart. 'But luckily for me, good old Trick stopped that.' He swung a fist. 'Pow, what a fight. Shame about the ribs though, I bet that hurt.'

'It was you in those photographs, on Cassie's film. It was you who attacked her in the darkroom.'

Pete reached into his bag and pulled out a handful of tea lights. 'Yet again, another fortunate event for me. I got the film, I got my first piece of art brought to life. Deconstruction

281

of Beauty.' He bent down, arranging the candles in front of Trick's painting. 'But she deserved that, Grace. You know it was her supplying the photographs to the newspaper? I found the emails on her computer.' He shook his head. 'Some people only think of themselves. You know, I got all her films. Everything she was hiding in her locker and in her room, so there would be no way of her selling any more. I did that to protect you, Grace.'

Grace stared at Trick's Bell Tower, at the way it rose up into the sky. The perspective was that of someone lying on the ground below, looking up.

That was why Pete had wanted Trick to jump from the window; so he would fall to his death and the final piece would be complete.

She looked once more at her own picture, 'Forever'. The figures embracing each other, a painting that was supposed to represent a future of love.

Then it struck her. Trick's wasn't the final piece at all.

It was hers.

Pete thought this gesture, the completion of The 100 Society, would be enough to make her love him.

Her heart pounding, she squeezed her eyes closed, desperately trying to think of a way to get her and Trick out of here. There was no doubt about it; if Trick didn't get help soon, he would be dead.

'Look,' she said finally. 'Let Trick go. He can still go downstairs and lay at the bottom of the tower, it'll be just the same. Then we can be together.' She swallowed before forcing out the next word. 'Forever.'

Pete paused. For a moment he seemed to consider Grace's suggestion, then he reached into his bag for more tea lights. 'The problem is, Grace, I know about you and Trick.'

'You know what about me and Trick?'

Grace clutched at Trick's hand, squeezing it as she willed him to hold on for a little longer.

'I saw you,' he said, his voice hard. '*Kissing*.' He spat the word, like he had said something dirty. 'It's my own fault, really. It had become something of a habit to watch you in your room. Why do you think I spent so much time running around that field?' He laughed and Grace's stomach turned.

'You spied on me?'

'Hey, don't worry. Most of the time you had nothing to worry about. This was pretty much the only time you did something that made me angry.' He sighed. 'Seems silly now, to have ruined all that work over a little anger.'

'What work?'

'My sculpture. I had a bit of a tantrum and threw it down the steps. All because of a little kiss.' Wiping his hands on his jeans, he looked at her. 'But as I said, it's OK. I understand that you've been confused and, once Trick's gone, you and I—'

'There is no you and I,' Grace cried, all her plans to play along falling away. She got to her feet, brandishing the knife. 'You disgust me – how can you not understand that?

I *hate* you for what you've done.' She was screaming now, tears streaming down her face. 'I hate you more than I've ever hated anyone.'

Pete's face crumpled. He looked as though he had just been stabbed through the heart.

'But . . .' he stuttered, his own eyes filling with tears. 'I did all this for you. Because I love you.'

'You can't love anyone,' she spat. 'You can't love anyone, because you're a psychopath.'

'You can't say that. You can't, because you kissed me. I felt it. It was so real.' Pete was crying now, too. She had only seen him cry once before, in the kitchen before she had kissed him.

But that had all been fake too, she realized now. He had to push her away so they could be reunited like this, so they could have their own Forever, at a time that suited Pete.

'It was the worst mistake of my life.'

Pete's hands fell to his sides. The wind howled outside and a sudden gust brought a shower of rain into the belfry, spattering Pete's face with tiny droplets. He didn't even move to wipe them away. 'Is that really how you feel?'

'That's how I feel. Now let us go.'

Pete reached for his bag, scooping it up before sweeping from the room.

Grace rushed after him, but Pete was faster and before she had the chance to grab the door it had slammed, the latch clicking as it secured into place on the outside.

284

Grace rattled the handle, but it didn't move. She ran her hand up and down the length of the door, but there was no latch on the inside.

They were trapped.

33

Grace ran back to where Trick was still slumped against
the wall.

'Trick? Hey?' she shook him slightly and he opened
his eyes.

'Hey,' he whispered. He licked his lips, his eyelids
drooping as his head started to slump.

Dropping the knife on the ground, Grace reached for
his shirt and lifted it. There was a lot of blood and in the
darkness she was unable to see exactly where he had been
stabbed. Gently, she wiped her hand across his skin and
soon she found it, the small puncture mark that was oozing
blood at an alarming rate.

'OK,' she said. 'Shirt off.' She started to pull it up and
Trick groaned. 'Suck it up, Turner,' she said, although her
voice was gentle.

'Is this *déjà vu*?' Trick muttered, a tiny smile playing across his lips.

'I think it might be.' Grace slipped his shirt over his head and pressed it against the wound. She took Trick's hand and held it in place. 'You need to hold this,' she said. When Trick's hand fell away, she replaced it firmly. 'Hey, Trick,' she shouted, firmer this time. 'Patrick? Open your eyes.'

He did. 'You need to get out of here,' he said, licking his lips again and turning his head. 'Pete's gone mad.'

'I know.' Grace angrily wiped away a tear. 'But I'm not going anywhere without you, OK?'

Trick nodded and Grace stood up. Her hands were sticky with Trick's blood. There must be a way to get out. She ran to the window and looked outside. She shouted, but her voice was instantly carried away by the wind, the rain dampening any volume she might have had.

When she turned back, Trick had slumped further on to the floor.

Grace rushed to where he lay. 'It's going to be OK,' she said, but there was no answer.

Behind her, a click announced the turning of a lock and the return of the person who had forced her on this journey. Grace's fear vanished as quickly as the hatred began to boil inside her.

How many more people had to die?

Turning to look into the eyes of the person stepping into the bell tower, she had her answer.

One.

Just one.

With a scream, she lunged forwards, grabbing at Pete. His eyes widened and he sidestepped, grasping Grace as she almost hurtled past him and out of the doorway. Just before he pulled her on to the floor with him, Grace saw the first plumes of smoke rising up from the tower, the fumes almost covering the smell of petrol.

'What have you done?' she cried, struggling to get back to her feet.

Pete pulled her back down and she fell against the floorboards, her head smashing against the wood. Stars burst before her eyes and for a moment she thought she was going to black out, but the sharp tang of smoke filling her nostrils brought her back. She opened her eyes to see Pete's face over hers, his weight heavy on her chest as he straddled her, pinning her arms back against the floor.

'I've finished it,' he said, moving her arms down until they were trapped beneath his knees. He was almost nothing but a shadow against the orange glow that filled the doorway, but even that was dimming as the smoke thickened outside.

The calmness in his voice terrified Grace. She bucked, kicking her legs as she tried to free herself.

'If you won't be with me forever through choice,' he spat, his now-free hands finding her throat, 'then you will be with me forever through force.' He stroked her jawline, positioning the thumb of his other hand over her larynx.

'You'll kill us all,' she cried, the last words to escape her throat before Pete's fingers tightened around it.

'That's the idea.'

Grace's eyes bulged and she started to kick again, trying to free her arms, but Pete's weight was too much.

There was no escape. She looked up, her eyes meeting his.

'Shh,' he soothed. 'It'll be over soon. Just let go. Just give yourself to me; I'm all you need.' He bent down and kissed her gaping mouth. 'Not Trick,' he whispered into her ear, 'not your brother, not your father.'

Her phone. Pete was the one who had blocked the numbers of her father and brother.

'They don't love you like I do.' He moved to kiss her again, but this time his weight shifted and Grace's right arm came free.

She grabbed one of his wrists, pulled at his hands, but her vision was fading, the room was starting to collapse in on itself.

'It was always going to be this way,' he said. 'I'm not stupid, Grace. I knew I wouldn't get away with this, but I wanted it to be your choice. I just wanted to hear you say you loved me before I finished Daniel's piece.' His hands tightened again and Grace felt herself and everything else start to slip away. 'The fire was always going to be the finale.'

Her hand reached up again, clawing pathetically at his face as the darkness closed in.

Then his hands loosened.

For a moment there was nothing.

No movement, no sound, no pain.

Was this death?

Then Grace coughed, a huge, guttural, choking fit that told her she was very much alive. When she looked up, coughing again because of the smoke billowing into the belfry, she saw Pete's eyes widening in shock, his hands clutching at something protruding from his belly.

The knife.

Grace twisted, pushing at Pete as she pulled herself from under him. Pete staggered backwards, his hands still on the handle of the knife.

'What did you do?' he cried, his voice almost a scream.

Grace turned to see Trick, still lying on the floor in the ever-expanding black puddle.

'I threw it,' Trick muttered. A smile played across his lips. 'Just a simple matter of physics.'

Pete looked down again in disbelief and he staggered backwards. 'It's not meant to end this way,' he shouted. 'I have to finish it.'

Grace moved after him as he stepped out on to the staircase, the smoke thickening beneath them and rising quickly.

Pete stepped down again, this time landing on the step that Grace had fallen into earlier. The boards that had been damaged by her elbow gave way and his foot disappeared through the rotten wood. He reached out, clutching at the wooden handrail and looking at her with pleading eyes.

'Grace, I did this because I love you. I have to complete all the pieces.' At the bottom of the tower there was a loud pop as something exploded. The staircase was burning and the flames had started to lick upwards.

'There was one piece you forgot about,' Grace said, her voice barely more than a croak. She reached into her pocket before pulling out the piece of clay sculpture. 'Remember what happened to this? What you did to it on the staircase?'

There was a flicker of confusion before Pete's mouth fell open. 'Grace, no—'

'Yes,' she shouted, drawing her leg back before kicking outwards, her foot hitting Pete's chest with enough force to knock him backwards, his arms pinwheeling with almost cartoon effect for a second or two before the rotten step released his foot.

At the last moment he turned, reaching out as he fell, but it was fruitless. He tumbled down the narrow staircase, his flailing limbs striking the wall and steps until he reached the broken section of handrail. One of his legs fell through first and, despite reaching out to grab hold of one of the intact parts, the rest of his body followed.

Without so much as a scream, Pete fell from the spiral staircase and plunged down into the smoke and flames.

34

It was far from over.

Grace raced back into the belfry, to where Trick was still clutching his shirt to his side. The top half of the room was filled with smoke, but the slit windows allowed a good amount of airflow. There was still a little time before the whole belfry was filled with the thick fumes.

Kneeling beside Trick, Grace could feel the heat of the fire through the floorboards. The staircase was wooden and their only escape. It wouldn't be long before the flames worked their way up and destroyed the floor beneath them.

She reached out to stroke Trick's hair. 'I'm so sorry I didn't believe you,' she said, managing little more than a whisper from her damaged throat. 'It's just, when I saw that tattoo, I thought . . .'

Trick wiped away one of her tears with his free hand.

'It's OK,' he croaked. 'But you have to know I only got that tattoo because I knew I could never let myself forget what we'd done to Daniel.'

'That's where you went the morning after Lost Souls? To get the tattoo?'

Nodding, he closed his eyes. 'I knew I should never be allowed to forgive myself.'

'It wasn't you, though.' Grace burrowed her head into his shoulder. 'It wasn't you.'

Another gust of wind blew through the belfry, bringing with it the sound of voices. Grace froze. 'Did you hear that?' She stood up and ran to the window. Far below, torch beams were swinging wildly across the churchyard as people ran towards the bell tower.

Leaning out of the window as far as she could, Grace cupped her hands around her mouth. 'Hey.' She tried to shout, but her damaged voice seemed to disappear into the rain. She leaned out even further, and shouted again. 'Hey, please, help us.'

This time the beams changed direction, swinging upwards. Grace winced as the light hit her eyes, but she continued to shout, waving her arms frantically.

The voices below grew louder and although Grace couldn't hear the words, she knew they were supposed to be reassuring.

Then the sky lit up, a blue flash that made Grace wince as she braced herself for the clap of thunder, but it didn't come. Instead, there was another flash, followed by another and another.

Help had arrived.

She turned back to Trick, his breathing shallower than ever. 'Trick, it's OK, we're going to be OK.'

He lifted a hand to give the thumbs up, before his arm collapsed back on top of him.

The commotion outside grew louder and within seconds came the sharp sound of metal against stone. In the darkness, Grace was unable to see much of what was going on until a floodlight, mounted somewhere out of sight, turned the night into something resembling daylight. Below, firefighters and police hurried back and forth, dragging hoses and positioning ladders. Thick smoke billowed out in steady streams from the slit windows beneath, the grey and black clouds dancing upwards in the artificial light.

Then, out of the chaos on the ground below came the top of a ladder, rising slowly up the outside wall. It scraped against the stone, screeching as it grew closer to Grace. Her heart leaped as it drew nearer, closer, just two metres away, until it stopped.

'It's not here yet,' she shouted down, unsure if the people below were able to hear.

Why weren't they extending it more? Why weren't they doing anything?

Then a horrible realization struck.

It wasn't long enough.

She turned back to Trick. 'It's going to be OK,' she said,

but this time there was less confidence in her voice and she wasn't even sure if he would be able to hear her over the wind and the roars of the flames below.

Pulling herself back into the belfry, she crouched down low to the ground. The floorboards were now decidedly hot and the smoke was getting lower with every second. She crawled back to Trick and although she kept her head low, she was still hacking from the fumes. How could it be so difficult to breathe when the smoke was still above her?

She reached Trick and grabbed his hand, sticky with blood. 'Trick?' she shouted, but there was no response. She slapped his face but he didn't so much as open his eyes.

'Trick?' She was barely able to get the word out before a new coughing fit erupted. She lowered herself further, placing her face against Trick's chest. She could just feel the lift of his ribcage, the fluttering of his heart, enough to know that he was still with her. But there was hardly any clean air left.

They were almost out of time.

Grace crawled back to the window, sure that if she was able to get just one lungful of clean air, she would be able to think clearly again. She pulled herself up, leaning out as she took a deep, clean breath. Beneath, something large, square and red was being laid out on the ground. The smoke that was rising up from the windows obscured her view somewhat and Grace choked again as she took in a lungful of the fumes, but she didn't turn away.

The red square started to expand and Grace watched as

it grew in size, a yellow circle appearing in the middle.

Her heart leaped.

'We have to jump,' she shouted, lowering herself back to the floor. She could barely see Trick now, the smoke was so thick. It was hot and her eyes streamed with tears, her throat burning with every breath she took, but she pulled herself along the wooden floor to Trick. In the middle of the room, the floorboards had started to smoke. Any moment now they would burst into flames and she and Trick would fall through, but Grace refused to give in.

She reached out, grabbing Trick's hand.

He didn't move as she dragged him, inch by inch, towards the window. He might be dead, but she couldn't think about that now. She had to get him out of here, even if all she could hope for was giving his parents something to bury.

It was more than Pete's parents would have.

By the time she reached the window, she could barely breathe, let alone lift Trick to the window.

'Please,' she sobbed, 'please someone help me.'

Trick's hand twitched in hers.

'Trick?' She shook his shoulders. 'Patrick Turner, you listen to me. If you want to live, if you want *me* to live, then you have to help me get you out of here. Because I'm not going anywhere without you. Do you hear me, Patrick?'

Trick's hand reached up and Grace moved it towards the window. 'That's it,' she cried, hacking against the smoke. 'Pull yourself up. You can do it.'

Trick's fingers clawed against the stone and Grace slipped her hands beneath his arms, pulling him up and through the window as he pushed with his feet.

Then her hands were empty.

She pulled herself up to the window, leaving streaks of Trick's blood on the stone as she leaned out. The jump pillow below was already clear and she was unable to see what had happened to Trick. Without a thought for the distance between her and the ground, she propelled herself through the window and into the clean, fresh air.

Falling had never felt so good.

Grace took one last breath before the darkness finally closed in.

She didn't even feel her body hit the pillow.

35

Grace blinked.

There was something on her face, something was suffocating her. She reached up and pushed away whatever was blocking her nose and mouth, but it was quickly replaced.

A face appeared above her, upside down. 'Grace? Are you with us?'

Why was someone shouting at her? Grace reached up again, pushing at whatever this person was trying to suffocate her with.

'It's oxygen, Grace. You need to leave it on.' A hand appeared and pulled at the mask, lifting it for Grace to see. This time when it was replaced, Grace found she was able to breathe.

She closed her eyes again, welcoming the coolness of

the rain against her face. It was lighter now and the wind had dropped, but the sky above was still dark.

The blue lights were still flashing, although Grace was unable to see where they were coming from. To her right, a large crowd of people in uniforms were huddled together, moving quickly around something. She squinted, trying to see what it was they were so interested in.

'Trick?'

She tried to sit up, but a hand pushed her back down. 'Don't try to move – we need to get you to the hospital.' The face reappeared, this time looking far more friendly. 'You've breathed in some nasty stuff, we need to get you checked out, OK?'

'Please, my friend. Trick?'

The paramedic frowned. 'Excuse me?'

'Trick.' Grace shook her head. 'Patrick. His name's Patrick.'

'They're doing all they can.'

'Please, don't let him die.' She lay back, suddenly sure that the darkness was about to take her again. 'I love him.' She closed her eyes, squeezing out fresh tears. 'I love him.'

Then the crowd surrounding Trick started to move. They were running and Grace could see Trick lying on a gurney just like hers, his arms fastened against his sides with the same red straps that were stopping her from jumping up and running to be with him.

'We're going to get you to the ambulance now too,' the

paramedic said. 'Just need to get the all clear.'

Grace looked around, for the first time noticing all the police. She recognised some of them from the entrance hall, although she couldn't see the one who had grabbed her arm.

'There's someone else inside,' Grace said. 'He's dead. He tried to kill us, but then he fell . . .'

The paramedic glanced at one of the police officers. 'I think you'd be better off waiting until you get to the hospital,' she said to Grace. 'There'll be plenty of time for questions and answers later.'

'How did you know we were in there?' she asked.

The paramedic turned and pointed through the crowd. 'That guy, apparently.'

Grace followed the direction in which the paramedic was pointing. There, on the outskirts of the crowd, stood Sylvester. He was listening to a policeman, nodding between drags of his cigarette as the officer read something to Sylvester from his notebook.

'Apparently he does a pretty good job of keeping an eye on things around here.'

Grace nodded. 'So I hear.'

The policeman patted Sylvester on the shoulder before pocketing his notebook. Sylvester turned, this time making eye contact with Grace.

Grace lifted her oxygen mask. 'Thank you,' she mouthed.

Sylvester lifted his hand to his head, offering Grace a small salute before dropping his cigarette to the ground.

He blew out a final stream of smoke before turning back to Clifton.

The paramedic replaced Grace's oxygen mask and beckoned over her colleague. Together, they started to push Grace's gurney towards the waiting ambulance.

Grace closed her eyes and inhaled, letting the oxygen fill her lungs.

When they passed the charred door of the tower, smoke still billowing from whatever was burning inside, Grace didn't even look up.

36

Grace's father folded his newspaper and placed it on her bedside table. 'I'll leave you now, hun. You get some sleep, OK?'

Grace smiled and nodded, closing her eyes as he leaned in to kiss her forehead. 'I will.'

'I love you.'

'You too.'

Jack grabbed Grace's hand. 'You take it easy, sis. You hear me?' His face was stern, but a smile played across his lips. 'And if those cops come back with any more questions, you tell them—'

'Jack,' Grace's father snapped a stern warning and Jack closed his mouth, winking at Grace.

'They're just doing their job.' Grace yawned. It was only four thirty, but it felt like midnight.

'See you tomorrow, sweetheart.'

'See you tomorrow. Bye, Jack.'

'Later, squirt.'

Grace turned to the window.

The storm of the previous day had given way and now, with the sun setting, the sky outside was a deep red, streaked with orange clouds.

She exhaled slowly, blinking away the sting of tears.

She knew she was lucky to be watching the sunset, especially when there were some who would never see the sky again.

Grace pushed her blanket back and swung her legs out of bed. The oxygen tube that ran beneath her nose was to be removed tomorrow if her doctor deemed her well enough, but she was allowed to take it off for short trips to the bathroom.

She stood up, slowly. The floor was cold beneath her feet and she curled her toes against the hard surface, savouring the feeling and wondering how long she would marvel at these everyday things before she started to take life for granted again. With a bandage on her twisted ankle, the walking was getting easier, although she still found herself gasping by the time she reached the corridor. She stopped to catch her breath before continuing to the next bay of beds. She peered through the double doors, checking that the curtains weren't pulled around Trick's bed.

He looked up and lifted a hand.

'Hey,' she mouthed through the glass.

'Hey,' he mouthed back. He beckoned her inside.

Grace pushed through the doors and walked to Trick's bed, drawing the curtains before plopping herself down in the chair next to him. Her breath came in short whistles and she inhaled deeply, before letting out a long wheeze.

'You sound like an old woman,' he said, before starting his own fit of coughing.

Grace smiled. 'Yeah, you're not sounding too great there yourself, buddy.'

He leaned back, wincing as he placed a hand over the dressing on his side. 'That's the worst thing about the cough,' he said. 'Chest pain. Feels like I've been stabbed.' He grinned at her, though his swollen mouth made it slightly lopsided.

'You're an idiot, Trick.'

'I know.' He reached out and took her hand. His smile disappeared. 'I know.'

They sat in silence, hands entwined while the sun set, filling the ward with long shadows.

'I miss him,' Grace said finally. She waited for a response, but none came. 'Pete, I mean.'

'I know who you mean.'

'Like, I know my Pete never really existed. But I miss the Pete I thought I knew. Does that make sense?'

'It makes perfect sense.'

Grace paused. 'Do you think it's all my fault?'

Trick looked at her. 'Of course not.'

'But if I'd never come up with The 100 Society idea,

304

would he still have tried it? Did the rest follow because of that?'

'Hey.' He squeezed her hand again until she looked at him. His eyes were fierce. 'Now you listen to me. Pete was sick in the head and he twisted something for his own gain. He wanted to have an excuse to live out these sick fantasies he had of hurting people. All this time he thought he was so smart, he thought he'd be able to fool everyone . . .'

'He did fool us though, for all those years.'

'Because he was a psychopath and psychopaths are very good at covering their dark side.'

Grace nodded. A nurse peered in through the curtains and tutted. 'You should be in bed,' she said to Grace, with a raised eyebrow.

'Just a while longer?'

The nurse smiled before drawing the curtains again.

A few more minutes passed before Grace spoke again. 'Do you think Faith and Cassie will ever get over what happened?'

Trick shrugged. 'They've got just as much chance as we have.' He looked away. 'Personally, I don't want to get over it. It's a part of me now and I have to learn to accept that.'

'It doesn't have to be like that.'

'It does.' He shook his head. 'I don't think I have the ability to let it go.'

'That's why you get the tattoos, isn't it?'

Trick nodded. 'There's something about the pain, something about the way the ink goes in and the blood

305

comes out . . .' He paused. 'It's a release. It's something I need to do.'

'You know, you don't have to carry these burdens with you for the rest of your life.' Grace leaned forwards, running a hand gently across his tattoos, down his arm. 'You're allowed to let go.'

He looked at her, his eyes brimming with tears. 'I'm too afraid.'

'Then let me help you.' Grace stood up and sat on the edge of his bed, his hand in hers. 'I won't leave you, I promise. You can let go of it all and I'll still be right here.'

Trick pulled her down beside him. She lay her head on his pillow, her face centimetres from his, and wiped away his tears with the palm of her hand.

'I don't think I can do this without you, Grace.'

'You don't have to,' she whispered. She wrapped her arms around him, pulling him into an embrace. For a moment she was reminded of her painting, lost in the fire. 'I'm with you now.'

'Forever?'

'Forever.'

Acknowledgments

Thanks to my wonderful agent, Stephanie Thwaites, for absolutely everything. Also to my editor, Naomi Greenwood, and all at Hodder who have helped sculpt *The 100 Society* into something I will always be proud of.

To my friends, who have encouraged, supported and celebrated with me every step of the way. Sophy Duarte, Naomi Doran, Beccy and Nathan, Jo and Kenny, Jirina and Steve, Simon and Mim. Also Ben, Marie, Matt and Rochelle. To John and Diane, your enthusiasm is never ending and for that I am forever grateful.

To all the bloggers: you guys are amazing and I thank each and every one of you for your support. Finally, my parents, Brenda and Mike Simson, for always reading my stories and poems, no matter how dark they got. I love you.

MEET CARLA SPRADBERY

 WHAT INSPIRED YOU TO WRITE *THE 100 SOCIETY*?

IT WAS INSPIRED BY AN ACTUAL PIECE OF GRAFFITI I SAW
IN LONDON. I ORIGINALLY INTENDED THE NOVEL TO BE A
SUPERNATURAL HORROR ABOUT A GRAFFITI DRAGON THAT
COMES TO LIFE, BUT THE IDEA GREW AND DEVELOPED INTO
THE 100 SOCIETY. MUCH BETTER THAN A PAINT-MONSTER,
I THINK!

 **IF YOU HAD A GRAFFITI TAG, WHAT WOULD IT
LOOK LIKE?**

IF I WAS TALENTED ENOUGH, I THINK IT WOULD BE THE TAG
USED IN *THE 100 SOCIETY* – A DRAGON CHASING ITS OWN
TAIL. I THOUGHT THE IDEA HAD COME FROM THIN AIR, BUT
RECENTLY FOUND SOME CHILDHOOD ARTWORK OF A RED
AND GOLD DRAGON CHASING ITS TAIL, JUST LIKE IN THE
BOOK. IT WAS A SURREAL EXPERIENCE TO DISCOVER THAT
I HAD WRITTEN ABOUT A LONG FORGOTTEN MEMORY!

**WHO WOULD BE YOUR DREAM CAST IF *THE 100
SOCIETY* WAS MADE INTO A FILM?**

I'D LOVE TO SEE *THE 100 SOCIETY* MADE INTO A FILM AND
WOULD HOPE IT COULD GIVE A NUMBER OF UNKNOWN
YOUNG ACTORS AND ACTRESSES THEIR BREAK. SAYING THAT,
I THINK BILL NIGHY WOULD MAKE AN EXCELLENT SYLVESTER.
AND I'M SURE WE COULD FIND A ROLE FOR BENEDICT
CUMBERBATCH ...

4 WHAT SONGS WOULD BE ON *THE 100 SOCIETY* SOUNDTRACK?

I WROTE THE NOVEL ALMOST EXCLUSIVELY TO FALL OUT BOY AND PANIC! AT THE DISCO ALBUMS, SO IT WOULD HAVE TO BE SONGS BY THOSE TWO BANDS.

5 WHO IS YOUR FAVOURITE CHARACTER FROM THE BOOK?

DEFINITELY TRICK. HE WAS SO MUCH FUN TO WRITE AND WAS THE MOST FULLY FORMED CHARACTER WHEN I FIRST CAME UP WITH THE IDEA FOR THE BOOK.

6 WHO WOULD BE AT YOUR DREAM DINNER PARTY?

DAVID MITCHELL, STEPHEN KING, BEN FOLDS (AND HOPEFULLY I'D GET HIM TO PLAY A FEW SONGS WHILE HE WAS THERE!), GILES COREN AND, ER, BENEDICT CUMBERBATCH ...

7 WHO IS YOUR FAVOURITE AUTHOR AND WHY?

STEPHEN KING. NEVER HAS AN AUTHOR THRILLED, SCARED AND INSPIRED ME AS MUCH AS HE HAS. HE IS THE REASON I WRITE, THE AUTHOR I COMPARE ALL OTHERS TO, AND THE REASON WHY I WILL FOREVER BE TERRIFIED OF CLOWNS AND STORM DRAINS. HE IS MY HERO AND I HOPE ONE DAY I WILL GET THE CHANCE TO SHAKE HIS HAND AND THANK HIM FOR HIS NOVELS.

IS THERE A BOOK YOU WISH YOU HAD WRITTEN?

TOO MANY TO LIST HERE, BUT YES! BASICALLY, ANYTHING BY STEPHEN KING. MOST RECENTLY, I WOULD SAY *CRUEL SUMMER* BY JAMES DAWSON. HE HAS A FANTASTIC POINT HORROR-ESQUE STYLE WHICH I ADORE.

9 WHERE IS YOUR FAVOURITE PLACE TO WRITE?

EITHER IN MY ARMCHAIR (TERRIBLE FOR MY POSTURE, I'M CERTAIN!), OR AT THE DINING-ROOM TABLE. WE HAVE AN OFFICE, BUT IT'S TOO CLUTTERED AND I NEED A CLEAR SPACE TO THINK CLEARLY!

10 WHAT ARE YOU CURRENTLY WORKING ON?

I'M WRITING A NEW NOVEL ABOUT TWO TEENS WHOSE (SEPARATE) LIVES FALL SPECTACULARLY APART ON NEW YEAR'S EVE. THE STORY IS ABOUT HOW OUR MEMORIES CAN BE INFLUENCED BY OUR FEELINGS AT THE TIME, AND WHAT MIGHT HAPPEN IF WE ARE ABLE TO REVISIT THOSE MEMORIES AS IF WATCHING THEM ON A HD TV SCREEN. OH, AND THERE'S A LITTLE BIT OF MURDER THROWN IN FOR GOOD MEASURE!

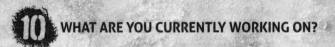

Follow Carla on Twitter @CarlaSpradbery